ACCLAIM FOR
EXPLETIVE DELETED

"Swearing is not big and it's not clever, as we're often told, but somehow this collection manages to be both. One in the eye for the prudes, but also one in the eye for those who doubt the power of short stories to amuse, stimulate and, occasionally, shock the jaded reader."

—John Connolly, author of *The Unquiet*

"A sharp, unapologetic collection of love, lewdness, and language."

—David Morrell, author of *Scavenger*

"No expletives have in fact been deleted from this nose-thumbing anthology ..."

—*Publishers Weekly*

"A dirty little collection of dirty little tales, *Expletive Deleted* is the most original—and interesting—anthology I've read in a long time. Placing the four-letter pariah of the English language under a microscope, these stories ride the razor's edge between crime and sex with a wicked half grin and come-hither eyes. I gave into it like a bad habit."

—Gregg Hurwitz, author of *The Crime Writer*

EXPLETIVE DELETED

EXPLETIVE DELETED

EDITED BY JEN JORDAN

BLEAK HOUSE BOOKS

MADISON | WISCONSIN

Published by Bleak House Books
a division of Big Earth Publishing
923 Williamson St.
Madison, WI 53703
www.bleakhousebooks.com

ISBN 13 (trade paper): 978-1-932557-56-5

FIRST TRADE PAPER EDITION

Library of Congress Cataloging-in-Publication Data has been applied for.

Printed in the United States of America

11 10 09 08 07   1 2 3 4 5 6 7 8 9 10

Set in Adobe Caslon Pro

Cover and book design by Von Bliss Design
www.vonbliss.com

This book is dedicated to my Dad, who taught me how to swear after he made me promise not to tell my mother (who already knew about every "fuck" and "hell" and "damn" that came out of his mouth).

SECTION FOUR

SECTION FIVE

SECTION SIX

MARK BILLINGHAM

is one of the UK's most acclaimed, popular and sweariest crime writers. His series of London-based novels featuring D.I. Tom Thorne has won him the Sherlock Award and the Theakston's Crime Novel Of The Year Award and he has been nominated five years in succession by the Christian Fellowship Of Strongly-Worded Letter Writers as Author Most Likely To Burn In The Fiery Pit Of Hell And Damnation. Mark also uses a good deal of profane and industrial language on stage when performing as a stand-up at London's Comedy Store. This is due more to a lack of material than any kind of political stance. He certainly does not believe that swearing is big or clever. If it was, he couldn't do it.

INTRODUCTION
MARK BILLINGHAM

"**MR.** Billingham,

My enjoyment of your recent 'novel' about a series of grisly murders was spoiled ... no *ruined* by the continual use of foul and disgusting language. I am not a 'prude' and neither am I easily offended. Indeed I purchased your so-called 'novel' having read the blurb on the back and looking forward to some good, old-fashioned mutilation and gore. But why, oh why must your characters employ such an industrial vocabulary? Repeated usage of the F-word, along with the dreaded C-word raising its ugly head now and again, made it simply impossible to continue and I was forced to lay aside your novel in favor of something that rose occasionally above the level of the gutter.

"In my experience, to fall back on the use of bad language usually indicates a paucity of imagination, and this often goes hand in hand with a reliance on scenes of a sexual nature. As you will imagine therefore, I was disappointed, though far from surprised, to see that several of your so-called characters engaged in pre-marital sex. On one particularly sordid occasion, your so-called 'detective' was involved in what I can only describe as an act of 'self-love.' Not that love of any sort plays much of a part in your vile and revolting book etc etc ..."

It's hard to believe, and not just because they seem so fond of using the expression "so-called," or know what the word "paucity" means, but this is typical of letters or e-mails I have received on many occasions in the last few years. The obvious response, and one which I have had to fight the temptation to fire straight back at these people, is pithy, not to say highly appropriate. But instead, I have simply seethed, or bitched about it at conventions, which is as close as I get to maintaining a dignified silence. After all, there seems little point trying to engage with people whose mindset is far more twisted and immovable even than my own.

No matter how many times I hear this kind of thing—and it is perhaps worth stating for the record, that the majority of these correspondents are (A) female and (B) American—I'm still shocked by the strength of feeling. Why should a few bad words and a spot of rumpy-pumpy ruffle anyone's feathers to this extent?

More to the point, why should it do so *in such a context?*

Fine. If your favored reading matter is no racier than the Bible (not that this doesn't have its fair share of "smitings" and "oaths" and assorted beardy types in flowing robes "knowing" one another all over the place) then you might well be shocked by the average medium/dark/dark-as-all-hell crime novel. If you like your murders solved by detectives called "Whiskas" or "Mr. Tibbles," then you have every right to be mildly offended by stuff you might find in one of my books. But ... if knowing full well what the subject matter of such books is, you are *still* shocked and disgusted by a little bad language, then frankly you are an idiot, whose sense of values is way overdue for a service. Just how skewed does your worldview have to be, before you find it acceptable to read about death and dismemberment but are offended if those who come close to it swear now and again? Or go home and have a drink to cope with the trauma? Or, heaven forbid, sleep with someone they haven't known for very long?

It has, on occasion, been suggested that my books, and those of other equally depraved writers, should be issued with warning stickers, like those on the front of many rap albums. You know the sort of thing:

WARNING.
THIS NOVEL ABOUT A SERIES OF BRUTAL SLAYINGS
ALSO CONTAINS CURSE-WORDS AND SCENES
INVOLVING TOILET PARTS.

I would be perfectly happy with this. As long as the people making these demands are forced to wear stickers themselves. These should be large, square and fluorescent. They should be stuck to their foreheads. They should read:

FUCK ALL IN HERE.

Every so often, they'll run a questionnaire, in a magazine or newspaper, in which a celebrity answers quirky questions, designed to give readers a snapshot of their personality. "How would you like to die?" "Have you ever been unfaithful?" Insightful stuff like that. Sometimes the subject will be asked "what is your favorite word?" Invariably, the answer will be something like "gossamer" or "bibulous" or—on one particularly nauseating occasion—"mittens." Not once have I seen anyone own up to loving what is perhaps the single most useful word in the English language.

Not once. Pussies!

You are about to read a collection of stories that goes a long way towards redressing the balance.

FUCK . . .

Come on now, put your hands together and give it up for our F-guest of honor. The King of curses; the Sultan of swearing. It's a cracking word, isn't it? A beautiful, evocative, *glorious* word, and one that cedes ground to no other—least of all "mittens" for crying out loud—when it comes to sheer versatility.

"Fuck you, you fucking big fucker."

It's a verb, it's a noun, it's a whatever-you-want. How can you not love a word like that? If on some level, you are unable to appreciate a sentence like the one above, then you have no poetry in your soul. In fact, I seriously wonder what *is* in the souls of those that so despise these four, wonderful letters. I've always suspected that those who make a song and dance about how offended they are by bad language, have pictures in their heads that would make Caligula go green and chuck up his chips. I'm convinced that many who claim to be disgusted by the depiction of honest, dirty lovemaking, go home and piss on each other while listening to Sting and wearing clown masks.

I am delighted that it was on hearing me rant about these kinds of double-standards, that Jennifer Jordan felt inspired to put *Expletive Deleted* together, but I know that many other writers trying to tell stories set, you know, in the *real world* receive the same sorts of criticism. It's wonderful that so many of them, sharing my sense of outrage, jumped at the chance to come on board and let rip.

Boy, have they ever let rip.

What a dark, disgusting and fabulous treat lies in store within the pages of this vile and appalling book …

From a seedy, New York hotel room to a somewhat grander one in Budapest; in African sunshine and Glaswegian rain, an astounding line-up of writers have taken the simplest and most tempting of briefs and run amok. There are paedophiles, pornstars and hit-men. There are set-ups and screw-ups; bank-jobs and blow-jobs. For reasons I don't begin to understand the rock group AC/DC appears twice, as does the television series "Lost," and for those who think "noir" demands a firearm or three, there are guns put into places where guns simply do not belong.

There is fuckage and fuckery a-plenty, and of course a lot of people get comprehensively fucked in one way or another. People, and things. I'm not sure that any animals come in for the stick they deserve, but that may be put right in a follow-up volume.

As for the word itself, yes it would be safe to say that it is writ large throughout, and with passion. Though at least one story features no bad language whatsoever, there is no shortage of those words that make some people hot under the collar. I have not actually done a count, but I reckon it would come somewhere between the last Harry Potter book and Brian De Palma's screenplay for *Scarface*. So, if anyone has been perverse enough to buy this collection *just so they can complain about it*, they had better make sure they have a lot of notepaper.

So, in a gratuitous orgy of bad language from both sides of the Atlantic, I say "bugger," "bollocks" and "fuck, yeah!" to the assortment of wonderfully sick puppies that have made this collection as great as it is. Some may have contributed stories in an effort to push back boundaries; to take their characters further into the shadows than they have gone before. Some may just think that sex and swearing is big and clever, which of course it is.

And some might simply have wanted to annoy the sorts of people who get upset by this type of thing and fire off holier-than-thou emails to mystery writers.

Which seems like a good enough reason to me.

—*Mark Billingham*

EXPLETIVE DELETED
SECTION ONE

LAURA LIPPMAN

was a journalist for twenty years, including twelve years at the *Evening Sun* and *The Sun* in Baltimore. Her mystery novels have won or been nominated for virtually every major prize given to North American crime writers, including the Edgar, the Anthony, the Nero Wolfe, the Agatha and the Shamus. She has published eight books in the Tess Monaghan series and, as of 2007, three stand-alones, *Every Secret Thing*, *To the Power of Three*, and *What the Dead Know*. She lives in Baltimore.

A GOOD **** SPOILED
LAURA LIPPMAN

IT began innocently enough.

Well, if not innocently—and Charlie Drake realized that some people would refuse to see the origins of any extra-marital affair as innocent—it began with tact and consideration. When Charlie Drake agreed to have an affair with his former administrative assistant, he began putting golf clubs in the trunk of his car every Thursday and Saturday, telling his wife he was going to shoot a couple holes. Yes, he really said "a couple holes," but then, he knew very little about golf at the time.

Luckily, neither did his wife, Marla. But she was enthusiastic about Charlie's new hobby, if only because it created a whole new category of potential gifts, and her family members were always keen for Christmas and birthday ideas for Charlie, who was notoriously difficult to shop for. And as the accessories began to flow—golf books, golf-themed clothing, golf gloves, golf hats, golf highball glasses—Charlie inevitably learned quite a bit about golf. He watched tournaments on television, and spoke knowingly of "Tiger" and "Singh," as well as the quirks of certain U.S. Open courses. He began to think of himself as a golfer who simply didn't golf. Which, as he gleaned from his friends who actually pursued the sport, might be the best of all possible worlds. Golf, they said, was their love and their obsession, and they all wished they had never taken it up.

*****

At any rate, this continued for two years and everyone—Charlie, Marla and Sylvia, his former administrative assistant—was very happy with this arrangement. But then Sylvia announced she wanted to go from mistress to wife. And given that Sylvia was terrifyingly good at making her pronouncements into reality, this was a rather unsettling turn of events for Charlie. After all, she had been the one who had engineered the affair in the first place, and even come up with the golf alibi. As he had noted on her annual evaluation, Sylvia was very goal-oriented.

"Look, I want to fuck you," Sylvia had said out of the blue, about six months after she started working for him. Okay, not totally out of the blue. She had tried a few more subtle things—pressing her breasts against his arm when going over a document, touching his hand, asking him if he needed her to go with him to conferences, even volunteering to pay her own way when told there was no money in the budget for her to attend. "We could even share a room," she said. It was when Charlie demurred at her offer that she said: "Look, I want to fuck you."

Charlie was 58 at the time, married 36 years, and not quite at ease in the world. He remembered a time when nice girls didn't—well, when they didn't do it so easily and they certainly didn't speak of it this way. Marla had been a nice girl, someone he met at college and courted according to the standards of the day, and while he remembered being wistful in the early days of his marriage, when everyone suddenly seemed to be having guilt-free sex all the time, AIDS had come along and he decided he was comfortable with his choices. Sure, he noticed pretty girls and thought about them, but he had never been jolted to act on those feelings. It seemed like a lot of trouble, frankly.

"Well, um, we can't," he told Sylvia.

"Why? Don't you like me?"

"Of course I like you, Sylvia, but you work for me. They have rules about that. Anita Hill and all."

"The point of an affair is that it's carried on in secret."

"And the point of embezzlement is to get away with stealing money, but I wouldn't put my job at risk that way. I plan to retire from this job in a few years."

"But you feel what I'm feeling, right? This incredible force between us?"

"Sure." It seemed only polite.

"So if I find a job with one of our competitors, then there would be nothing to stop us, right? This is just about the sexual harassment rules?"

"Sure," he said, not thinking her serious. Then, just in case she was: "But you can't take your Rolodex, you know. Company policy."

***

A month later, he was called for a reference on Sylvia and he gave her the good one she deserved, then took her out to lunch to wish her well. She put her hand on his arm.

"So can we now?"

"Can we what?"

"Fuck?"

"Oh." He still wasn't comfortable with that word. "Well, no. I mean, as of this moment, you're still my employee. Technically. So, no."

"What about next week?"

"Well, my calendar is pretty full—"

"You don't have anything on Thursday." Sylvia did know his calendar.

"That's true."

"We can go to my apartment. It's not far."

"You know, Sylvia, when you're starting a new job, you really shouldn't take long lunches. Not at first."

"So it's going to be a *long* lunch." She all but growled these words at him, confusing Charlie. He was pretty sure that he hadn't committed himself to anything, yet somehow Sylvia thought he had. He had used the company's sexual harassment policy as a polite way to rebuff her, and now it turned out she had taken his excuse at face-value. The thing was, he did not find Sylvia particularly attractive. She had thick legs, far too thick for the short skirts she favored, and she was a little hairy for his taste. Still, she dressed as if she believed herself a knock-out and he did not want to disabuse her of this notion.

(And did Charlie, who was 56, with thinning hair and a protruding stomach, ever wonder what Sylvia saw in him? No.)

"I'm not sure how I could get away," he said at last.

"I've already thought that out. If you told people you were playing golf, you could get away Thursdays at lunch. You know how many men at the company play golf. And then we could have Saturdays, too. Long Saturdays, with nothing but fucking."

He winced. "Sylvia, I really don't like that word."

"You'll like the way I do it."

He did, actually. Sylvia applied herself to Charlie's needs with the same brisk efficiency she had brought to being his administrative assistant, far more interested in his needs than her own. He made a few rules, mostly about discretion—no e-mails, as few calls as possible, nothing in public, ever—but otherwise he let Sylvia call the shots, which she did with a lot of enthusiasm. Before he knew it, two years had gone by, and he was putting his golf clubs in his car twice a week (except when it rained, which wasn't often, not in this desert climate) and he thought everyone was happy. In fact, Marla even took to bragging a bit that Charlie seemed more easy-going and relaxed since he had started golfing, but he wasn't obsessive about it like most men. So Marla was happy and Charlie was happy and Sylvia—well, Sylvia was not happy, as it turned out.

"When are you going to marry me?" she asked abruptly one day, right in the middle of something that Charlie particularly liked, which distressed him, as it dimmed the pleasure, having it interrupted, and this question was an especially jarring interruption, being wholly unanticipated.

"What?"

"I'm in love with you, Charlie. I'm tired of sneaking around like this."

"We don't sneak around anywhere."

"Exactly. For two years, you've been coming over here, having your fun, but what's in it for me? We never go anywhere outside this apartment, I don't even get to go to lunch with you, or celebrate my birthday. I want to *marry* you, Charlie."

"You do?"

"I looooooooooooove you." Sylvia, who clearly was not going to finish tending to him, threw herself across her side of the bed and began to cry.

"You do?" Charlie rather liked their current arrangement and, given that Sylvia had more or less engineered it, he had assumed it was as she wanted it.

"Of course. I want you to leave Marla and marry me."

"But I don't—" he had started to say he didn't want to leave Marla and marry Sylvia, but he realized this was probably not tactful. "I just don't know how to tell Marla. It will break her heart. We've been together 38 years."

"I've given it some thought." Her tears had dried with suspicious speed. "You have to choose. For the next month, I'm not going to see you at all. In fact, I'm not going to see you again until you tell Marla what we have."

"Okay." Charlie laid back, and waited for Sylvia to continue.

"Starting now, Charlie."

"Now? I mean, I'm already here. Why not Saturday?"

"Now."

***

Two days later, as Charlie was puttering around the house, wondering what to do with himself, Marla asked: "Aren't you going to play golf?"

"What?" Then he remembered. "Oh, yeah. I guess so." He put on his golf gear, gathered up his clubs and headed out. But to where? How should he kill the next five hours? He started to head to the movies, but he passed the club on his way out to the multiplex and thought that it looked almost fun. He pulled in, and inquired about getting a lesson. It was harder than it looked, but not impossible, and the pro said the advantage of being a beginner was that he had no bad habits.

"You're awfully tan," Marla said, two weeks later.

"Am I?" He looked at his arms, which were reddish-brown, while his upper arms were still ghostly white. "You know, I changed suntan lotion. I was using a really high SPF, it kept out all the rays."

"When I paid the credit card bill, I noticed you were spending a lot more money at the country club. Are you sneaking in extra games?"

"I'm playing faster," he said, "so I have time to have drinks at the bar, or even a meal. In fact, I might start going out on Sundays, too. Would you mind?"

"Oh I've been a golf widow all this time," Marla said: "What's another day. As long—" she smiled playfully "as long as it's really golf and not another woman."

Charlie was stung by Marla's joke. He had always been a faithful husband. That is, he had been a faithful husband for 36 years, and then there had been an interruption, one of relatively short duration given the length of their marriage, and now he was faithful again, so it seemed unfair for Marla to tease him this way.

"Well, if you want to come along and take a lesson yourself, you're welcome to. You might enjoy it."

"But you always said golf was a terribly jealous mistress, that you wouldn't advise anyone you know taking it up because it gets such a horrible hold on you."

"Did I? Well, if you can't beat 'em, join 'em."

***

Marla came to the club the next day. She had a surprising aptitude for golf and it gave her extra confidence to see that Charlie was not much better than she, despite his two years of his experience. She liked the club, too, although she was puzzled that Charlie didn't seem to know many people. "I kind of keep to myself," he said.

The balance of the two months passed quickly, so quickly and pleasantly that he found himself surprised when Sylvia called.

"Well?" she asked.

"Well?" he echoed.

"Did you tell her?"

"Her? Oh, Marla. No. No. I just couldn't."

"If you don't tell her, you'll never see me again."

"I guess that's only fair."

"What?" Sylvia's voice, never her best asset, screeched perilously high.

"I accept your conditions. I can't leave Marla, and therefore I can't see you." Really, he thought, when would he have time? He was playing so much golf now, and while Marla seldom came to the club on Thursdays, she accompanied him on Saturdays and Sundays.

"But you *love* me."

"Yes, but Marla is the mother of my children."

"Who are now grown and living in other cities and barely remember to call you except on your birthday."

"And she's a 57-year-old woman. It would be rather mean, just throwing her out in the world at this age, never having worked and all. Plus, a divorce would bankrupt me."

"A passion like ours is a once-in-a-lifetime event."

"It is?"

"What?" she screeched again.

"I mean, it *is*. We have known a great passion. But that's precisely because we haven't been married. Marriage is different, Sylvia. You'll just have to take my word on that."

This apparently was the wrong thing to say, as she began to sob in earnest. "But I would be married to you. And I love you. I can't live without you."

"Oh, I'm not much of a catch. Really. You'll get over it."

"I'm almost forty! I've sacrificed two crucial years, being with you on your terms."

Charlie thought that was unfair, since the terms had been Sylvia's from the start. But all he said was: "I'm sorry. I didn't mean to lead you on. And I won't anymore."

He thought that would end matters, but Sylvia was a remarkably focused woman. She continued to call—the office, not his home, which indicated to Charlie that she was not yet ready to

wreak the havoc she was threatening. So Marla remained oblivious and their golf continued to improve, but his new assistant was
beginning to suspect what was up and he knew he had to figure
out a way to make it end. But given that he wasn't the one who had
made it start, he didn't see how he could.

✳✳✳

On Thursday, just as he was getting ready to leave the office for
what was now his weekly mid-day nine, Sylvia called again, crying
and threatening to hurt herself.

"I was just on my way out," he said.

"Where do you have to go?"

"Golf," he said.

"Oh, I see." Her laugh was brittle. "So you have someone new
already. Your current assistant? I guess your principles have fallen
a notch."

"No, I really play golf now."

"Charlie, I'm not your wife. Your stupid lie won't work on me.
It's not even your lie, remember?"

"No, no, there's no one else. I've, well, reformed! It's like a pen-
ance to me. I've chosen my loveless marriage and golf over the
great passion of my life. It's the right thing to do."

He thought she would find this suitably romantic, but it only
seemed to enrage her more.

"I'm going to go over to your house and tell Marla that you're
cheating."

"Don't do that, Sylvia. It's not even true."

"You cheated with me, didn't you? And a tiger doesn't change
his stripes."

Charlie wanted to say that he was not so much a tiger as a
housecat who had been captured by a petulant child. True, it had

been hard to break with Sylvia once things had started. She was very good at a lot of things that Marla seldom did, and never conducted with enthusiasm. But it had not been his idea. And, confronted with an ultimatum, he had honored her condition. He hadn't tried to have it both ways. He was beginning to think Sylvia was unreliable.

"Meet me at my apartment right now, or I'll call Marla."

He did, and it was a dreary time, all tears and screaming and no attentions paid to him whatsoever, not even after he held her and stroked her hair and said he did love her.

"You should be getting back to work," he said at last, hoping to find any excuse to stop holding her.

She shook her head. "My position was eliminated two weeks ago. I'm out of work."

"Is that why you're so desperate to get married?"

She wailed like a banshee, not that he really knew what a banshee sounded like. Something scary and shrill. "*No*. I love you, Charlie. I want to be your wife for that reason alone. But the last month, with all this going on, I haven't been at my best, and they had a bad quarter, so I was a sitting duck. In a sense, I've lost my job *because* of you, Charlie. I'm unemployed and I'm alone. I've hit rock bottom."

"You could always come back to the company. You left on good terms and I'd give you a strong reference."

"But then we couldn't be together."

"Yes." He was not so clever that he had thought of this in advance, but now he saw it would solve everything.

"And that's the one thing I could never bear."

Charlie, his hand on her hair, looked out the window. It was such a beautiful day, a little cooler than usual, but still sunny. If he left now—but, no, he would have to go back to the office. He wouldn't get to play golf at all today.

"Who is she, Charlie?"

"Who?"

"The other woman."

"There is no other woman."

"Stop lying, or I really will go to Marla. I'll drive over there right now, while you're at work. After all, I don't have a job to go to."

She was crazy, she was bluffing. She was so crazy that even if she wasn't bluffing, he could probably persuade Marla that she was a lunatic. After all, what proof did she have? He had never allowed the use of any camera, digital or video, although Sylvia had suggested it from time to time. There were no e-mails. He *never* called her. And he was careful to leave his DNA, as he thought of it, only in the appropriate places, although this included some places that Marla believed inappropriate. He had learned much from the former president and the various television shows on crime scene investigations.

"Look, if it's money you need—"

"I don't want money! I want you!"

And so it began all over again, the crying and the wailing, only this time there was no calming her. She was obsessed with the identity of his new mistress, adamant that he tell her everything, enraged by his insistence that he really did play golf in his spare time. Finally, he thought to take her down to the garage beneath her apartment, and show her the clubs in the trunk of his car.

"So what?" she said. "You always carried your clubs."

"But I know what they are now," he said, removing a driver. "See this one, it's—"

"I know what's going on and I'm done, I tell you. The minute you leave here, I'm going to go upstairs and call Marla. It's her or me. Stop *fucking* with me, Charlie."

"I really wish you wouldn't use that word, Sylvia. It's coarse."

"Oh, you don't like hearing it, but you sure like doing it. Fuck! Fuck, fuck, fuck, fucking!"

She stood in front of him, hands on her hips. Over the course of their two-year affair she had not become particularly more attractive, although she had learned to use a depilatory on her upper lip. What would happen if she went to Marla? She would probably stay with him, but it would be dreary, with counseling and recriminations. And they really were happier than ever, united by their love of golf, comfortable in their routines. He couldn't bear to see it end.

"I can't have that, Sylvia. I just can't."

"Then choose."

"I already have."

No, he didn't hit her with the driver. He wouldn't have risked it for one thing, having learned that it was rare to have a club that felt so right in one's grip and also having absorbed a little superstition about the game. Also, there would have been blood and it was impossible to clean every trace of blood from one's trunk, according to those television shows. Instead, he pushed her, gently but firmly and she fell back into the trunk, which he closed and latched. He then drove back to the office, parking in a remote place where Sylvia's thumping, which was growing fainter, would not draw any attention. At home that night, he ate dinner with Marla, marveling over the Greg Norman shiraz that she served with the salmon. "Do you hear something out in the garage?" she asked at one point. "A knocking noise?" "No," he said.

It was Marla's book club night and after she left, he went out to the garage and circled his car for a few minutes, thinking. Ultimately, he figured out how to attach a garden hose from the exhaust through a cracked window and into the backseat, where he pressed it into the crevice of the seat, which could be released to create a larger carrying space, like a hatchback, but only from within the car proper. Sylvia's voice was weaker, but still edged with fury. He ignored her. Marla was always gone for at least three hours on book club night and he figured that would be long enough.

***

It would be several weeks before Sylvia Nichols' body was found in a patch of wilderness near a state park. While clearly a murder, it was considered a baffling case from the beginning. How had a woman been killed by carbon monoxide poisoning, then dumped at so remote a site? Why had she been killed? Homicide police, noting the large volume of calls from her home phone to Charlie's work number questioned him, of course, but he was able to say with complete sincerity that she was a former employee who was keen to get a job back since being let go, and he hadn't been able to help her despite her increasing hysteria. DNA evidence indicated she had not had sex of any sort in the hours before her death. Credit card slips bore out the fact that Charlie was a regular at the local country club, and his other hours were accounted for. Even Marla laughed at the idea of her husband having an affair, saying he was far too busy with golf to have time for another woman.

"Although I'm the one who broke 90 first," she said. "Which is funny, given that Charlie has a two-year head start on me."

"It's a terrible mistress, golf," Charlie said.

"I don't play, but they say it's the worst you can have," the homicide detective said.

"Just about," Charlie said.

JASON STARR

is the author of eight fucking crime novels published in ten fucking languages, including Barry Award-winner *Tough Luck*, and Anthony Award-winner *Twisted City*. He also writes fucking screenplays, including adaptations of his own books, and has co-written two fucking novels with Ken Bruen for Hard Case Crime, *Bust* and *Slide*. He's at work on an original fucking graphic novel for DC Comics and his latest novel *The Follower* is now available from fucking St. Martin's Press. He was born and raised in Brooklyn and now lives in fucking Manhattan.

LUCKY BASTARD
JASON STARR

I was in the bar at the Mansfield Hotel on Forty-fourth Street, nursing my fourth or fifth scotch on the rocks, when I smelled her. Every guy smelled her. I didn't know what kind of perfume she was wearing, but she was wearing a ton of it and it worked.

I looked over, expecting a big letdown. After all, a lot of women smelled great, but how many lived up to it?

This woman did.

She was probably the best-looking woman I'd ever seen. Okay, I was drunk and I could barely sit up straight but there was no doubt she was a knockout—tall, blonde, Jessica Rabbit shape with great lips in a tight red dress under a real mink jacket and bright red fuck-me pumps. You get the picture. She was one of those women you just can't stop staring at, and while you're looking at her with your mouth sagging open you can't stop thinking about the lucky guy who gets to see that body naked in bed every night when you're home with your miserable, nasty, post-menopausal wife who treats you like dogshit.

And, trust me, I wasn't the only guy who felt this way. Every other horny, frustrated, defeated, married, middle-aged man in the bar couldn't take their eyes off of this goddess. We watched her sit at the far end of the bar ordering a drink—something green that came in a long skinny glass. We were all waiting for one thing—the mink coat to come off, and come off it did. I don't think anybody made a sound but we might as well have shouted,

"Holy fuck!" because we were all thinking it. I won't even bother describing her body. Just picture the best-looking women you've ever seen and mix them all together and that'll give you some idea. I remember seeing a few guys shaking their heads in total awe and frustration, as if thinking that a woman this good-looking shouldn't be allowed to exist. It just wasn't fair to put us through this kind of pain.

I took a swig of my drink, still thinking about the lucky bastard who got to see what this woman looked like naked every night, and then looked at her again and saw her smiling at me. I thought I had to be making a mistake—maybe some Ken doll type was behind me or next to me. But I looked around and, nope, I was the only one there. I smiled back and my body heated up when she headed in my direction. Then I nearly shit my pants when she sidled up next to me and went, "Can I join you?"

I still couldn't believe this was happening. She had to be making a mistake, confusing me with somebody else, though it would've been hard to confuse me with the type of the guy she'd be interested in. I lied on my driver's license, said I was five-five, but I was five-four and a half. I'd been bald since college and the last time I bothered to weigh myself I was in the two hundred pound range. I was fifty-four years old but looked late sixties. To put it in simple terms, I wasn't a pretty sight.

But she was. She was one of those rare women who look better close up than far away. Her breasts, pushing against the dress, looked so good I wanted to reach out and grab them. And her perfume was driving me nuts. If it wasn't called Mating Call it should've been.

"Yeah, sit down," I managed to say, although my mouth was suddenly so dry it was hard to get my tongue to work properly.

"I'm Jenny," she said, extending her hand.

"Jerry," I said.

I held her hand. Her skin was so damn soft and smooth I could only imagine how soft and smooth the rest of her was.

"Jenny and Jerry," she said. "That's so funny ... we rhyme!"

Okay, so there didn't seem to be much going on in the brain department, but what did I care? When you looked as good as she looked you didn't need a brain. She could've had her brain removed and it wouldn't've mattered.

"Sorry to interrupt," she said.

"You're not interrupting," I said. My mouth was still dry and tasted like a Band-Aid. I took a gulp of scotch, but it didn't help.

"Do you come here a lot?"

At least she didn't say "often," right?

"Once in a while," I lied. I actually hit the Mansfield bar once or twice a week. "I work in Garment Center and sometimes I come by here after work."

"You're a designer?" Her eyes were sparkling.

"No, I'm a furrier," I lied. Actually, my company was a wholesaler of men's outerwear and we didn't deal in fur, but I had a feeling that the idea of me being a furrier would impress her.

"Wow, fur," she said. "I love fur."

Proud of myself for pulling "the fur card," I said, "I can tell. I noticed your coat when you walked in."

"Is that all you noticed?"

"That and some other things."

She smiled. We had a great rapport going. We were like Bogart and Bacall. We had chemistry.

"A furrier, huh? That can come in very handy. Can you get good discounts?"

"Considering I own the company, yeah."

I was actually the assistant manager of my company, but I figured I was on a roll so what the hell?

"You know what I noticed when I came in?" she asked.

"What?" I asked.

"You," she said.

I wanted to pinch myself. Stuff like this just didn't happen to Jerry Friedman.

I don't know how I kept my cool, but I managed to say, "What did you notice?"

"How adorable you are," she said, "but kind of sad too. I said to myself, there's a rich and successful guy, but he's sitting there, alone, drinking on a Thursday night. There has to be something missing in his life."

"You thought about all that, huh?"

"Am I right?"

I knew she wanted me to say yes, so I said, "Yes."

She leaned across the table, letting me smell more of her perfume and giving me a better view of her cleavage, and said, "Let me tell you my situation. I was supposed to get married last week in L.A., but I caught my fiancé cheating on me."

"Someone cheated on *you?*"

"It was worse than that—he said it had been going on for three years. Naturally I was devastated. I flew to New York, to try to forget about the situation, and I just arrived at the hotel an hour ago. I'm still hurting a lot over the breakup and nothing would make me happier than to get even with him. So what do you say? Are you up for it?"

It was like I was in a real-life *Penthouse Forum.* It was my Lotto-winning moment—after years of losing and disappointment, my numbers had finally come in. Of course I thought there was something weird about her coming on so strong to a guy like me, but what was I going to do, complain about it? Let's face it—my life sucked. My career was going nowhere and the only thing I looked forward to anymore was going out drinking, usually alone. Miriam and I had a few good years together, but she'd gradually turned into a nightmare. She was nasty and irritable most of time; she definitely had some kind of undiagnosed personality disorder. We didn't have kids and we didn't go on vacations or go out a lot. We went to work every day and came home and that was about it. I knew if I turned down an opportunity like this I'd regret it forever and I had enough regrets in my life.

"I'm up for anything," I said.

"Wonderful?" she said. "I have a suite on the top floor. Ready?"

When I left with Jenny the guys in the bar looked at me in total awe and I knew exactly what they were thinking: *That lucky bastard.*

When the elevator doors closed Jenny started kissing me. I'd never kissed a woman so beautiful. It was like I was kissing for the first time. I didn't know what to do.

In the room, we kissed some more, then she started undressing me. When I was naked she told me to lie in bed and then she did a strip tease in front of me. Her body was incredible and she was wearing the sexiest lingerie I'd ever seen outside of a Victoria's Secret catalogue. It was the male fantasy to end all male fantasies.

I was worried that after all the alcohol I'd had and with no Viagra on me that I wouldn't be able to get it up. It would be just like me to blow my one shot at screwing the most beautiful woman I'd ever seen because of a limp dick. But there were no problem at all on that front. Houston, we had lift-off.

Then, when her panties came down, revealing her neatly shaved landing-strip bush, she climbed on top of me. I could describe the sex but there would be no point. Watch any porno movie and that'll give you a good idea of what it was like. It was loud and dirty and raunchy. We were cursing at each other and we did every kind of sex you can do, in positions I never knew existed.

Afterward, lying next to her, drenched in sweat, I wanted to do it all over again, but she was already up, putting her clothes on.

"What? No second round?" I said smiling.

"I think you better get dressed," Jenny said. "Relax, have a drink from the mini-bar, and I'll explain the situation to you."

Suddenly she didn't sound like the ditz she'd sounded like twenty minutes ago.

"Situation?" I said. "What situation?"

"Put your fucking clothes on," she said.

I did as I was told, took the bottle of beer she'd opened for me, then said, "So what's the problem? Did I do something wrong?"

I wondered, Did I come too fast? Yeah, probably, but that didn't explain her pissed off attitude.

"I'm a professional escort," she said.

"You are?" I don't know why, but this actually came as a shock to me. She looked slutty, yeah, but I didn't think she was *that* slutty.

"I normally get paid a thousand bucks a shot for screwing losers like you."

The loser part hit home hard. It stung. I'd thought she actually liked me.

"Look," I said, if you expect me to pay you for this it's not gonna happen."

"Oh, you're gonna pay all right. One way or the other, I mean." She was fully dressed. "You see, I wasn't working alone. Your wife's detective hired me."

"My wife's what?"

"She thought you were cheating on her and she hired a detective to follow you around. Is that so unbelievable?"

Actually, it was kind of flattering. I didn't think Miriam cared enough about me to hire a detective, but it made a lot of sense. I'd been out a lot lately, drinking after work. She'd probably been getting suspicious, afraid I'd finally gotten sick of her crap and was going to leave her for a younger woman.

"So let me get this straight," I said. "My wife's detective hired you to screw me?"

"Yes."

"What's the detective's name?"

"I can't tell you that."

"So what does this have to do with you?"

"Lots of detectives hire escorts to screw the person their client's suspicious about. It makes their lives easier."

"The hell're you talking about?"

"The detective wanted to catch you cheating on her. And you got caught, hook, line and sinker."

"This is entrapment," I said. I didn't know if this was true or not—I wasn't a fucking lawyer—but it sounded good.

"Maybe," Jenny said, "but that won't help your marriage once I tell the detective and the detective tells your wife."

"I'll deny everything."

"People saw us in bar; they saw us leaving together. The surveillance camera in the elevator will have some nice footage of you kissing me. Face it, you're screwed ... unless you want to make a side deal with me."

"Side deal?

"I can go collect my thousand bucks from the detective. Not bad for five minutes work, right? I can either take one thousand from him or you can pay me ten thousand tomorrow—I tell him you were faithful, not interested in me."

It's funny, the things a guy will think about at the most tense moments, when his whole life is on the verge of going down the shitter. My marriage was on the line, my security, my future, but I was thinking, Five minutes? You kidding me? I lasted at least ten.

I snapped out of it, said, "Are you crazy? Ten thousand dollars?"

"If you don't give me the money, your marriage is over. Do you really want that to happen?"

I thought about this. Yeah, Miriam had been treating me like shit for years. Yeah, I had been thinking about calling it quits, especially lately. But did I actually want my marriage to end?

"What if I call the cops?"

"And tell them what? That you had sex with an escort? I'll say you picked me up at the bar. How would that look when your wife finds out?"

"But I don't have ten thousand dollars." I was sweating, like I was getting fucked all over again. In a way, I guess I was.

"Bullshit," she said. "You own a company."

"I lied. I'm not the owner."

"That's your problem, not mine."

"I can't give you money I don't have."

"Then I'm telling the detective that you picked me up at the bar and fucked me."

"You're full of shit."

"Ten grand," she said. "There's a parking lot on Forty-sixth between Ninth and Tenth, north side of the street. Be there tomorrow at six p.m. Don't try anything because I won't be there alone. Just have the money in a briefcase or a bag—something concealed. See you there."

She left.

I stayed in the room for a while, then I got myself together and went down and took a cab home to my apartment uptown.

Miriam was asleep, thank God. The last thing I needed was one of our nightly fights. I stayed up, watching TV, trying to decide what the hell to do. I didn't have ten grand. For years we'd been living on a shoestring, paycheck to paycheck, and it was a struggle to come up with the rent money every month. We had 2,200 dollars in a savings account, which was supposed to go for our mutual thirtieth anniversary present next year—a widescreen LCD TV.

I weighed my options. I could tell Miriam the truth, put it all on the table. But if she was angry enough to hire a detective I doubted she'd forgive me for cheating on her. She'd leave me or demand a divorce and I didn't want to go down that road, not at the stage in my life when I was thinking about retirement, reducing stress. I could do nothing, call Jenny's bluff, but what if she wasn't bluffing? But if I gave her the ten grand—ten grand I didn't have—there was no guarantee she wouldn't go to the detective anyway and cash in twice.

I decided I had no choice but to make some kind of payment to Jenny. The next day, during my lunch break, I withdrew two thousand dollars, hoping that double what the detective was paying her would be enough to get her off my back. I had no idea what I'd tell Miriam when our anniversary came, but at least I had some time before I had to deal with that one.

At six p.m. I showed up at the parking lot off Ninth Avenue. Sure enough Jenny was there with some muscle-head guy. She was wearing jeans and a cut-off T-shirt and dungaree jacket, but she looked as good as she had last night. She smelled just as good too, wearing more of that Mating Call stuff.

"Where's the money?" she asked.

I took out the two thousand dollars and said, "Look, this is all the money I have in the world. It's all you're gonna get so I suggest you take it."

"You were supposed to bring ten thousand," she said. "That was the deal."

"I don't have ten thousand."

"He's lying," muscle-head said. "He's got money."

He grabbed me, pushed me to the concrete. Then he reached into my pocket and took out my wallet.

"Eleven bucks," he said to Jenny. Then he kicked me in the ribs and said, "Where the fuck's the rest, douche bag?"

"It doesn't matter," Jenny said. "We got two grand off of him. Let's just get the hell out of here before somebody sees us."

Muscle-head kicked me once more and then they left.

I lay there for a long time, people walking right by me, I guess figuring I was homeless or a passed-out drunk. Finally I was able to stand up. My ribs hurt like hell but I didn't think they were broken.

When I got home Miriam was in another one of her moods. First she laid into me for forgetting to pick up milk and toilet paper, then she noticed I was in pain and said, "What the hell happened to you?"

I told her that I had gotten mugged on the way home and the mugger had kicked me a few times because I didn't give him my wallet. She called me "an idiot." I didn't feel like hearing any more, so I locked myself in the bedroom and came out when dinner was ready.

It was her usual meatloaf and mashed potatoes. It tasted like crap, but I ate it anyway.

Midway through the meal, I decided I had to tell her about Jenny. For all I knew Jenny had already gone to the detective to try to get paid twice. My only chance of saving my marriage was beating Jenny to the punch and breaking the news to Miriam myself.

"There's something I have to tell you," I said.

In a calm, controlled voice I told her what had happened last night—how I'd gotten drunk and how the gorgeous blonde came over to me and seduced me. I told her it was the stupidest thing I'd ever done in my life and that it didn't mean anything to me and I begged her for forgiveness.

When I was through Miriam stared at me for a few seconds and then she started laughing.

"You really expect me to believe that some gorgeous blonde picked you up at a bar?" Miriam asked.

"She did," I said.

"That's the funniest thing I've ever heard. Are you sure that mugger didn't bang you on the head? Maybe you should go to the hospital and get checked for a concussion."

She laughed again.

"I don't care if you believe me or not," I said, "it's true. So you can fire that detective."

"Detective? What detective?"

The meatloaf and potatoes churned in my stomach and I winced on the reflux. Then I said, "The detective you hired to follow me."

"Maybe you really do have brain damage. Why on earth would I hire a detective to follow *you*?"

It hit home what a total fool I'd been. Miriam didn't care enough about me to hire a detective and when Jenny came into the bar she'd noticed me all right. She'd noticed the ugly drunk sad sack with the thick wedding band who was an easy target for a sex blackmail scam.

"What's so funny?" Miriam asked.

"Nothing," I said. "Nothing at all."

I had another sleepless night. Not because of my bruised ribs or because Miriam was snoring like a goddamn horse. It was because of Jenny. I couldn't stop thinking about her. Not about how she'd used me, but about how great it had felt when she came over to me at my table and started hitting on me. The scary thing was that, despite everything, all the hell and humiliation she'd put me through, I knew I would've gone up to that room with her all over again.

SARAH WEINMAN

writes crime fiction columns for the *Los Angeles Times* and the *Baltimore Sun*, has had short stories published in *Ellery Queen's Mystery Magazine*, *Alfred Hitchock's Mystery Magazine* and several anthologies, and is the proprietor of Confessions of an Idiosyncratic Mind (at www.sarahweinman.com), hailed by *USA Today* as "a respected resource for commentary on crime fiction." She lives in Manhattan and stopped being a fan of Mr. Softee when the truck decided to take up permanent residence outside her apartment window.

LOOKOUT
SARAH WEINMAN

CINDY Mackey was eight years old and there was nothing she loved more in the entire world than ice cream. So when she heard the familiar refrain of the Mr. Softee truck, she ran to find her mother.

"The ice cream man is here! Can I have some money?"

She tugged at her mother's skirt until she had her answer.

"Yes, dear," said Cindy's mother with a heavy sigh. "Will a dollar be enough?"

Cindy shook her head. "Mom, you *know* the price went up the last time Mr. Softee was here. I have to have two dollars!"

She knew her mother didn't like it, but she didn't care. She wanted the money right now, getting more impatient as her mother fished around in her skirt pockets and took out two crumpled bills.

"Here you go. But be back here in fifteen minutes exactly. Do you understand me?"

"But—"

"Do you understand me, Cindy Mackey? I need you to say so."

"Yes, Mommy." Before her mother could add any more dire warnings, she raced out of the house.

After ice cream, Cindy loved being outside. Summer was here and it was too hot to stay indoors, with only her mother and her constant nagging for company. Cindy, sit down. Cindy, clear the table. Cindy, did you do all of your homework? She was sick of it. She thought being away from stupid school would make her mother stop, but it wasn't working. She hoped the taste of ice cream would wash everything away.

She hoped that fifteen minutes was enough time to be away from her mother. Or maybe it would be like the last time the ice cream man came, when Cindy stayed out for twenty minutes and her mother never even noticed. Could she do that again?

She saw the Mr. Softee truck parked on the corner and waved to the driver. Taking out the crumpled dollar bills, Cindy hoped she'd find out.

✳✳✳

He'd been watching her for weeks.

Oh, there were plenty of other children who were more pliant and trusting, but there was something about the girl that really made him take notice.

It wasn't the hair; he hated little red-haired girls because their tempers usually matched. And it wasn't her looks, plain at best and more often bordering on homely.

It was the way she ate ice cream. Others licked tentatively, unsure if the taste of chocolate or vanilla or strawberry was really as good as they remembered. But this one devoured each bite greedily, as if it might be the last she'd ever have.

One time she was so excited and hungry that she finished the entire cone in less than one minute. He timed it because the truck jingle was on a 10 second loop and six of them had passed from the time she began to eat.

He hadn't been able to take his eyes off her after that. Her ice cream habits filled his dreams, and one morning he woke up in a sweat, wondering if he should feel guilty or determined.

Instead, he chose to wait. And by doing so, he was rewarded every time she came back with another pair of crumpled bills to buy another cone of ice cream.

Like now.

"Hi there, Mr. Softee!" He liked how she called him that, even though they both knew he was only the driver.

"What's your flavor today?"

"I had strawberry the last time. I think I'll try chocolate."

A thrill shot through him. Chocolate was his favorite.

"But I'll have to take it with me," she continued. The thrill disappeared.

He tried not to let it show, concentrating on giving her enough ice cream on the cone so that it was on the precipice of falling onto the ground. There was no better ice cream cone than one on the verge of free fall.

He took one last look at his creation: absolutely perfect.

He hoped she would remember it as fondly as he would.

"Here you go," he said to Cindy, handing her the cone.

***

She knew she shouldn't worry. Cindy hadn't even been gone ten minutes.

But she'd spent most of her life trusting her instincts, and now they told her something was amiss.

The ice cream truck had appeared in the neighborhood at the beginning of the summer. The driver—she refused to think of him by name—had to earn money somehow, and all the protests in the world hadn't deterred him from moving back here. There was nothing she or her neighbors could do, even though she was certain something horrible would happen.

The first time Cindy had wanted to buy ice cream, she'd insisted on going along. The look on his face when he handed a cone to Cindy chilled her from then on.

But Cindy was adamant: she didn't want her mother watching her all the time. She was a big girl, she'd come back right away, what was the problem? And they argued so much already that finally, she caved in, taking her frustrations out on her fingernails.

She hoped her instincts were wrong. The last time, she'd been sure of something terrible when the minutes passed and there was no Cindy.

But nothing had happened. Cindy returned, ice cream in hand, and chided her for getting upset.

"I came back in time! You said fifteen minutes!"

"I know, honey, but when you weren't here, I worried—"

"But the Mr. Softee man could see me!"

She hadn't wanted to explain. It would be too complicated for Cindy to understand.

But the girl loved her ice cream and she was so damn stubborn. She knew she should treat her daughter more kindly and not nag her so much about everything. But she couldn't help it. She didn't want her daughter to suffer the fate of others she'd seen on TV. Like the little blond girl who'd asked her mother for money for ice cream, run to get it, and disappeared without a trace.

Or like her best friend Susan.

Three more minutes passed. Still two under the time limit, but it was more than enough. The sun beat down on her when she stepped outside. Lord, it was so hot this summer. How could anyone stand it? No wonder all the kids wanted to eat so much ice cream.

She heard the jingle get louder and louder.

The damn thing should be outlawed.

***

He couldn't remember when she began to haunt him. Not consciously, of course, because he was certain she had no idea he even existed as a man.

Maribel. A lovely name, innocent and knowing at the same time.

He first noticed her a few months ago, when she and her daughter moved to the neighborhood. He watched as she tried to discipline the child, to cement valuable concepts of right and wrong even though hardly any of them took. After each lost argument, Maribel would hold her face in her hands and cry in the hopes that no one would pay attention to her.

Such dignity and poise! He could barely contain himself.

But he lived by his vows and knew he could never breach them. He'd taken the cloth and chosen to serve God; no woman, however desirable, could be his undoing.

Still, he continued to watch, hoping he could keep his secret thoughts buried deep.

Then one morning she sat down in the confession booth. "Forgive me, Father, for I have sinned."

At first, he hadn't known what to say. She was here, only inches away from him. But he soon recovered.

"Pray tell your troubles and ease your mind," he said in his most soothing voice.

"I struck my daughter this morning. She wanted to go outside and play and I wouldn't let her, so she got upset and I hit her."

Her final words, said with a slight hitch. He understood her plight and sorrow more than she could ever realize, for her story brought back memories of being young, struck by his own father after breaking something in the house.

He wanted to rip open the confession veil and hold her.

He knew he could not.

"Say this blessing and repeat it throughout the day. God will absolve you."

He struggled not to say the Hail Mary along with her. Only experience and strong will kept him from joining in. When she had completed it, he bade her goodbye.

She'd hardly said anything to him, but he felt something change. And he found he could do little else besides preparing his sermons and watching her go about her life.

Now he sat on his front porch. The air conditioning had broken and as hot as it was, he needed to sit outside.

Then he heard a scream.

Maribel's scream.

"Cindy! Where has she gone? What have you done with my daughter?"

***

Every time she came to clean his apartment, she was always shocked by his frail appearance. He couldn't be more than fifty-five, but he seemed so much older.

Did he even realize this? Could she tell him?

She shrugged. It wasn't her place to tell Father Lowry what to do. He was a powerful man with a devoted following. Let one of them say how awful he looked. She was only the cleaning woman.

Still, she couldn't help but notice that in spite of his failing health, his eyes were unnaturally bright, and he sat with the best posture she'd ever seen. She was no Catholic—she didn't get the whole notion of original sin—but she would stay by him as long as she possibly could, under any circumstances. Even if those circumstances consisted of vacuuming, doing his laundry and occasionally speaking to him when spoken to.

Because she had a key to his apartment, occasionally she'd sneak in when he wasn't home, usually during the Sunday sermon. At first she'd been stupid and tried to steal his belongings, but found she couldn't go through with it. She liked the apartment too much, the opportunity to feel his presence and find out who he might have been.

And perhaps learn a secret or two.

Ridiculous, she chided herself, to rummage through his things. But speaking to him at length was out of the question. They lived in two different worlds. This way, she could find out about his innermost thoughts without actually having to ask uncomfortable questions.

She looked forward to Sunday mornings more than anything.

Especially after she'd found the picture secreted away.

It was of the lady neighbor. Why did he have her picture? She wasn't beautiful at all. And her child was the worst-behaved little girl she'd ever seen. Why would Father Lowry ever be attracted to this woman?

But she never asked, and never would. Just delighted in knowing he had a secret, and a big one at that.

She hated cleaning apartments when it was so hot. And he didn't even have air-conditioning. How could anyone survive without it? She thought she would keel over, but kept on cleaning regardless.

When she finished, she opened the glass window to the front porch, where Father Lowry sat. He seemed more animated than usual. In fact, he actually was saying something to her.

"Can you go for help? Do something?"

What could he possibly mean? "What happened?" she asked.

"Cindy Mackey is missing."

She still didn't understand. Father Lowry was looking at her like she was some idiot, but she couldn't help it. The words "Cindy Mackey" and "missing" simply didn't go together.

"Her mother's been searching for her for over an hour and can't find her. She nearly took the ice cream vendor's head off with accusations."

Why are you telling me this? she thought. Wouldn't you rather be talking to *her*?

"Were they true?"

Father Lowry shook his head. "I know that man. He wouldn't hurt anyone, let alone a child."

She smirked. He really did live in his own world. Didn't he know the Mr. Softee man only lived in the community by default, because no one else wanted him and his record?

But she pretended to agree. "I understand."

He regarded her with something resembling kindly affection. "You're almost finished?"

"Yes, thank you."

She left in a hurry, wishing she could have stolen something to quell the itchy feeling inside.

***

Why was she running out of the house? This wasn't good.

He'd been following his sister for weeks now, wondering if she suspected something. He'd been so angry when she'd started working for the priest. He didn't want her hanging around company like that. Then she'd be sure to find things out.

Things he would much rather keep hidden.

He never much liked her. They fought viciously as children, beating each other up over the most trivial things. And most of the time, Bonnie won. He'd never forgiven her.

She'd been the cherished child, the adored one. He'd spent most of his time hanging around in his room, collecting bugs and plotting revenge, with no one the wiser.

He kept the car at a reasonable distance. She hadn't suspected his surveillance and there was no way he was about to blow it now. He needed to know what she knew.

When she'd told him she was going to work for the priest, he'd made it clear what a dumb idea that would be.

"Cleaning houses, Bonnie? You've got a college degree. Why the hell would you want to do that?"

She shrugged. "It gets me out of the house. No one else wants to hire me right now, and Father Lowry needs someone to help him out."

"You just want to spend more time with that freak," he sneered.

She threw a pillow at him. Bonnie was twenty-three and he twenty-two, but they fought just as hard as they had as kids.

It didn't matter that he spent three times a week at the gym. Bonnie still won.

He drove around in discreet circles, trying to vary the route slightly around the row of houses. That's when he saw the woman approach the car.

"Please, you have to help me!"

Jesus, she sounded hysterical. Her voice hurt his ears.

He rolled down the window. ""What seems to be the matter, ma'am?" He hoped it sounded suitably polite and professional.

"My daughter is missing!"The rest of the woman's words were muffled because she couldn't stop crying. He hated women who cried.

"I gave her money to buy some ice cream and told her to be back in fifteen minutes. When she didn't return after a half an hour, I went out to look for her and she wasn't there! She was gone! It's that horrible driver, I just know it is!"

She was making him twitch. He had to do something.

"We'll do everything in our power to find your daughter, ma'am." He handed her a sheet of paper. "Write down everything you know. Her height, weight, what she was wearing, anything that might help us when we locate her."

She scribbled things down in a fury, and he hoped he'd be able to read her handwriting. But he was in a hurry and her chicken scratches would have to do.

And now Bonnie was out of his line of sight. It annoyed him that he was stuck here and he couldn't check if she'd gone back home where he could deal with her properly.

Finally, after what seemed like ages, the woman finished writing. She handed the report back to him.

"You have to find my daughter!" she wailed.

"Don't worry, ma'am. We'll do everything we can. Please come to the station later this afternoon."

Without responding, she ran back to her house. Probably to call some more people or something. Not that he cared, because he had two important things to do:

Find Bonnie and shut her up, and get rid of the lump in the trunk.

***

Cindy Mackey thought this might be the best possible ice cream cone ever. She gobbled it down and wished she hadn't, but it had tasted so good!

She waved goodbye to the ice cream man and wondered if she should go home yet. But she didn't want to. She wanted to see if the other man would drive by.

The first time she saw him she wondered why he drove in the police car but didn't have his siren on. Didn't all policemen want to let people know they were around? Or was he not working?

Then she saw him another time, and another. Driving slowly in circles, like he was watching someone.

Just like she was watching him.

But this time she would talk to him. She had to. She wanted to know why he was always going round and round. Didn't it make him dizzy?

When the police car came round to start another loop, she waved at him frantically.

He rolled down the window.

"Officer Gleason!" she squealed. He was her favorite. He came to school to talk to her class sometimes, to tell them what it was like to be a policeman in their little town. She loved to hear him talk about it.

"Well hello there, ma'am," the policeman said. Cindy giggled. She was too young to be called "ma'am."

"Why do you ride around in circles?"

He smiled at her. "Want to find out for yourself?"

She nodded, bouncing up and down. She knew she looked like her friend Andrea's little puppy but she was so excited.

"But here's the thing. You have to get in the trunk."

"Why?"

He grinned. "Because it's even more fun that way, and you're lucky. You're small enough to fit."

He got out of the car and opened the trunk. She got in and he slammed it shut.

When she felt the car move, she wondered why it didn't seem so much fun. Then she understood: because it was so much hotter in the trunk than it was outside.

And her ice cream was gone.

KEVIN WIGNALL

is the author of four novels, two of which have been optioned for film, including the most recent, *Who is Conrad Hirst?*. He's done good things and a few bad things, but there are no bodies, and if there were you wouldn't find them.

THE PREACHER
KEVIN WIGNALL

HECTOR could see that one apology wasn't going to be enough. Either that or the old man hadn't really believed his first apology, which was understandable because it hadn't been genuine. But then, Hector had only been flippant because he'd thought the old man had to be joking. Because who took offense over stuff like that in this day and age? Hector's grandmother was nearly ninety and she could probably teach this old guy some new words. Even so ...

"Hey look, I really am sorry, man, I didn't realize. I'll be more careful." He didn't get a response so he looked across at him.

"Just keep your eyes on the road."

Hector faced forward and made a show of looking out at the night-time streets.

Sidney, the old man, had the feeling he and the young punk wouldn't become friends. It wasn't just the cursing and the profanity, it was an air the punk had about him, like no standard was too low. And he just didn't shut up, either—he just never ran out of things to say.

Of course, Mr. Costello had asked Sidney to take him under his wing, felt he just needed a little guidance, that he'd come on with the right role model, so here they were, driving out to Nolan's house to sort out a little company business. And because Mr. Costello had asked him to take the punk along, he was taking the punk along, that's the guy he was.

He could tell the punk was thinking about something now, that he was itching to speak yet again.

Hector had kept turning the word over in his mind, the word that had upset the old man. Having said that, the old man was such a stickler, he probably got upset if someone pronounced "oregano" in the wrong way. But the word that had actually upset him also upset a lot of people, and the more he thought about it, that hardly seemed fair, because it was a good word.

"You know," said Hector, "that word I just used, you know, the word you didn't like, I mean, the F word ..."

"I know which word you mean," snapped Sidney.

"Yeah, well that one. I mean, why is it a bad word? I don't mean, why is it like a curse word, I mean, why do people use it to talk about bad things, because it's a good thing. You know, to fu ... What I'm saying is, to do that thing is a good thing, enjoyable, so why do people use the word to describe bad things?"

It was a twenty minute drive to Nolan's place, forty minutes there and back, and Sidney wasn't convinced he'd be able to do the whole trip without shooting the punk just to shut him up. He wouldn't mind if he said anything that made the slightest bit of sense, but it was all this rambling stream-of-consciousness weirdness.

"Are you on drugs? I mean, are you high right now?"

Hector laughed and said, "I'm serious, man. You know it's like ... well, let's call it the C word, you know, to describe a woman's er ..."

"I *know* which word you mean."

"I would hope so," said Hector with a knowing smile that made Sidney want to slap his face. If the punk hadn't been driving he'd have done just that. "It's a bad word, the worst word, but it describes one of the greatest things ever. Haven't you ever wondered, why that is?"

"No, Hector, I haven't, just like your parents probably never wondered why you didn't get into Harvard." Sidney thought he'd try to change the subject and said, "How d'you end up with a name like Hector, anyway?"

"My dad was half Spanish."

"Which half?"

"On his mother's side, obviously." He glanced across at the old man and said, "My name's Murphy." The old man nodded his understanding and pointed forward, telling him to keep his eyes on the road.

The old man was senile, that was clearly the problem. Or else he'd done loads of coke or something back in the day. He acted all prim and proper, but these guys were all young in the '70s and he'd seen *Casino*, he'd seen *Scarface*—they were all the biggest cokeheads.

"Oh, man, this friend of mine had a cousin called Tamara and she'd get wasted at parties when she was, like, sixteen, and let us play Tamara's Ti … Well, I won't say the word, I know you don't like words like that, but I'm referring to her, you know, her bre …" Hector wasn't sure if even breasts would be out of bounds. "Her chest things, packets, whatever."

Sidney was staring at him, dumbstruck. It was bad enough when his nonsense was actually related to the here and now, but this new story had apparently been plucked out of the ether.

"I know the word you're looking for, but that still doesn't make it any clearer. What on God's good earth are you talking about?"

"Give me a minute, man. This game. See, she'd strip naked to the waist and lay on a table and let all us guys snort coke right off her … you know, the things we were just talking about." He was overcome briefly by the memory of the last such party, the summer before last. "And she was loaded up top, if you know what I'm saying. She was *nice*."

"Why would you tell me that story?" Sidney was wondering if this kid had frazzled something in his brain and had lost any sense of discernment or understanding of what might be an appropriate story for the company he was in. "Seriously, what is it about me that made you think I might want to hear that story? Better than that, tell me what suddenly inspired you to share it with me! I'm curious, Hector, I really would like to know ... Actually, forget that, I don't want to know what's going on in your mind, but I'd like to know why you thought that was an appropriate story to tell on this occasion."

Hector had changed his mind. Clearly, the old man hadn't done enough drugs back in the day. If he had, he wouldn't be quite so uptight now. And man, was he uptight.

"It's just a story, you know. Just something I thought of. I mean, isn't that what we're supposed to do? Like, we're two buddies on a job together, talking about stuff, swapping stories."

"You hear me telling any stories?"

"I bet you could tell some stories, things you did back in the day." He was about to give the old man a playful punch on the arm but didn't, thinking he probably wouldn't go in for that kind of thing, either. Besides, he was old, really old, and a playful punch on the arm could be bad news—it could cause a blood clot or something serious like that.

"Back in the day! You don't know what you're talking about. And we're not buddies, and we're not on a job together—you're tagging along to watch me, to learn some people skills. That'll actually involve you watching and keeping your mouth shut."

"I'm all eyes and ears, no mouth, trust me." With an afterthought, he said, "Does that mean no stories at all?"

Sidney had to hand it to him, the kid was persistent. "It means no stories like that one. I have a daughter who's sixteen."

"Is her name Tamara?"

"If her name was Tamara I'd be chopping you into pieces in a dumpster right now."

"Hey man, I was only joking." Though clearly, it was completely wasted because the old man's sense of humor had been sucked out of his nose by aliens or something—they probably had it in a jar on their home planet right now, realizing they'd stolen the wrong one. "I knew Tamara wasn't your daughter. For one, she's eighteen now, not sixteen, and she's my friend's cousin, you know."

"I was joking too," said Sidney, realizing that even the broadest brush strokes of humor were wasted on the punk. "I haven't chopped anyone up in a dumpster in nearly twenty years."

Now they were getting somewhere. "You really did that!"

"No, I'm still joking." He remembered what Mr. Costello had said about showing him the ropes, giving him the right moral guidelines. "Hector, you have to understand that we're in a serious business, and you don't run a serious business on threats and violence. Sure, sometimes threats and violence are necessary, just to make people understand how serious you are about your business ethic, but it is always the option of last resort."

Hector waited a couple of beats, wondering if the old man was finished. For someone who didn't like talking, he was good at churning out the boring speeches. God help them all when his daughter got married. On the good side, he guessed the old man was talking about the job, Nolan—the option of last resort.

"Can I do him?"

It was pointless, thought Sidney. He didn't know if there was such a thing as a clinical moron, but this kid Hector was about as close as anyone was ever likely to get.

"Can you do who?"

"Nolan. The option of last resort."

"Kid, you don't know what you're talking about. You just leave everything to me when we get to Nolan's place. You just watch and learn, remember?"

"Sure, I remember," said Hector. It was pretty frustrating though, knowing he'd have to watch this fossil blow Nolan's brains out when he was itching to do it himself. That was how people learned, by picking up the gun and pulling the trigger.

"I had someone pull a gun on me once. Threatened to shoot me in the ... well, you know, he threatened to shoot me so I wouldn't ever have kids, in the groin-type area."

The guy with the gun had clearly been a generation too late, but Sidney decided to play this one straight, giving the punk the benefit of the doubt, offering him the opportunity to give a little background. "So he wasn't a friend?"

"He's not a friend anymore," said Hector. "He was my best friend until he pulled a gun on me. Never seen him since, and if I saw him again, I'd pop a cap in his ... well, I'd hurt him. He was a motherfu ... He wasn't nice, if you know what I'm saying."

"What did you do?"

This guy was just like his parents. Hector couldn't believe it. Old people were always just too quick to jump on top of them. What did you do? You must have done something. There's always two sides to every story. Always the same thing.

"I didn't do anything. Why would you assume I'd done something?"

"Hector, I'm not a cop, I'm just asking what happened. If it helps, why did your friend pull a gun on you?"

"It was nothing. I was doing his girlfriend, that's all."

"You were *doing* his girlfriend?"

"Yeah, you know, I was ... that word, the word I apologized for, I was ..."

"Hector, I know what you mean. I was just questioning how that constitutes nothing at all." The kid look baffled and Sidney wondered if he was just so completely out of step, that morals had disappeared completely. He hated to think any of his own children would end up like this. "Do you consider it normal to date your friend's girl?"

"I wasn't dating her, I was ..."

"Hector, I know!"

"Well, yeah." The old man obviously thought he'd been around the block a couple of times, but Hector could clearly teach him a thing or two. "Let me tell you, this has always been my policy and I've had more girls in more ways than you could imagine. See, for one thing, you don't have any of the responsibility—no taking them out, no buying them stuff. For another, it's easier, you know, because there's only one other guy. With a single girl, you're up against all the other guys in the world. So ask yourself, why be in competition with every guy when you can just be in competition with just one?"

The punk looked pleased with himself, like he was only one step away from being awarded the Nobel Prize in some newly created category. Sidney waited, thinking he'd own up to it being another not very funny joke, but he kept looking smug and in the end, Sidney said, "What about loyalty and honor, doesn't that mean anything to you?"

"Of course! I'm the most honorable and loyal guy you'll ever meet." Hector didn't know where the old man was getting off—what was he doing trying to connect girls and stuff with loyalty and honor. It just didn't make any sense.

Sidney thought of his wife and daughter and how much he'd rather be with them right now, not heading out to Nolan's place with this deranged punk. Still, he'd be back with them soon enough, and he knew one thing, if either one of them ever had to deal with someone like Hector, he wouldn't be responsible for his actions.

He could see Nolan's house on the tree-lined street up ahead of them so he said quickly, "That joke I made about the dumpster. It wasn't a joke, it was 1983, and if you're ever so much as in the same room as my daughter, I won't even hesitate."

"You're pretty scary," said Hector, flattering the old man, because in truth, he reckoned it was all front, like a lot of these guys from the past.

"I know," said Sidney, but he wondered if Hector had the slightest idea how scary he'd been and could still be. "It's that house on the left. Pull over."

"Nice place," said Hector as he parked, looking across the lawn at the double-fronted house with ivy growing all the way to the roof.

"Remember …"

"I know, listen and learn."

They got out of the car and walked up the path, then up the three steps to the front door. Hector was faster up the steps and rang the bell, then cursed under his breath because he knew the old man would get all precious about it. Sidney let it go, the punk was just eager, but he couldn't see him ever coming to anything.

Nolan opened the door. He was in his shirt sleeves and was either wearing contacts or just didn't bother with his glasses in the house. He stared at Hector first, but then fixed on Sidney with the shock of recognition and said fearfully, "You're the preacher."

Hector looked at the old man. He'd heard a couple of people talk about a guy called the preacher, but he'd never realized they were talking about him. The old man had just nodded in response and now Nolan looked like he was about to cry and wet himself all at the same time.

"Please, I'll do anything, I'm begging you please." He put his hand up, changing his plea, as he said, "Okay, but look not here, not in front of my family."

This was cool, thought Hector, the old man was the preacher and this guy Nolan was about to be dog food.

"Mr. Nolan, you don't understand," said Sidney, reaching inside his jacket.

Nolan started sobbing, his words almost inaudible, but something about mercy. What was it with people nowadays, thought Sidney, that they never listened? He held the envelope, fat and pleasing in the hand, out towards Nolan, who looked at it like Sidney had just offered him a pineapple.

"What's this?"

"Mr. Nolan, if you'd let me finish, Mr. Costello wanted me to tell you that there had been a misunderstanding and that he's very sorry for any distress this might have caused to you or your family. He's been completely happy with your legal work on his behalf, he completely understands if you won't want to work with him in the future, and this is just a small compensation. We're really very sorry."

Sidney might as well have let Hector do the talking because Nolan was staring at him like he'd explained the visit in Swahili. He took the envelope in slow motion and opened it to look at the bundle of notes inside. He looked up again, and stared in confusion at Sidney.

He laughed then, and said, "I thought, I mean ..."

"I know," said Sidney, sympathetically. He heard someone coming down the stairs behind Nolan then, and said quietly, "Dry your eyes, Mr. Nolan."

Nolan took a handkerchief and dried his eyes and blew his nose, and looked grateful to Sidney for thinking about how he'd look in front of his family.

Hector was struggling to connect here, like the aliens had been and sucked something out of *his* brain and suddenly nothing made sense. He'd just heard the old man named as the preacher, one of the most fearsome men ever talked about, and they'd come all the way out here to apologize to someone! What next, helping old ladies across the road?

Then he got distracted. The old man and Nolan were saying something to each other when the most beautiful girl appeared on the stairs in the hallway, dressed in one of those skinny-rib t-shirts—they did it for him every time, and she didn't have much going on up there, but she was *nice*.

Sidney saw the girl and heard Hector's tongue hit the floor, even though she had to be fourteen at most. He really was a sick puppy. "Okay, Mr. Nolan, we have to be going. Once again, sorry for the distress."

"Thank you. Thank you very much."

"Let's go, Hector."

The door closed quickly and the two of them headed back to the car. Hector wasn't happy. Not only had they not killed anyone, or even given anyone a beating, just as things had been getting interesting, the old man had called it a day.

"That was one beautiful piece of ..."

"Don't say it, Hector."

Sidney took his gun out and gave Hector a sharp little crack across the top of the head.

"Fu ... Fiddle! What did you do that for!"

"You're a degenerate. I'm trying to knock some decency into that thick skull of yours."

Hector got into the car, rubbing his head, but couldn't help laughing. "My grandfather used to do that. Not with a gun obviously, but he used to crack me on the head and say he'd knock some sense into me."

He pulled away and Sidney said, "I'm guessing he either hit you too hard, or not hard enough."

Hector laughed. It was all on a pretty weird wavelength but the old man was actually pretty funny, even if it was a pain in the posterior that he couldn't curse or use profanity around him, or talk about sex or drugs. Had he just *thought* the word posterior? That was something—he was even censoring his thoughts around the old man.

"Say, anyway, why do they call you the preacher?"

Sidney looked at him and said, "Take a wild guess," and the punk started to laugh. Sidney laughed too. He wasn't sure they were both laughing at the same joke, but they were both laughing at the same time, and he guessed that was a start. Maybe he'd show him the ropes yet.

EXPLETIVE DELETED
SECTION TWO

FUCK

OLEN STEINHAUER'S

most recent novel, *Victory Square*, ends a five-book sequence of thrillers chronicling the Cold War from the perspective of a small and entirely fictional Eastern European country. He lives in Budapest.

HUNGARIAN LESSONS
OLEN STEINHAUER

AGOTA was the Real Queen Bitch of Vaci Street—that's how she marketed herself to the Ukrainian pimps when she arrived in Budapest. She was from the western Hungarian plains, six feet tall, and an ounce creamier than the other whores who traipsed the after-hours tourist strip. She stood out, and when Mikhail first approached her—he later admitted—Agota terrified him. Mikhail, a roughneck from Kiev with three bullet scars, wasn't easy to scare.

So he beat her, then hooked her on heroin. But Agota cleaned herself up after a year of running the old scam: Find a lone male tourist, perhaps two, walking Vaci Street at night, and pretend you're just a pretty suburban girl out window shopping. Strike up a conversation—in English, of course—and ask if he wants to buy you a drink; you know a very intimate place, just around the corner. Doesn't matter what you order, the bill is always somewhere between five hundred and a thousand dollars. And when he complains, the bald Ukrainians with tattooed necks come out from the back and escort him to the closest ATM.

That's the easy mark, because no matter how many guidebooks explain this scam in precise detail, boys from London or Los Angeles want to believe they're so damned irresistible that a beautiful, six-foot stranger would just be gagging for it.

Of course there was plenty of fucking too, because when you're so striking, and working for a man as connected as Mikhail, there are plenty of fat politicians with spare Marriott suites on the

Danube, rooms they use when their families are off at Lake Balaton or in Vienna buying knick knacks. A girl like Agota quickly became a favorite, with regular Gabors who loved climbing up each inch of her body, and the more astute Gabors who brought her in to help seal an international coal export treaty, or acquire the Chinese computer delegation's cut-rate mainframes used to run the Defense Ministry's lighting system.

Suffice to say that, by the time I met her, Agota was on intimate terms with people I'd only seen in newspapers or on television, and she probably knew them better than their own families did.

***

I'd come in from the suburbs to have dinner with my new Hungarian publishers—Pidkora Editions—to discuss marketing plans. Viktor, the head publisher, wanted me to do a national tour of bookstores, but didn't seem to realize I couldn't read— or speak—Hungarian. I needed to make this clear. But what I thought would be a small on-expenses dinner at the Marriott with Viktor and my editor, Erika, turned out to be an elaborate banquet for "International Presses and Linguistics with an Emphasis on the Fictional Crime"—that's the literal translation. In fact, after a dinner of paprika chicken that sat in my stomach like lead, the real purpose became clear: It was just an excuse for Viktor, the publisher, to stand at a podium and address (in painful monotone) a conference room half-full of government ministers. Because in a small country you can do this. Get conference space at a foreign hotel, slap an obtuse name on it, and the Prime Minister might even sit at your table.

I learned later that it was all about subsidies, which Viktor's company was in desperate need of.

I sat at one of twenty round, white-draped tables with Erika and Andras (the Minister of Finance, it turned out) and the six-foot "friend" he'd brought along named Agota. While Viktor spoke in his dull, flowery Hungarian at the front of the room, beneath a PIDKORA EDITIONS KFT sign, I stared at the back of Agota's head, her black mane glittering in the spotlights whenever she shifted or laughed politely at what I assumed were Viktor's jokes. I'd never quite seen anything like her. My girlfriend was back in the suburbs, so a little overt staring didn't seem much of a crime.

I joined the applause when Viktor finally ran out of things to say and listened to Erika's translated explanation of the speech. Agota turned back to the table, smiled and held the Finance Minister's hand, then looked at me very intensely. My feet went cold, and I couldn't hear what Erika was telling me, though I nodded, blinked, smiled—all the signs that I was, in fact, right there with her.

After shaking an inordinate number of hands, Viktor joined us at the table and shook my hand as well, though I wasn't sure why. Then he began to explain why and how he was going to make me the most famous foreign novelist in Hungary—"More famouser than Dan Brown!" he said, laughing. He was drunk. He said they'd make my readings into big events, with newspaper notices and maybe even a television spot. That all sounded great, but I still didn't speak Hungarian. I told him so, and though his smile didn't change, I could see the elation fade from his eyes.

On the other side of the table, Agota translated the conversation for the Finance Minister, whose hand sometimes appeared at the edge of the table, just over her groin. Viktor said some urgent Hungarian words to Erika, who shrugged and answered just as urgently. He looked at me. "You don't speak Hungarian?"

"No, and I've said that over and over again."

"Well, you must learn!" he said, raising his champagne. "How long have you been here in Budapest?"

"Three years."

A quick intake of breath as he realized that if I hadn't learned it in three years, chances were I didn't give a damn about the language. "We can get you a teacher." He turned to Erika.

"Yes," said Erika, trying to display confidence she didn't feel.

Then Agota leaned forward, and all eyes turned to her. "I have a friend," she said in her thick, cumbersome accent. "He learned Hungarian in only two months. Can you imagine?" She smiled, and we all smiled with her.

"A school?" I asked.

She looked puzzled.

"He went to a school?"

"Oh! No," she said. "I taught him. We were very close."

The Finance Minister moved his roaming hand from her groin back to his own and cleared his throat, but smiled.

Then Viktor said something to her in Hungarian, and it seemed—surprisingly—to surprise her. Agota bit the tip of a long red thumbnail and shook her head no, then answered him. But Viktor, drunk and full of himself, pressed. Agota smiled over at me as my publisher chattered on, and I felt myself flushing. I leaned over to Erika. "What's going on?"

"He's trying to buy you lessons."

Just then the Finance Minister threw his silk napkin on the table and, red-faced, said something rough to Viktor, who suddenly went mute. The minister stood and tugged Agota's arm; she slowly stood as well. "It was very nice to meet you," she said to me, then they walked off, Agota towering over the black-suited minister, who walked like a duck.

I glared at Viktor. "What the hell did you say to piss him off?"

He lit a Kent. "Fucking Fidesz fascist."

Fidesz was the ruling political party of the moment, arguably nationalist, that was always taking heat from lefties like my publisher. "But what did you *say*, Viktor?"

"I just tried to hire her for some lessons."

"You know what you did," said Erika.

"What did I do?"

Erika turned to me with a sour expression. "She's a whore. Agota is. And the minister thought he wanted to buy her for the night."

"Oh," I said. While the possibility had occurred to me, I'm just naïve enough not to believe the whispers of my intuition. I didn't really care about the nationalist Finance Minister, but Agota: "She understood, right? *She* knew you weren't trying to buy her for sex."

Viktor blew a smoke ring. "I don't care *what* the slut thought. Sleeping with the fucking fascists."

***

The chicken paprika with potato noodles, mixed with the embarrassment that followed, gave me an overwhelming urge to shit. So I excused myself and wandered through a sea of suits to the exit, and in the corridor found the men's room, a long stone-tiled expanse with high bronze sinks and something that might have been the Hungarian national anthem playing quietly over speakers. A wall separated the motion-detector urinals from the rest of the room, and the bronze stall doors went all the way to the floor.

I've always felt you can tell a lot about a place by the way they design and keep their bathrooms, and the Marriott, by this estimation, was all about style and power. It made one—well, it made *me* feel as if there wasn't anything in this world I couldn't have, or do, if I really set my mind to it. Then I opened a stall door—silent, well oiled hinges—and found the Finance Minister sitting on the toilet, pants around his ankles, and Agota bowed between his legs, sucking his cock.

I froze for just an instant, but long enough to know from the smell that the guy was shitting while he was getting his blowjob. Only after he let out a wild-eyed Magyar yelp and I slammed the door shut did the filthiness of this really hit me, and I leaped to the farthest stall and closed myself inside.

I heard his voice—angry, determined—but not hers. I imagine he told her to not stop, because she didn't, and soon he let out that international male gasp of orgasm. I made sure the door to my stall was locked as I covered my ears and did my own business. Even through my paprika-stained fingers I could hear them leave the stall quietly, then the bathroom door open and shut. I released my ears. Then I heard a tap on my stall door.

"Hello?"

It was Agota.

At first I didn't answer—I didn't want any part in this—but she tapped again and spoke in a very soft, almost maternal voice. "Mister More-Famous-Than-Dan-Brown?"

Which made me laugh. I said, "Agota, I'm sorry. I didn't know you were in there."

"Want to unlock the door?"

"Let me finish first."

"It's only fair, isn't it?"

She was right, and she was wrong, but I unlocked the door anyway. She opened it and stood smiling down at me. From my low angle her legs seemed very long. Then I noticed something. I touched my cheek. "You've got something. There."

She wiped some of the Finance Minister's sperm from her cheek and looked at it, raising the corner of her lip in an expression of disgust. Then she went over to the bronze sinks and began washing up. "He's upset, you know."

"It was an honest mistake."

"I told him I'd talk to you."

"About what?"

"You're a famous writer."

"I'm not famous."

She shrugged into the mirror, eyes on me. "A writer, we'll say. He's afraid you'll write about it."

"Why would I do that?"

She dried herself with a towel and turned to face me, leaning against the sink and crossing her ankles. "He's a politician. He doesn't want press. Is that so hard to understand?"

"Okay," I said, reaching for the toilet paper. "I won't write about it. I promise."

"He's a politician. He doesn't believe promises."

I looked at the paper in my hand, then at her.

"Go ahead," she told me.

So I crouched and cleaned myself as well, trying to talk around my embarrassment. "I, uh—I think the minister should remember I'm not a politician. He can take my word. I'm not interested in writing about it."

"I know you're honest," said Agota. She opened up a very tiny purse I hadn't noticed before and removed a clear plastic sack of cocaine. "But he doesn't know that. And he's too important to take chances on the honesty of an American." She shook the bag. "Your president used to do a lot of this, didn't he?"

"Back in the day, sure."

"And you, Mister Most Famous? Did you do this in the day?"

At that point I was zipping up my drawers. I didn't want to sound like a schmuck. "Sure, I've snorted in my time."

"Let's do a few lines. It'll make everything else easier."

At the sink next to her, I washed my hands. "What do you mean, everything else?"

She handed me the towel. "You're going to have some fun."

"Why do I need to be coked up to have fun?"

She leaned close, pressed her damp cheek against mine and kissed my ear. It says something that I didn't pull back. Then she whispered: "Trust me, you'll like it. Let's go upstairs first."

She took my hand and led me out of the bathroom. In the corridor we turned right instead of left, where more politicians and publishers were smoking outside the conference room. A few peered jealously at me being led off to the elevators with the most beautiful woman at that conference. I peered back at them as well, vaguely hoping someone—dull Viktor, perhaps—would come and interrupt.

In the mirrored elevator she smiled again and straightened the tie my girlfriend had helped me with before I came into town. I suddenly wondered what time it was, and what she was doing. What was on TV now that it was (I checked my mobile) ten-thirty?

And why on Earth, standing in an elevator mirrored with bronze trim—with *her*—was I thinking about television schedules?

"Lost," I said involuntarily.

"What?" She touched my shoulder with her long nails.

"The TV show. *Lost*. I usually watch it about now."

"Hmm," she said with the vague scorn of the uninitiated. "Television."

I followed her down a pastel-toned ninth-floor corridor with doors spaced out enough for me to know they led to suites, not the tiny hotel rooms of my past. That's when I started to become frightened. I still couldn't figure out how going to a room with this woman was going to ensure my silence. And then I did. Behind one of these doors, someone was going to kill me.

"Wait," I said.

She stopped, pivoting on a stiletto heel. That smile again. "Yes?"

"I'm not going anywhere, understand? I'm going back downstairs."

"You don't trust me?"

"I don't *know* you."

She walked up to me, bent close, and kissed my lips. She did something with her tongue that I still don't understand, but the effect was wonderful. "I want you," she whispered. "I honestly do. And this way I can have you." She gave me another of those kisses. "I like writers."

"But the minister."

"He's fine with it. And don't worry; I'm clean."

She took my hand and placed it on her ass, encouraging me to squeeze. My knees weren't working right anymore.

* * *

As expected, 920 was an enormous suite with three rooms. And it was empty. I locked the door as she went to a fully-stocked oak bar and poured a vermouth for herself, then looked questioningly at me.

"Vodka," I said.

"Very good." She miraculously produced a bottle of chilled Ketel One she poured into a martini glass. "Come on, relax," she said as she took the cocaine out of her purse again and began laying out lines on the glass coffee table.

I sat across from her and watched her expertly use a razor blade on that white powder. She rolled a fifty-Euro bill into a tight straw and held it out to me.

"The famous writer first."

Looking back, I still can't see how I didn't flee. Yes, Agota was immensely attractive; and yes, that Columbian was of interest. But this wasn't my world. I spent my life in the suburbs of Budapest with my girlfriend and our dog, typing out little fantasies on my laptop and emailing them to New York for the all-too-seldom wire to my bank account. That really was my life in a nutshell. I sometimes wrote about this other world, the world of money, but I didn't feel comfortable in it—I didn't *know* it. I'd also just seen a government minister getting his cock sucked in the shitter—I knew the minister was scared. How could I not see the rest coming?

Fact is, I didn't want to see it coming.

The first line went down hard because, in truth, I'd done coke only once before, at a friend's mother's tea party. I'd stood around, sniffing maniacally, saying, "Has it hit me yet? Has it hit me yet?" much to the annoyance of my friend. But by the second line I saw how easy it could be, and just how fine you could feel. Agota did a few lines and used a remote control to turn on some music from hidden speakers—Sinatra sang "My Way," which made me yawn and then laugh with glee.

Agota, sniffing, came to join me on the leather sofa.

"What a song," I said.

"Yes." She started helping me with my pants.

✳✳✳

That's the last thing I remember. I assume it was something in the drink, because the cocaine, I'm sure, was good shit. I woke naked in the vast Marriott bed, alone. No Agota, just the soft lilt of more music coming from the lounge—Dean Martin singing a Christmas jingle. Though my dick and tongue were sore, I wasn't hungover or otherwise impaired, and that's how I was able to hop up in a panic and run around collecting my clothes. I checked my phone—my girlfriend had called seven times but had left only one message. She hoped I was having a good time—this was her way of saying, "Come home now." It was five in the morning, and through the blinds the sun was reflecting against the Buda-side castle, glimmering off the Danube. What a gorgeous city.

I wanted to remember what had happened, but couldn't. If I'd been drugged, I at least wanted to know what happened before I passed out. In all honesty I wanted to remember the sex, because at least that would be something. But I'd worry about that later. I dressed quickly and rushed to leave, then saw, taped to the back of the door, a Maxell DVD case with a single word scrawled on it:

QUIET

Inside was a store-bought rewritable DVD. I brought it over to the plasma television, under which was a DVD player. I tracked down all the remotes and began to watch.

The production quality was good. I saw myself and Agota enter the room. I locked the door and she poured my vodka, then we started on the coke. She really was achingly beautiful—that's the first thing I noticed—and that body. Wow. Then I realized this was shot at many different angles, and edited together semiprofessionally. I began looking around the room. I didn't see any cameras, but knew they were there. Then "My Way." On the screen Agota joined me on the couch and unzipped my fly. And I didn't pass out. I helped her with her clothes, and then it began.

We did things that I really wish I remembered, because I'd never done them before. Things I'd only seen in after-hours movies. And the cocaine just kept coming. I snorted it out of her ass crack, she snorted it off my balls. We put our faces everywhere and our organs, it seemed, could be given pleasure by anything. I was astounded, if only because I'd never witnessed myself so damned energetic. And I'd never been with a woman with so much energy. It was simultaneously thrilling and horrifying, if that makes any sense. I didn't yet feel the shame I'd feel when I returned to my girlfriend, nor the horror that faced me in the bathroom. I was just excited, and had to shift my pants around because of my uncomfortable, sore erection.

We didn't only fuck, which was nice. Once, we stopped and drank and lay intertwined, her magnificent thighs wrapped around my stomach, and talked. That's when she told me she was known, on the street, as the Real Queen Bitch. She told me about Mikhail, her pimp, and when I became upset that the man beat her, she said, "But he's just like all pimps, you know? He's not so bad." She was very relaxed and comfortable and open about her past, and I told her a little about myself, the places I'd lived, and how I wanted to be an Important Writer someday. She fingered my balls and said, "I know you will be."

Then we snorted another line and went back to it. Who *was* this man I was watching? A goddamned superhero.

As we were wrapping things up, Agota asked if I wanted another vodka. That's probably the one that knocked me out. Not that I would've given a fuck at that point, after having spent two hours doing all that. Amazing. The video ended with her handing me the vodka and me leaning close to kiss her, saying in my erudite way, "Wow."

Giddily, she said, "Want those Hungarian lessons now?"

Cut to black.

This was a way to keep me quiet, but a rather generous way. The minister had given me one hell of a night, and for that generosity he expected silence, or the video would make the rounds. Which was fine by me. I had no desire to utter a word about what I'd seen. But I needed to cover my tracks and, realizing I stank of sex, undressed again and went to the bathroom for a shower.

The suite's bathroom was much like the ones downstairs, stone tiles edged in bronze. But unlike downstairs, the tiles were speckled in red, and there was a stink here more pungent than the smell of myself, which made me immediately queasy. I looked down and saw why: Agota was on the floor, naked, split open from the neck to the groin, her sticky organs spilling out all over the tiles, the way an overcooked pan of Jiffy-Pop will explode popcorn all over the stove.

I choked, then stumbled back, and vomited on the lounge carpet.

A half hour later I'd made it out into the corridor. I hadn't showered; all I'd done was dress again and collect my phone and that DVD, but it seemed to take forever, and then, heading down in the elevator, where I was nearly sick again, it hit me: My fingerprints were everywhere. *Everywhere.* So I hammered the buttons to take me back up to the ninth floor. But it was too late. I had to go to the lobby first.

The doors opened, and as I waited for them to shut again a short, extremely hairy middle-aged man stepped in wearing a tie and jeans. He smiled at me, started to press #9, then realized it was already lit.

"Get lost?" he said with an extremely heavy Slavic accent.

"Uh, yes. No, just forgot something."

The doors slid shut.

The man smelled heavily of some rank cologne, and as the elevator rose again, he started humming to himself. It took me a moment, then I looked at him in the mirrored walls. "Is that 'My Way'?"

The man brightened. "*Da!* You like Sinatra?"

I nodded but didn't say anything; I didn't want to get into a conversation.

He said, "He is truly the king. You know? A voice like that, the way with the woman. Yes. The most exceptional man."

We were passing the fifth floor; I inhaled.

The man winked at me in the mirrored wall. "I'm Mikhail. You're Olen?"

My first reaction was that Agota had been right: I was a famous writer, and even a stranger in the Marriott knew my face. But no. This was Agota's pimp, Mikhail, the one who slapped her around now and then, "like all pimps, you know?"

"You all right, Olen?"

I tried to look at him, but my eyes were too wet to see a thing.

"Don't worry," he said, and placed a hand on my shoulder; I flinched. "Mikhail take care of everything. You go home."

"But, I—"

"I know, I know," said Mikhail as the doors opened onto the ninth floor corridor. I saw a blur of pastel. "The fingerprints. No worries, my friend. Mikhail is here to take care of everything." He stepped out of the elevator and held the door open as it knocked against his palm. "You go home, right? Take a bath. You stink."

He took his hand away and tapped his forehead in a kind of salute as the doors closed and I was faced with a reflection of myself.

***

Agota's mutilated corpse made the front page of most major papers in Hungary that day, and even the Austrian *Kurier* did a piece on the dangerous world of Eastern prostitution. But no matter how much conjecture—and there was a lot—popped up, no one seemed notice that obscure American writer living in their midst with shaking hands whenever the murder was brought up. Luckily, my girlfriend doesn't read newspapers.

She was still asleep when I returned home. I showered while our dog sat on the wet bathroom floor staring up at me. Accusingly. And when I slipped into bed beside her, I had my story established: Viktor insisted on keeping me out, showing me what a big man he was by giving me a tour of local strip clubs. I threw in a fight he had with my editor over his choice of drinking establishments, and that added verisimilitude. You see, I know my job.

And my job meant that, six months later, in the middle of a sweltering summer, I found myself on my first book tour. Viktor paid for an intensive Hungarian tutorial run by a pretty girl from Esztergom, but I made sure not to learn anything about her personal life, and she reacted to my coldness by giving me lousy lessons. So by the time of the tour I still couldn't speak the language, and Erika, my editor, had to come along as translator. It was awkward, and the potential readers were unimpressed by this, but it did work to some degree. I sat to the side as she read out passages, then we focused on the question-and-answer sessions, where I was asked mostly about Hungary. Why was I there? Wasn't the fictional country really just Hungary in disguise? When I told them no, they seemed rather disappointed, and when I told them the early books were based more on Romania, they were just annoyed.

Then in a bookstore in the old part of Debrecen, I got a question from a man in the back of the crowd I couldn't see. He said in English: "I think maybe a young American gets into a lot of trouble in a town like Budapest, no?"

Slavic accent. It was Mikhail.

"I don't get out much," I said. Erika translated (the answer received a few smiles), then I pointed to a fat woman who wanted to know why I didn't set my stories in Hungary; didn't I *like* my adopted home?

Afterward, people came up and spoke to me and handed me business cards—I again kicked myself for not printing up any for myself—and then I was faced with Mikhail. His thick black eyebrows kept shifting over his bright eyes as he said, "Maybe we can have the talk?"

We talked in the bookstore's bathroom—a dusty one-stall brick room—and he said he needed my help.

"I don't know how I can help you, Mikhail."

"I would like to go to the America."

"Well, have a nice trip."

"But," he said, shrugging genially, "there are problems. They don't want to give Mikhail visa."

"I can't help you with that. I can't even get my girlfriend a visa."

He shook his head, smiling. "You are the famous writer. Agota tell me that before she die. Mister More-Famous-Than-Dan-Brown, I think you can help me."

The mention of Agota's name fucked with my knees, but in a different way than her kiss had. "Honestly, Mikhail. I can't help you. What about that Finance Minister? You've got friends in the government."

Mikhail pursed his lips and exhaled, almost a whistle. "You don't read the papers, no? Fidesz voted out of power. The new guys, they got their own pimps." Then he patted me on the shoulder. "I have faith in you. On Monday I go for to apply again. And I expect to have visa. But if for some reason Mikhail has no visa, then I will have DVD party. You understand?"

***

I thoroughly pissed off the entire staff of Pidkora Editions Kft when I cancelled the rest of the tour and rushed back to Budapest and walked into the US Embassy that Friday afternoon. I didn't look good; I was sweating a lot, and the young man in the suit—Rodger, I think his name was—asked if I needed a towel to dry off my face. Of course, he had no idea who I was. I listed off my books and the prizes I'd been nominated for, but he didn't even blink. It was like talking to a wall.

"What can I do for you, Mister—" He looked down at the piece of paper I'd had to fill out at the security check. "Mister Steinhaver."

"Hauer. Steinhauer."

"Right. Well, what is it you need?"

I'd rehearsed the story on the train. I had a good friend, see, and he needed to go to America in order to meet with some of his friends. They were going to help me research my next book. "It's set to be published in five countries."

"What's it about?"

"You know, Russian Mafia, that kind of thing. Balkan Mafia too." I'd said that because, even though I had no interest in the subject, at parties it was the only thing people suggested I write about. But Rodger's eyes didn't shift from mine.

"Yes. Interesting." Not even trying to sound like he meant that. He looked at the other sheet I'd given him, the one with Mikhail's full name and a photocopy of his passport. "Well, you see Mister Steinhauer, this Mikhail Yekhanurov, he's a Ukrainian citizen. He needs to apply for a visa in Kiev."

I nodded, very seriously. "There's a time element here. I'm dealing with publisher schedules, that sort of thing. Isn't there any way ..."

"I'm afraid there isn't."

I wasn't too upset by this. I'd tried, and I'd tried honestly. Mikhail couldn't fault me that. But that night at the Negro bar by the Basillica, where some trance DJ was blowing out the speakers, he did fault me. He sat in a leather booth flanked by two bald Ukrainians with neck tattoos. "Mikhail, he tell you to try. You not try."

"I try, I tried," I said quickly. "But I'm *not* famous, and the rules are the rules."

"So you come to Kiev with me."

"What?" I said, cupping my ear. But I'd heard. I said, "No. Absolutely not."

"Is beautiful town, you know?"

"I don't have a visa for the Ukraine."

Mikhail leaned forward, heavy brows narrowing, then leaned back and let out a large, rather beautiful laugh. His companions laughed less prettily, and he slapped the table. He pointed at me. "I like you. I do. And that's why I tell you now, it's too late."

Despite his tone, I was shaking again, my knees going bad. "What's too late?"

"Oh," he shrugged. "The video. I send it off yesterday to MTV1. Tonight, I hear, will be the report."

No, not Music Television 1, but *Magyar Televízió* 1. The state television station.

I gripped the edge of the table. "What? But you—"

He held up a hand. "They offer the good money. You might want to leave the Hungary."

I was close to passing out. The throbbing music, the blood rushing to my head, and this laughing Ukrainian. I didn't understand a thing.

On Hungarian television they feel freer to show nudity than, say, back in the States, so I knew they would show most of the DVD. I didn't wait to find out, because an hour after that meeting in the Negro I was on a train heading out of Nyugati Station to Vienna. Riding through the dark countryside, I called my girlfriend and told her I was still in Debrecen, which she had no reason to disbelieve until the special was aired. I didn't know what else to say. By midnight I arrived at my Vienna hotel and started writing this.

***

The first draft of the story finishes with the above paragraph, and that's what I mailed to the Hungarian police Saturday morning. A confession and a statement of innocence, if that's what you can call it. I booked myself on the next free flight to New York on Tuesday night and stayed in my room for three days, going out only to buy schnitzels and vodka. I watched Austrian television that made no sense because my German is lousy. Then, on Tuesday morning, there was a knock on my door. The Austrian police had come to fetch me.

It all came out in the trial, though I learned of it in a Vienna police station, where a visiting Hungarian policeman had a chat with me. He was an old man with a kind face, but his English was rough and brutal, which seemed like a sign to me. So I wept and insisted that I'd never hurt Agota. No matter what they saw on that video, they had to believe that I hadn't killed her. Okay, I'd snorted some coke off her ass, yes, but that was it.

Tamás, as he told me his name was, pulled up a steel chair and sat in front of me. "What is the video?" he said.

"The one they showed on TV."

Tamás smiled a little, then shook his head. "Mister Steinhauer, you must explain to me this."

So I did, again, everything I've already put on paper here, and that was when he started to laugh. No, there had been no television special on my sexual deviance. "You think you are that famous?" said Tamás. "Andras Papp, Finance Minister—*he*—yes, that is famous man. It is you. The story what you send us. It ruin his career."

"But Mikhail," I began, then got quiet. Finally, I asked, "What's going on?"

By the time we returned to Budapest in a Hungarian paddy-wagon, I had my answer. Forced into a corner by the accusations my story had given light to, Andras Papp, Fidesz Finance Minister (no, the elections hadn't changed a thing—Mikhail knew how ignorant I was), insisted that this sinister American novelist had invented a story about him to help his faltering literary career. Then I had killed a woman and framed Andras Papp for murder, and for getting blowjobs while on the john.

Of course, no one believed Andras Papp, and a week later he was sacked.

Then put on trial.

And convicted of murder.

And me? I became, for a few months, more famous than Dan Brown—in Hungary, at least. In his new, slick office overlooking the Danube, just before a board-of-directors meeting, Viktor presented me with some incomprehensible certificate saying that I was the biggest selling writer in the 10-year history of Pidkora Editions Kft. "What did I tell you, Olen? I made you very famous!"

He was also ecstatic because the new Finance Minister had promised extensive subsidies for the company. But I was doubtful about everything. I felt like shit, and all I wanted was to return home to the country where I believed I understood things. I said, "I don't think you made me famous, Viktor. I think I made you famous."

But nothing could dampen his good mood. "You think so?" He checked his watch. "Time to go."

I followed him down the hall to where the board of directors would meet. Just outside the door stood a small man with thick eyebrows grinning wildly at me.

"Hello, Mikhail."

He clasped my shoulders with manly affection, and at that moment I hated this country with more intensity than I thought possible. "You look sad, my friend! Why? You tell me. Anything Mikhail can do for you, he do!"

I shrugged him off, and on the way to the elevator muttered, "You could find me a new girlfriend, you fuck."

OTIS TWELVE

won the 2006 Debut Dagger Award for his novel, *Imp: Being the Lost Notebooks of Rufus Wilmot Griswold in the Matter of the Death of Edgar Allan Poe*, a Gothic-Noir study of the mysterious last, lost week of Edgar Allan Poe's life that brings the crime, horror and art of a violent age to life. His current project is a Psychedelic-Gothic tale entitled *The Romance of Certain Old Clothes*. Twelve's short fiction has appeared in *Crimespree Magazine*, *North American Review*, *The Reader*, and *The Templeton Prize Anthology* (2005). Otis regularly attains total enlightenment—usually on Tuesdays—before lunch— for brief nano-seconds—then he forgets. Fuck.

FLUFF
OTIS TWELVE

"TAKE that cock out of your mouth, Sarah, and talk to me."

I said it as nice as I could. It was a rather awkward social situation, so I kept my voice soft, barely a whisper, at first. "Take that cock out of your mouth, Sarah, and talk to me."

She was on her knees with her eyes closed, working away at the guy's dick. There was a lot of commotion as the tech crew set up lights in the tile kitchen down a short hall. A CD player was blaring out some music. The song was "Beautiful Day" by U2. It wasn't a beautiful day. It was a crappy day.

I'd been kicked out of my shit-hole studio apartment in West Hollywood. I was having my period. My car smelled like frying vomit. My teeth hurt and the meth was running low. I'd snuck in through the dry-rotted patio doors of a faux-adobe house in fucking Reseda and I was on all fours, trying not to be seen, watching a topless old pal suck dick. It was a crappy day.

✳✳✳

Mommy's been really tired. I haven't been getting any sleep. I shouldn't be telling you this—using language like this. You're just a kid. A little ten-year-old sick kid. But I don't know if you're going to wake up ever again.

I want to tell you what happened. How much your mommy loves you. I know I've been a piece of shit as a mother. I know, and

I'm so sorry. They took you away from me, and maybe that was for the best. I tried my best. Maybe God wanted it this way. If I were any other kind of mommy—any better type with an apron and a sheet of cookies fresh out of the oven—well, maybe you're blessed that I am the way I am. And fuck, they didn't take you away from me because I had a dirty mouth. Oh, that's kind of funny.

✳✳✳

Anyway, I was trying to get the stupid bitch's attention. I knelt down on the floor right behind her.

"Sarah, really. Stop with the cock and talk to me."

I knew Sarah's eyes were shut. Blowjobs have shitty scenery. This is the voice of experience. I've tried that particular line of work myself.

I just wanted some information. I knew Sarah's mind was wandering—probably thinking about vintage clothing, or a hot dog at Pink's, or last night's episode of "Lost," or China Ruby nail lacquer, or trying to remember to buy toilet paper on the way home. When you're a fluff girl, it's just another day at the office.

I could have reached over and tapped her on the shoulder. But I think it's rude to touch people without permission. I leaned over until my mouth was about six inches from her ear.

"Sarah. Dammit, I've got to talk to you!"

She snapped her head around when she finally heard me. There was a slurping sound and a percussive pop as the purpled head sprang out of her cheek. "Ginny? What the fuck?"

"Ow!" The guy attached to the damp erection seemed upset. His dick was oscillating like a bent car antenna.

"Pop Goes the Weasel, Timmy."

"You not supposed to be here. You're like …" Timmy's face strained as he looked for a word inside his shaved, too-small head.

"You're like … You're like not supposed to be here." He hadn't found anything on the search.

"Shut up, Timmy. Take your boner elsewhere. The grownups have to talk."

"But, I …" Timmy might have been trying to look angry, but his eyes were too close together. It wasn't a big deal. Timmy never got a close up, at least not one involving his face.

"Money shot time! On set for the money shot!" The voice came from the kitchen.

"Get to work, Timmy," I said.

Sarah grabbed his rod and gave it a couple quick pumps, like she was adjusting a kid's collar on their way out the door. "You're ready. Get in there."

He dropped the bathrobe off his shoulders and put his best "Italian" look on his square face—that's what he called it—"the Italian." I thought he looked like a drugged donkey, but people tell me I'm just a critical person.

In the narrow hallway he had to turn sideways to get past the soundman. It was a tight squeeze. "Keep your prick off my microphone, asshole. Fuckin' secretor."

There was an over-the-hill blond with huge boobs waiting for him, perched on a cheap dinette table. Her legs were spread. A make-up girl was backing away from her freshly powdered, shaved pussy. Brazilian wax-jobs were the rage, but the glare was always a problem. Every art faces its own set of challenges.

"Whatta' you doing here, Ginny?" Sarah pulled an antibacterial wipe out of her purse and dabbed at her lips. "How's your kid? I hear he's sick."

"Real sick. You seen Peter?"

"Fuck." Sarah wiped her hands with the throwaway towelette. "What you wanna' see him for, Ginny? There's been enough trouble, ain't there?"

"I heard he was shooting here today."

"Good way to put it." Sarah laughed. Her boobs bounced. Well, the left breast did. The right tit was frozen hard like it was superglued to her ribcage. Probably was.

"Is he here?"

"No. He came last night. Ha! Get it?"

"Fuckin' funny, Sarah. Last night?" I really wasn't into any joking around.

Sarah's Crest Whitening-Strip smile faded quick. "Yeah. Yeah. Last night. Peter did a cream pie around, well, two this morning. Jewel was half out of it—'Ludes again. No big deal. They called Pete in before she totally passed out. Did it all in close-up. She mighta' been comatose. Who'd notice? The angle was good. I fluffed him. He was in and out in half an hour." She looked at me and paused for a heartbeat, waiting to see if I got the pun.

"Where'd he go?'

"Jeeze, you're sure in a mood."

"Where'd he go?"

"Shit, Ginny. I can't tell you that."

"Why the fuck not? Listen, Sarah. You owe me."

"The restraining order. Pete'll blacklist me like he did you."

"Blacklist? You stupid …"

There was a crescendo of orgasmic moaning from the kitchen, then a scream. "Fucking dumbshit!" Timmy was in pain. "You burnt me with the fucking light!"

"That wasn't the light, dip shit. I just touched your sack with the lens. It's cold, that's all."

"It felt hot."

"Jesus H. Cumshot, shut the fuck up, assholes. Timmy! Fuck. Ah shit! There it goes." It was Randy Glans, former actor and bodybuilder, now award winning director and soon—judging by the tremor in his voice—to be full-blown, indictable, multiple-dismembered-victims roid-rage mass murderer. "Fluff! Sarah, need a fluff in here!"

"I can't tell you where he is, Ginny. You know that."

"Sarah, get your tits in here!"

"I gotta work, Ginny." Sarah headed towards the crowded dinette set.

"Sarah!" I grabbed her arm and stopped her. That's when Randy, looking down the hallway from the kitchen, saw me.

"Fuck!" Randy was roaring.

"I can't, Ginny." Sarah twisted out of my grip and headed towards Timmy's limp dick.

"Ginny Clemm, get your ass off my set!"

"Fuck you, Randy." I wasn't going to take any shit from him. Hell, he wasn't much of a director. His website was barely making money. Randy had picked the wrong niche—"Nasty Grandma's Funky XXX Kitchen"—a limited market.

One of the gophers—a big Samoan with an ugly tattoo covering half his face—started towards me. I was on my feet and out of there before he could get past Sarah in the tight confines of the little hallway.

Sarah hadn't been any help, but I grabbed her purse as I stood up, and I figured that would do the trick. I got into my car and got the hell out of there.

***

Your hand is so cold. I wish I could make you warm, sweetheart. You need a haircut. There doesn't seem to be much of you left. I hope it's not too late. Seems like it took me a long time to figure out how to be a good mom.

I wish things had been different. I'll always love you. The things I did might have been crazy or awful or whatever, but I'll always love you. Someday maybe you'll understand. Geeze, that sounds like something my mother used to say to me.

Having a kid is tough. No. No. You're the best kid ever. Don't get me wrong, sweetie. It's just that the responsibility and shit is … Let me rub your hands. Mommy will rub your hands. It won't be long, now.

***

I sped out of the little back street maze onto Oxnard, then over to Reseda Boulevard and up to Victory. I headed east until I saw the Sepulveda off-leash dog park. I pulled in and parked next to a Hummer. There was a guy unloading about six Russian Wolfhounds from the passenger side. He gave me a dirty look. Fucking fag. I flipped him off. He headed through the gates into the park.

I remember rolling my window down just a bit. It was a big-time San Fernando Valley hot day. The air smelled like trucker's breath, solvent, and old dog shit—a typical summer afternoon. That's why I like the fire season best. When the hills are burning, the smoke aroma covers all the chemical decay that usually fills the Los Angeles air. There's something natural about brushfire smoke. Reminds me of burning leaves in a small Iowa town—not that I've ever spent an autumn on the prairies, but I saw it in a movie once—whatever—I like fire season. It smells healthier.

***

If you wake up, honey—when you wake up—when you get all better, sweetie, I'll take you to Iowa, and we'll burn leaves. I know. I know. It won't happen. After what I've done, maybe I won't even get to see you again.

Maybe you can just dream about me. Maybe that will be enough. My poor little man, maybe you can just live on the dreams.

Are you dreaming now? Your eyes are flickering under your little lashes. God knows I just want you to keep dreaming a little while longer.

***

Sarah's cell phone was in her purse. That was the prize I was looking for. She and Peter had a thing. Don't know why he was going out with her. I mean, Peter was kind of a porn legend. What the fuck did he want with a fluff-girl? What am I saying? He went for me once, didn't he?

Men liked to be fluffed. Suck their cocks. Tell 'em how big and strong they are. Stay on your knees and worship them. Then they can perform their functions—stupid fucking sperm machines. I spent a lot of time on my knees with Peter. Hey, that's kind of funny, too.

Maybe it's that men aren't threatened by women who work on their knees. They should be. After Peter broke up with me, and after that day in court when CPS declared me "unfit," I was on my knees again. And that smart ass—I don't remember his name now—had his cock in my mouth. It was some small studio shoot in Van Nuys. I remember—just another day at work. And that dumb shit said, "I love you, baby." That's what he said, "I love you, baby."

I don't know why that pissed me off, but it did. I damned near bit his dick off. They really bleed a lot—penises, that is. I was surprised by that. He was screaming, and I was chewing. They drug me off him after somebody hit me with a chair. That's what they told me. Mostly I remember the taste of that blood.

They kicked me out of the business. That wasn't such a surprise. And everybody got AIDS tested. The industry is so very health conscious these days. That's when I found out. The guy was HIV positive. Isn't that funny? I saved so many other lives that day, and they end up blacklisting me.

Sarah, who was my friend back then, told me, "It's like a Freudian thing, Ginny—'Vaginal Dental Alan Alda,' or something—a pussy full of teeth. It's some kind of primal fear that all guys got. They can't work with some girl who got the taste for chomping off their tools."

"I'd never do it again," I insisted.

"That's not how they figure it. They think you're like a dog that's gone wild with the smell of fresh meat." Sarah smiled. "And, sweet cheeks, they'll wither up just thinking about your lips close to their willies. Tough break."

Everything was tougher. I ended up getting a job as a waitress at TGI-Friday's in Northridge. Shit, I'd rather suck cocks.

***

I'm sorry, honey. You look so peaceful there. It'll be okay. The doctors are going to save you. It's a good thing the County took you. I knew you were sick. But I didn't have any insurance, and I couldn't seem to get any of the Indian residents in the ER's to pay us any attention. You remember?

At least when you got into foster care, they got you some help. I just hope it isn't too late, sweetie. I did what I could. Mommy tried all the straight ways to help.

Is your pillow okay? Let me rub your neck. Mommy tried. You know that, honey. Mommy tried. Then I hoped they'd save you. I should have known. There are some things only a mother can do.

***

When I got Sarah's cell phone out of her purse, the first thing I did was check the in-coming calls list. There it was. Peter's name was right on top. I knew it would be. I hit "Send" and listened as it rang. Once … Twice … Three times … "Please God, let him answer."

"Hello, babe."

"Hello, Peter."

"Wait. Who is this? Is this you, Sarah?" It was a stupid question. Peter was stupid. It was easier to recognize with a little emotional distance.

"It's me. It's Ginny, Peter. Don't hang up. Please." I worked at keeping my voice calm.

"I don't want to talk to you, Ginny."

"I know, Peter. But I need …"

"You went crazy at my apartment the other night. Fucking screaming out in the middle of Balboa …"

"I needed to talk to …"

"And I let you in like a good guy, and what do you do?"

"I was wrong, Peter. I want to …"

"You were fucking crazy."

"I'm sorry, Peter. You're absolutely, one hundred percent right. I was …"

"And you took my wallet. Did you take my wallet?"

"Yes, Peter. I took your wallet."

"You crazy bitch. You took my wallet."

"I need to talk to you about your son."

"I pay child support through the County office, Ginny. That's it."

"I know. Peter, you do the best you can."

"Don't know why I should still pay when the State's got him now and everything.'

"Yeah. It doesn't seem fair."

"So … Fuck you."

"Yes, Peter. Fuck me. I was wrong."

"What's the matter, Ginny? You're not screaming at me."

"No, Peter. I'm trying to apologize."

At that point there was a long pause. For a second my heart almost stopped. I waited for him to say something. I started to think I'd lost signal, so I got out of the car. Still nothing. I got down on my knees. I knelt down right on the asphalt between my car and the Hummer. There was a pile of dog shit about six feet in front of me. I thought I'd lost.

"Peter. Please, let me apologize." I said it with all the little-girl love I could muster. Like the seventeen year-old I was when I first met him—when I'd first gone down on him professionally. "Peter, listen to me. I want to return your wallet. I want to apologize. I want to tell you I understand how hard all this has been on you." I paused. My knees hurt.

Then after what seemed like forever, "It has been real hard on me."

"I've been awful."

"You were such a bitch. No abortion. We could have had fun. And you put my name on the birth certificate. I could have asked for a DNA test on that. It was big of me to just pay."

"Yes, Peter. You were a real man. A stand up guy."

"I'll say I was."

"You did good."

"I'll say."

"You're the sweetest man, Peter."

"I could have killed you. You were lucky I only slapped you."

"I deserved it."

"Getting AIDS and everything. I got tested. They wouldn't let me work for six months. I had to do some of that real off-the-books stuff down in Venice. Stupid bitch."

"I was so fucking stupid."

The queen with the six wolfhounds came back from the park. He looked at me on my knees next to my car. I gave him the finger. He went around to the other side with his pack of dogs.

"You broke my stereo, too."

"Let me make it all up to you, Peter."

"You going to pay for the damages."

"I'll pay, Peter."

"And give me back my wallet. It's got all my credit cards and my driver's license and shit. Hey, have you been using my credit cards? Don't bother. I cancelled them real quick."

"I haven't tried to use them."

"Did you take all the money? Fuck, I had two grand in my wallet, Ginny. Did you … ?"

"I've still got all the money, Peter."

"Okay. Well … ah … um … So you still got my wallet?"

"Yes."

"All the cards?"

"Yes."

"The money?"

"I've got all the money, Peter."

"And my driver's license. You got that? Because it's a real hassle to drive all the way over to the DMV and stand in line and shit—waste a whole day. You got my license?"

"Yes, Peter."

"And?"

"I want to give it back, Peter. I was very stupid. I was acting crazy."

"You were acting crazy. Even for you. Real fucking crazy."

"I'm sorry, Peter."

The Hummer's engine started up. The breeze blew the exhaust right into my face. I almost choked. I remember wishing I had a big pile of leaves to burn. I wanted that clean smoke in my nose. He backed out of the parking spot. I didn't move. I stayed there on my knees—on the phone—with Peter.

"I just want my wallet back."

"I'll give it to you."

"When?"

"Tonight."

"Where?"

"At Children's Hospital."

"That's where he's at, isn't it?"

"Yeah."

"He's not doing too good, is he?"

"No, Peter."

"That's too bad."

"He's dying, Peter."

"That's really too bad, Ginny. I feel for you."

My knees were hurting real bad. The asphalt was hot and there were scattered chunks of rock in it driving into my bones. The pain helped me concentrate. "Thank you, Peter."

"So, do I meet you at the hospital?"

"Yes, Peter."

"I'm not going up to see him or anything. You know that. Don't be thinking you can trick me or talk me into seeing him. I can't stand hospitals and sick people and death and everything. So don't start thinking you'll talk me into going up to see him."

"Peter, it would be wonderful if you could say goodbye. He is your son. It would be such a sweet thing—such a nice gesture. I promised him that you'd visit."

"Don't be thinking that. See, I know you. That's what you're planning on doing. I'll go down there, and you'll try to get me up there to see the kid."

"You know me so well, Peter. I promise I'll only ask you once. It would be such a wonderful thing if he could say goodbye to his father. But I promise. No scene. If you want to go up, you can. If not. Well, you're in charge of what you do, Peter."

"Promise."

"Promise."

"So around eight?"

"Make it nine thirty."

"Nine thirty in the lobby?"

"No, meet me in the parking lot. It's right on Sunset and Lyman. I'll be there."

"Why not in the lobby?"

"I always sneak out and have a cigarette about then. Have to sneak those. Not even supposed to smoke on the medical center campus at all. I'll be in my old beater."

"You shouldn't be smoking. What with your health problems and all."

"I know."

"Well, okay. I'll see you at Children's Hospital at nine-thirty. Bring the wallet and no fucking around begging me to do shit."

"I promise."

"Okay."

"Okay."

"Goodbye." The connection was broken with his farewell. He wasn't interested in my goodbye. My legs were stiff when I stood up, and my kneecaps felt like they had been beaten with ball bats. A fluff-girl should be used to that.

***

Your mommy has never been really smart. But don't let that worry you. I used to do real well in school, and my teachers told me that I scored real well on those tests they give the kids in fourth grade. They said I was gifted.

It was all that shit that happened with that stupid "Uncle" Billy from Escondido who used to visit us when I was little. He told me all about kneeling down in church, and God, and other stuff in my bedroom.

Well, you're way too young to understand that. Anyway, I didn't do too well in school after all that. But I think I used to be smart, so you should be okay after you get all better. Hang on, honey. Stay with me, sweet little boy. I just know you'll be okay. Mommies know.

***

I had to get down on my knees one more time—over at a little storefront on Melrose, not far from the Hollywood Freeway. Eel is a funny guy. I don't mean like laugh at him funny. I mean any guy named Eel is, well—slimy. He fit his name. Eel sells shit documents, permits, fake papers for illegals—whatever—whoever.

"So, you gonna pay off, Ginny?"

"Like I promised, Eel."

"A good one. A real sweet job now."

I was on his cock before he finished the sentence. Didn't take too long, either. Men are so easy when they're amateurs. I was cleaning myself up with Sarah's anti-bacterial towelettes, sitting down on a real nice leather chair, when Eel came back into the room with the manila envelope.

"Here you go, Ginny." He tossed the lumpy envelope on the coffee table. The package clattered on the glass top and slid to a stop right in front of me. "You sure that's all you wanted? Just to add that one thing? Hell, I could make you a whole new one easy. A new photo—a new name—new birthday or expiration date—seems kind of stupid to just check that one little box."

"No. Thanks, Eel. That's all I needed. And the …"

"It's in the envelope. All ready to go. Rusty grip, but it works fine. Be careful. Don't be hurting yourself."

"Like anyone would care," I said.

"I would, Ginny. I like you." Eel said it like he meant it. Like I said, he was a funny guy.

"Thanks, Eel. See ya'." I stood up. I even thought about kissing him. I don't know why. I walked out into the early evening. The L.A. heat was still shimmering off the blacktop where my car was parked. The air smelled like old hairspray and burnt metal. Fire season was still a month off. The Santa Anas would bring the smoke back to the valley. "I'll be gone by then." I remember saying that out loud.

***

I wish I could give you some water. Your lips are so dry and cracked. I know, so are mine. The meth takes the moisture right out of me.

You have such lovely, curly hair. Let me push it back out of your eyes. When you get better and open those eyes, I want you to see everything clearly. I love you. Hang on, precious. Hang on.

***

It was right around eight forty-five when I pulled into the parking lot. Not the one by the hospital, but one a little further east, over by Sunset and Virgil. I sat in the old clunker listening to KSCR. They've got a program called "Licorice Slices"—all sorts of tunes. They call it ear candy. I listened to some spacey stuff with jangly, repetitious guitars and a spinning organ part like a drone, called "Missing Piece"—very appropriate. I kept my eye on the dashboard clock. At exactly nine twenty-five I got out of the car and walked over to the hospital. I stood out on the Sunset side of the lot there and lit up a cigarette.

Peter showed up pretty much on time.

"You got my wallet."

"Hello, Peter."

"Don't be hugging me or shit." He kept his distance like a dog that had been kicked once too many times. "I just want my wallet."

"I know, Peter."

"Then, you got my wallet?"

"Yes, Peter. Here it is." I held out the tooled leather wallet in my left hand.

Peter took a quick step towards me, snatched it out of my hand, and stepped back two quick little paces. He never took his eyes off me.

"I'm not going to act crazy, Peter."

"Okay." He was holding the wallet in his hand. He was suspicious. Frozen. Hyper-vigilant. "Okay?"

"It's all right, Peter. All the money's there. Count it."

"Really?" He opened the wallet. There it was—two thousand twenty-one dollars. "No. I won't count it. I trust you." He was lying. Truth is, Peter wasn't too good at counting. "And my driver's license? Yeah, there it is."

"I told you. I just want all our fighting to stop, Peter."

"Cool. I hear that."

"Now, do you want to go up and say goodbye to your son?"

"I told you I couldn't do that." Peter stepped back another step. His eyes were locked on me. He stuck his wallet in his hip pocket. He wanted both hands free in case I went psycho on him without warning.

I made a real show of taking a deep breath. I held it for a second, and then I let it go in a loud sigh. "That's fine, Peter. I understand."

There was a pause. He looked at me. I looked at him. A tricked-out Japanese car accelerated away from the light on Sunset. The driver put it through the gears, and the machine wound away into the distance like a maddened insect.

"So?" Peter's shoulders relaxed.

"It's okay, Peter."

"I'd visit him if I could, Ginny. I would."

"I understand. I know if you could, you'd go to him."

"It's just that ..."

"You don't have to explain, Peter. Goodnight."

"Okay. Well, thanks for giving me my stuff back. I mean the cash and not having to go to the DMV and waste the day and all. Thanks."

"Goodbye, Peter."

"Okay, Ginny. I hope everything works out."

"It will." I sighed again. I wanted to get all the tense air out of my lungs. I wanted to be very relaxed when it happened.

Peter turned around and took a single step towards his car. A bus diesel engine roared towards us on Hillhurst. I don't think anyone heard anything other than the din of that bus. I don't think Peter heard anything at all. It was all so supersonic.

I raised my right hand. Eel's gun was warm. I'd had it sitting on the black vinyl seat in my car and the rusty grip had absorbed all of the L.A. summer. That was good. I didn't want this to be cold.

Peter took a step away. I took two quick steps up behind him. The bus was very loud. The barrel of the gun was about three inches from his lovely curly hair. I pulled the trigger.

It was all so supersonic.

***

I came straight up here to see you, honey. I wanted you to know that you might not have the best mother in the world, but the one you have could not love you more. I would have given you one of my kidneys if I could have. But with HIV and everything, they won't let me.

I used to dream about getting you better and then getting you back. I guess that was just another stupid dream of mine. I'll just have to settle for you getting better. I love you, little Petey.

I can hear some people talking to your foster parents out in the hall. Your father must be here to see you. I'd better leave. You just get well. And when you feel up to it, remember how much your mommy loves you and how lucky you are that they mark "organ donor" right there on people's driver's licenses so that if anything bad happens suddenly to them, the doctors know what to do.

Your dad always wanted to help you, too. He was just a little afraid. So, mommy helped daddy do the right thing. Someday in heaven you can thank him.

Me? Look for me somewhere out in Iowa. Look for a woman burning a big pile of leaves in front of her tiny little white house. I'll be standing right in the smoke—so that I can smell it and remember. Yeah, I'll be standing straight up.

I won't ever kneel down again.

RUSSEL D MCLEAN

writes short stories, some of which contain objectionable language. Several of these have made their way into *Alfred Hitchcock's Mystery Magazine*, The Thrilling Detective website and a variety of other markets. He has edited other people's objectionable stories at www.crimescenescotland.com. This irregular e-zine focuses mainly on dark, noir fiction and these days exists as a hub for reviews, interviews and articles. Last anyone heard, Russel was alive and well and working on a top secret project from his fortress of solitude, located somewhere in the city of Dundee, Scotland.

PEDRO PAUL
RUSSEL D MCLEAN

FRIDAY: 7:54 a.m.

The two coppers perched on the edge of the sofa. Rick sat in one of the comfy chairs, watching them closely. His heart was beating hard in his chest, but he told himself he had nothing to worry about. They were just here to make sure Chantelle was okay. Chantelle was in the bedroom talking to a third female copper.

"Do you want to tell me again where you found her?" asked the male copper. He had a deep, hard-man voice, which seemed at odds with his friar-tuck haircut, little round face and wireframe glasses.

"I told ye's, she was sleepwalking. Walking around on the streets."

Lynn—who was sitting in the other comfy chair—reached across the gap between them and touched his arm gently. He thought maybe this was a new start for him. Maybe the world was trying to tell him something. What Lynn had been talking about the day before, maybe she was right. Maybe they belonged together. Maybe this was where he was meant to be. After all Chantelle had never really had a daddy. Lynn didn't talk about him, whoever he was. Sometimes that made Rick wonder if she even knew.

The male copper consulted his notes and then recited where Rick said he had found Chantelle. "You know there was a murder last night near that address?"

Rick tried to look at least a little surprised.

The female copper chimed in. "Paul McCay," she said. "Unemployed. He's lived round here for a few years, now."

Rick looked at Lynn. She was hugging herself, wrapping her arms around her stomach. She looked oddly distressed, her face white, her breathing fast and shallow.

"Are you okay?" asked the female officer, trying for sympathetic but not managing it.

Rick said, "Ye mean Pedro Paul."

"Pedro Paul?" asked the male copper.

TUESDAY 10:34 p.m.

"Whozat sadsack in the corner?"

Rick let his eyes slowly pan along the outstretched arm. Finally his eyes tripped off the end of Stott's fingernails and bounced to the far corner of the pub where an exclusion zone seemed to have been placed around the pile of rags that passed for a man. The only way you knew the sadsack was alive was that his arm moved every so often, lifting his pint off the table up to his face and back down again.

"Pedro Paul," he said.

"Pedro Paul?"

"Aye," said Rick. "Cos he's a pedrophile, see, a kiddie-fiddler."

Stott nodded. "Nae wonder aw they fuckers are steering clear, aye?"

"Aye, well," said Rick. They weren't steering clear because they were afraid of Pedro Paul. No, they were afraid of the coppers. Last time someone had just pushed Pedro Paul out their way, the pigs had been round in thirty seconds flat, kicking arse and taking names. No, they weren't out stopping fucks like Pedro. They were defending them, stepping in when decent people were only defending themselves against the filth and evil in this world.

Stott turned back to the bar, got in two more pints. He didn't ask any more about Pedro Paul. Instead, he asked Rick about whether he was still seeing that bird on the side, the one who lived down the street, the one with the wee bairn and, more importantly, the big tits.

Rick said aye, he was still seeing her. But he had to add, "Still on the sly, ken?"

"Gill doesnae ken?"

"No," said Rick. "And you'll keep yer big gob shut, aye? Say anything and I'll do ye."

"What am I gonnae say?" said Stott. He looked strange, not quite relaxed. His head kept turning over his shoulder, looking back at where Pedro was sitting.

Rick thought maybe he shouldn't have said anything about Pedro Paul at all, just claimed he was some filthy old tramp nobody knew who'd just popped in for a pint. It could have explained why everyone was avoiding the fuck by saying he stunk of piss. But part of him had known what Rick's reaction would be, wanted to watch the fireworks, see Pedro Pete get what was coming to him.

He wasn't about to be disappointed.

They talked for another ten minutes. Two friends bullshitting. It felt good, Rick had to admit that. Too long since they'd had a pint together, too long since they'd told *that* joke, the one with the three men at the bar comparing their wives to beautiful birds and this wee Glasgow fella sidling up and saying he called his wife Thrush because she was like an irritating cunt. Stott told it better than Rick ever could and it sent ripples of deep, knowing laughter up and down the bar. Stott had moved to Glasgow a year earlier, got himself a job as a bouncer. He'd got himself out of this shithole. Maybe doing doorwork wasn't the greatest job in the world but it beat all the knockbacks Rick was taking. The job market round town was poor at the best of times, but it was getting so even McDonalds had knocked Rick back for employment.

By the time Pedro Paul had finished his pint, Rick had gotten used to Stott's pattern, the way the bigger man's shaved head kept turning at regular intervals to check whether the ragged pervert was moving yet. He'd been thinking ever since Rick had told him about Pedro's perversions, and he looked ready to just down his pint the minute he got a hint that Pedro was going to make a move.

Finally, Pedro got up and walked outside. Stott downed his pint. Rick tried to do the same, but couldn't manage it. He left it, half-drunk, on the bar and followed Stott out the bar.

They followed Pedro down the street. He turned off up a close, away from CCTV. Heading back to the same grotty council block where Rick lived with Gill and where Lynn—she of the big tits and the wee bairn—lived just down the way.

Stott ran ahead, caught up with Pedro before they left the tight shadows of the close. He laid a beefy hand on the other man's shoulder, spun Pedro round so he could look down into the pale face with its sunken grey eyes. "You're a pervert," said Stott.

Pedro didn't say anything. He stepped backwards.

Rick watched all this, leaning back against a wall, hoping the shadows would hide him from view. As much as he had encouraged all of this, he felt ashamed for watching.

On the opposite side of the close, a light came on in a second floor window. Looking up, Rick saw a figure outlined, looking out.

Stott punched Pedro once in the face. The crack of the pervert's nose breaking echoed down the close, bouncing off the walls.

Pedro fell on his arse. Stott kicked him in the chest, knocking Pedro onto his back. Stott bent down and grabbed Pedro's shirt, pulling the fucker back to his feet. Pedro's body was limp, a puppet with its strings cut. Stott let Pedro go, dropping him to the ground. He didn't care about realisation. He wasn't scared of this pathetic sadsack excuse for a human being.

Stott trotted over to Rick, said, "You want a go?"

Rick just stood there like an eejit, his jaw flapping uselessly.

Blue lights flashed down the far end of the close. Stott looked up at the window where the silhouette had been standing. "Stupid fuckin' bitch!" he shouted. "He was the fuckin' criminal, a pervert! If the polis were really daeing their job, they'd be the ones kicking his arse!"

He grabbed Rick roughly by the shoulders, pulled him out of the shadows. They ran up the other end of the close, jumped a wall. Behind them, they heard the shouts of Police officers but they knew these streets, knew where they were going. The fuzz, with their heavy gear weighing them down, had no chance.

THURSDAY: 9:59 a.m.

Two days later and Rick was finally beginning to relax, pretending like it had been a bad dream. He wasn't a bad guy, didn't get in brawls, didn't want to fight, didn't want to hurt anyone even a sick fuck like Pedro Paul. But all the same, he'd been there, he'd stood back and watched while Stott kicked the crap out of the old bastard. Only now that Rick had gone back home to Glasgow it was starting to feel distant; like the half memory of some bad dream.

Lynn came back into the bedroom. She was wearing pyjama bottoms and a white top. She pulled off the top, and her large breasts swung loose, tantalising and beautiful. She climbed into bed beside Rick. "She's away, noo," she told Rick. "Off tae play wi' some of the other bairns."

Rick relaxed, reached to the bedside table and grabbed a pack of cigarettes. He felt uncomfortable without his fags, hated Lynn's rule of no smoking while the bairn was in the house. He understood it, of course, knew why she was militant. Smoking killed you, pure and simple. He thought if he was growing up now he'd never have started. The wee bairn—her name was Chantelle and she was far too innocent to have really grown up around these parts of the city—had the kinds of chances he wished he had all over again. She could be anything she wanted to be. She didn't have to grow up and get stuck, just living from day to day with no real job, no real opportunity. No chance to change and grow and experience anything except drink, sex and illness. He understood why Lynn doted on the girl. She was an opportunity for Lynn to leave some kind of mark on the world. Amazing breasts aside, Lynn never had the chance to impress anyone with her skills, her passions, her thoughts. But Chantelle had all those chances still ahead of her and it was only natural her mother would want her to have all the chances she had never been given or never thought to take.

Rick smoked the cigarette slowly, tipping the ash into the glass ashtray on the bedside table. Lynn lay under the sheets, her head on his chest, her big, blonde hair tickling underneath his chin. She didn't say anything, let him finish his smoke.

When he was done, he pulled away from her and she rolled onto her side. He was feeling horny, ready for another go. He moved in to kiss her but she pulled away. She wasn't teasing him. He could see from the way her features were set there was something else on her mind.

"What the fuck're we daeing?" she asked.

"What?"

"I mean, aw this sneaking aroond, behind yer girlfriend's back, like its aw a big secret or something."

He took a breath. He'd been waiting for this. Sooner or later, he'd known they'd be having this talk. Women always overthink sex, he told himself. They never see it for what it is.

"I mean, she's no your wife, right? Just yer bidey-in, ken? Its no like you cannae leave her or anything. Nae kids, nae ring."

Rick thought about this. She had a point, but then he liked living with Gillian. She was like his safety net, the one thing he could keep counting on day after day. She wasn't as wild in bed as Lynn, didn't do any of that kinky crap that Lynn liked—especially things like with the ice cubes: that had been a fucking revelation for Rick—and she tended to get on his back about the little things, the stuff Rick never thought mattered that much. But part of him found that reassuring, part of him knew that he liked having Gill waiting for him at home. He liked the stability of their arrangement. He knew he wouldn't care if she had her own bit on the side if that was what made her happy, just as long as she was there.

But he didn't say any of that to Lynn. Instead he said, "It's not the best time to be thinking of stuff like that."

"Why not?"

"It just isn't," he said.

"Ye're round here practically aw the fuckin' time," she said, her voice harsh and accusing, her face suddenly ugly even through all the makeup. "Everybody fuckin' knows except her and if she does-nae realise, she's a fuckin' eejit!"

Rick pulled back the covers, got out of bed.

"Where're ye going?"

"Back to Gill," he said. "The fuck away from here."

She got out of bed, too, grabbed the ashtray from the table and threw it at his head. "Fuck you!" she screamed. The ashtray missed Rick's head by inches, thumped against the wall. The glass was too thick to shatter and Rick didn't dare imagine the kind of damage it would have done if it had been on target.

Rick got dressed calmly while she stood at the other side of the bed, her lithe body humming with anger. He could almost hear it if he listened closely enough, the kind of sound a taut string makes when you brush your fingers against it.

She said, softly, "Get the fuck out, then ye cunt."

When Rick got outside, he was still doing up his shirt. He looked down the walkway—Lynn's flat being on the raised part of the estate—and saw Pedro Paul staring at him, wide eyed like Rick was still naked. But then Pedro darted round the corner. He was scared, likely, after the events a few nights previously. Maybe he would use this to get revenge, try and mess up Rick's life with what he knew or at least what he could imply. But Rick wasn't worried. Even if Pedro told people, who was going to listen to a kiddie-fiddler bastard?

THURSDAY: 5:57 p.m.

Rick clicked onto Channel 4. "The Simpsons" were about to start. He hoped it was a later one, perhaps. At least he hoped it wouldn't be about little Lisa and her problems. For all the complaining that kid did, she came from a pretty good life. For all the moaning about how poor the Simpsons were, they always seemed to have plenty of money to a man like Rick. He thought maybe he'd like to see the one where Homer and his boss get stuck in a mountain cabin together. As long as there wasn't any moral, he'd be happy.

Gill came through with a tray. She passed it to him and he laid it on his lap. He smelt the Findus Curry, delighted in the aroma. He remembered watching that documentary where some shithead ate McDonald's food for 30 days. He knew what was going on. The food snobs were trying to take away the few simple pleasures in life just because they liked to fucking cook everything and couldn't be arsed actually paying for it.

Yeah, it was junk food discrimination.

The doorbell rang,

"Got it," shouted Gill in a sing-song kind of way, but flat, like she didn't really want to answer the door but knew she was expected to at least offer.

When Lynn walked into the living room, Rick's heart stopped. He stood up feeling instantly guilty. Sweat broke out all over his body. He felt it most around his balls, the same way he always did when he got scared or nervous, like there was some special gland down there that was working overtime.

She'd been crying. Her mascara was streaked black down her face and her eyes were roadmap-red, the blood vessels cracking. She was wearing jeans and an old t-shirt. No bra, Rick noticed and felt a little ashamed for it.

He thought to himself that now he was in the shit. There was a look of sheer, outright horror and anger in her face. Her breasts heaved as she struggled to draw breath. She was here to fuck him over. Aye, he thought, this is her revenge. This is where she makes my life a pisshole.

He wondered whether it had been worthwhile, whether the sacrifice was worth the size of her tits and just being able to have them for a little while.

But she didn't start screaming, didn't start accusing him of anything.

Instead, when Gill came into the room, Lynn grabbed her and the two women held each other. Lynn wept openly. She gripped tightly to Gill as if afraid to let go.

Gill looked at Rick, still holding Lynn close, and said, "You havenae seen Chantelle?"

"What? No."

Gill moved Lynn to the sofa. Lynn sat down. She said, "I'm sorry," in a meek wee voice. She sat forward, held up her head with her hands. Gill left the room.

Rick moved to the sofa, sat down next to Lynn. "Its no that late, maybe she's just with her friends." He was thinking to himself that it was incredible how much this woman loved her bairn. He wouldn't have thought twice about a child of his unless it was missing for the whole night.

Lynn looked up and shook her head.

"No," she said. "Chantelle's always on time. Always. Never late. She's a dependable wee bairn, a good wee girl." She shuddered gently, and Rick was afraid she'd go into some kind of crying fit and worried about how he would cope with that. "We had an argument. Aboot some fuckin' toy, ken? I wouldnae buy it for her and she didnae get that I just don't have any money. She said it, said she was gonnae run away and I laughed at that. And now ..."

Lynn wiped at her teary eyes. The mascara smudged her face. She looked at Rick and said, "She always liked ye, you know? She mightae come here. But she's no wi' her friends. She's no wi' nobody." She shuddered and started crying again. Rick, without thinking, put his hand around her shoulder.

She looked at him, stopped crying and kissed him on the lips. It wasn't erotic, it was desperate, like by making physical contact she could somehow get rid of all the pain and fear that was inside of her.

He thought about Chantelle. She was a sweet wee girl. Long, dark hair. Big, brown eyes that always seemed far too intelligent for a girl so young. About a month ago, he remembered he'd been sleeping over at Lynn's while Gill was away visiting her mother. Chantelle had been unable to sleep and come through, interrupting them. Rick had been angry at first but you couldn't stay angry at a wee girl like Chantelle for long and so he had finally gone to her room and read her a story until she fell asleep. It had been a story about a handsome knight saving an innocent princess from the clutches of an evil dragon.

He thought about earlier that morning, coming out of Lynn's place.

He saw Pedro Paul's face, the eyes wide and angry, the lips parted slightly so you could see the teeth that were stained and yellow. In his mind, he thought Pedro Paul had looked like the evil dragon in the story.

He kissed Lynn, just to let her know everything would be okay.

Gill said, "What the fuck is this?"

Rick looked up, remembered where he was. He tried to say something, but Gill beat him to the punch. "Get out of here," she said, her eyes fixed on him. She didn't blame Lynn. She couldn't blame Lynn, not considering the reason she was here. But she could blame Rick. Rick was a horn dog. Rick was a shitheel.

She said it again. "Get out of here." Then, she added: "You shitebag."

He stood up. He tried to catch her eye, but she wasn't playing that game. He walked past her. On his way out the door, he thought about slamming it. Instead, feeling ashamed, he closed it quietly.

He thought about when Stott had attacked Pedro Paul. Rick had stood in the shadows, watching. He hadn't been involved, but then maybe just watching something was every bit as blameworthy as if he'd got in a few punches of his own.

Pedro Paul didn't know who Stott was. But he would have known Rick. Knew him now, at least, if he hadn't before. Pedro Paul had been there outside of Lynn's place. Pedro Paul must have known Lynn had a daughter.

Pedro Paul must have wanted revenge. He must have seen Rick in the shadows that night. He must have wanted revenge.

Rick ran down steps, to street level. He walked along the High Street, cursing and swearing. Kids in caps and hoodies looked at him, their expressions somewhere between fear and laughter. Loonies were to be laughed at on the streets, but sometimes you had to be careful. Sometimes the loonies fought back.

He turned things over in his mind, kept seeing Chantelle alone in some room somewhere. There was no real light source. Except when the door opened and the thing shuffled inside. In silhouette, it looked like some deranged creature from Night of the Living Dead. It moved slowly, deliberately. It took its time because it knew Chantelle was going nowhere. It was the dragon from the story, except this dragon was real and it terrified him completely.

Rick saw all of this from Chantelle's eyes, looking up at the creature. He felt the horror and revulsion she would be feeling. He wanted to crawl away when the dragon reached down. He wanted to scream, almost did right there in the middle of the High Street. Standing outside Woolies, he felt tears in his eyes.

And then he saw the dragon's face. And it was human.

The face belonged to Pedro Paul.

THURSDAY: 8.42 p.m.

Rick had been drinking. But all the drink in the world couldn't push those images out of his mind.

He drank alone at the bar. People kept clear of him. Maybe they sensed his thoughts. He didn't care. He just cared about the drink, feeling the alcohol soak into his system. He wasn't a natural drunk. He tried to be, because what real man couldn't hold his liquor? But if he was honest, the sensation of drunkenness wasn't one that came to him naturally.

Finally, he felt he'd drunk enough. Mere Dutch courage wasn't enough for what he had to do. He had to go above and beyond the call. As he slid off the stool, he thought to himself that maybe he'd overdone it, that he'd slipped one too many over the line. His legs felt unsteady and he wasn't sure about the feeling that his muscles had been replaced by cotton wool.

But outside, in the cool of the night air, he felt his strength return. His conviction was absolute. He knew what he had to do. He knew that in an ideal world he would call the police, let them deal with this. But this was real life and for people like Rick, the coppers were at best incompetent fools and at worst the enemy.

He walked the streets, his fists clenched by his sides. He walked back to the estate, walked confidently to Pedro Paul's door. Someone had scrawled graffiti over across it, telling Pedro what he go do with himself.

Rick read the graffiti and smiled.

He rapped hard on the door.

There was no reply.

He rapped hard again.

"Open up, yah cunt!" he yelled.

He kicked the door. It was flimsy; cheap materials that gave way under his onslaught. He stumbled inside. He found himself in the entrance hall. The place smelt of human sweat; like being stuck in an old man's armpit. Rick's stomach did flips. He walked down the hall.

He found the living room. Newspapers, remains of fish suppers, council tax bills, all thrown about the place like Pedro Paul just didn't give a crap how he lived. Rick waded through the mess. He had expected the fireplace and maybe the walls to be decorated with pictures of young children. He was sorely disappointed. There were no decorations. It was four walls and a few creature comforts; nothing more. Even looking at the telly, Rick saw it wasn't plugged in. The plug had been broken, bare wire trailing out the back of the telly, connecting to nothing. It was almost as though Pedro Paul had placed it in the corner of the room because he was expected to have one there. It was covered in dust.

He moved through to the bedroom. He looked at the single bed stuffed in the corner. The curtains were closed. There was someone lying beneath the covers. Even from here, Rick could make out the shape of a child. Dark hair spilled from beneath the covers and onto the pillow. Rick clenched his fists. "Sick cunt," he whispered. He crept forward, looked over the bed, saw the sleeping child's face more clearly.

His stomach churned. Vomit in his throat. He swallowed it back down. It sloshed about inside his stomach. He looked at the face again, felt tears in his eyes.

Chantelle.

He heard someone in the corridor. He moved out of the bedroom, made sure he shut the door quietly behind him.

Pedro Paul stood in the hall, holding two fish suppers. He looked shocked to see Rick, took a step backwards.

Rick tried to say something, but his throat was tight. His fists were still clenched. He felt his nails bite into the skin of his palms. He didn't care.

"Get outae mah hoose," said Pedro Paul.

Rick stepped forward.

"I know you," said Pedro. "You're the one who's cheatin' on his girlfriend wi' Lynn."

Rick ran forward, rugby tackled Pedro Paul.

The tightly wrapped fish suppers burst open. The smell of grease and vinegar exploded into the air, assaulted Rick's nostrils. Rick landed on Pedro, made sure his knee was up, crushing the pervert's privates.

Pedro yelped. Rick forced his hand across the man's mouth. "Ye'll wake the bairn," he said.

Pedro Paul bit down on Rick's hand. Rick bit his lip to stop from screaming. He crushed his knee down again hard on the other man's crotch. He pulled his hand away. Pedro Paul's bite was strong. Flesh ripped from between Rick's thumb and forefinger. Pedro Paul spat it out.

Rick stood up. "Right," he said. He crushed his heel into Pedro's stomach. Then he kicked up, caught the bastard under the chin. Pedro Paul rolled away. Rick felt the blood dripping from the wound in his hand. He held up his hand, examined the wound with a childlike curiosity. He was aware of a dull sensation there, but it didn't hurt like he would have thought.

He looked at Pedro Paul. The bastard was on his hands and knees, scrambling past Rick on his way towards the bedroom. Rick thought to himself that Pedro was a stupid bastard. Anyone with half a brain would have tried to get out. Maybe it was a sign of how sick Pedro Paul really was that all he could think of was going to the wee girl in the bedroom.

Rick grabbed Pedro by the hair, pulled him away from the bedroom door and across into the living room. Pedro crawled away from Rick, realising now that he had to find a way out.

"Get outtae mah hoose," Pedro said, in the kitchen now, pulling himself up to his feet by grabbing the worktop and levering his shaking body upright. His nose was bleeding badly, and his mouth was dripping with blood. Rick wondered whose it really was, mindful of his hand still throbbing as the blood pumped out between his thumb and forefinger.

Pedro pulled open a drawer. He reached in, took out a bread knife; long blade with a serrated edge. He held it out before him. His arm trembled wildly.

Rick stepped forward.

"Get outtae mah fuckin' hoose."

Rick reached out, Pedro Paul was too slow, couldn't move in time. Rick grabbed the pervert's wrist. He twisted. Pedro howled. The knife fell to the floor.

"She was innocent," said Rick. He let go of Pedro, let the bastard stumble away. He knelt down, scooped up the knife. "You sick bastard. Do you even know what you're doing? Do you know what you've taken away from her?"

Pedro Paul was leaning against the sink now. He slipped. Dishes clattered as the worktop vibrated. "Aw, Christ, I'm sorry," he said, his voice trembling with pain and fear. "I couldnae help it, what I did tae her ... I'm a changed man, I ..."

Rick stepped forward, holding the knife. He felt calm, now. He felt relaxed. This, he thought, this is justice. "You'll never dae that to anyone again," he told the bastard. "You should never have done it tae her."

The act itself was quick, almost anticlimactic. Pedro didn't squeal, or struggle. The fight was gone from him and he seemed to accept the inevitability of his own death as Rick plunged the knife into the bastard's throat. He caught an artery and blood sprayed.

Part of him was surprised he didn't flinch more, like they did on the TV.

When it was over and the pervert lay dead on the floor, Rick went through to the bedroom. He pulled the covers back and saw that Chantelle was lying, fully clothed, beneath the blankets. He picked her up, held her close and whispered in her ear that everything was alright. When she started to wake up, he shushed her and told her to keep her eyes closed. He didn't want her to see Pedro's body as they left. She had been through enough. And whatever he had done to her, she was still a child. Rick prayed the bastard hadn't taken that away from her.

THURSDAY: 9:04 p.m.

He knocked on the door. He was quiet, afraid he would wake the sleeping child he carried over his left shoulder. She wriggled, gently, and he thought she might wake up. He waited until she was still once more before he knocked again.

When Lynn finally answered, the sadness he had seen in hger face earlier had turned to a harsh anger. When she saw Chantelle, her jaw dropped and her face softened. She lifted one hand to her mouth as though to stop herself crying out. He passed Chantelle over to her, stood in the doorway, watched as Lynn took her baby away. He waited. He could have waited forever.

She came out of the child's bedroom maybe five minutes later. She looked at Rick with wide eyes, tried to ask him a question.

He stepped inside, shaking his head. He couldn't tell her what he had found. He couldn't bring himself to tell Lynn what had happened to her little angel. Instead he wrapped his arms around her, and he held her close. He let her cry. He absorbed her tears.

He thought to himself that justice was done.

FRIDAY 7:56 a.m.

The cop with the glasses and the round head said, "Pedro Paul?"

"Because he's a kiddie fiddler," Rick explained. "A pedrophile."

The male copper looked confused, like maybe he didn't know the word. But then it seemed to click and he nodded, sagely. He looked almost sad. "First we knew about this," he said.

"But he's been in jail."

The male copper shook his head. "As far as I'm aware, sir, he did do jail time. For assault. He used to batter his girlfriend, as I understand."

"Aye, but he didnae deserve tae be fuckin' killed." That was Lynn speaking, now. "Ye say that's where they found her? Near that cunt's place?"

"Yes."

Lynn took a deep breath. She turned to Rick. "He wasnae a kiddie fiddler," she said. "He was Chantelle's daddy." She looked sad. "For everything that cunt did tae me, he never lifted a finger tae her. He loved the bairn."

Rick felt sick to his stomach. He saw Pedro Paul in the kitchen, waving the knife, his face covered in blood. He flashed further back, remembered ramming his knee into the bastard's privates.

"Sir?" asked the male copper. "Are you alright?"

His stomach flipped. He puked onto the floor. It was almost effortless, but after it was over he felt like he'd run a marathon. He tried to stand up. But he could only take a few steps forward before he fell to his knees.

He thought about the family life he'd envisioned earlier. He'd been a hero, then. He'd been a knight in shining armour. He'd slain the fucking dragon.

Except there never was a dragon. Chantelle had been upset with her mum. She'd run off. She'd been angry with all the forceful short-term hate a child can muster. And while part of Rick would have loved her to have come to him, she had gone to her daddy. Her mum didn't allow Chantelle to speak to her dad so it must have seemed the perfect revenge to the wee bairn.

Rick cried like a bairn himself. His stomach kept flipping but he couldn't find anything else to bring up.

Someone said something. A hand landed on his shoulder.

Finally he collapsed completely to the floor. He sunk into the carpet.

And behind his eyelids he saw Pedro Paul laid on the kitchen floor, his sightless eyes asking Rick why this had happened? What had he done to deserve this? And Rick asked the same questions right back.

SCOTT WOLVEN

is the author of *Controlled Burn* (Scribner). Wolven's stories have appeared in the *Best American Mystery Stories* series (Houghton Mifflin) six years in a row, including 2007, selected by guest editor Carl Hiaasen and series editor Otto Penzler. Special thanks go out to CFC and best brother Will.

ST. GABRIEL
SCOTT WOLVEN

For DMC

THERE are violent hurricanes all the time, in my world.

Five men tried to kill my younger brother over some logging rights money, but he lived. By the time I got to the hospital in Spokane, he was sitting up and eating solid food. Recovering. He talked to me about what had happened to him. The five men set him up, to rip him off. They hadn't counted on his dog being so tough. He never went anywhere without his dog and she'd saved his life that night in the woods. She was dead. I got on the phone and the guys I knew in the Pacific Northwest and across Montana, guys who owed me favors, guys who sometimes paid me to move the index finger of my right hand less than an inch, depending on where the barrel was pointing—lots of eyes started to look for this group of five men. I took my brother home to Bozeman, to keep recovering.

***

The cost of pain and revenge finally dipped into a range I could afford. I got a late night call, and when it was all said and done, there were Montana state police questions about five men and their sudden death with my name as the answer and the court decided my house should be made of concrete and steel for about eight years or more. That I should wear an orange jumpsuit. Very little proof let me get off light. Three of the men were shot from three football fields away, most likely the result of hunting accidents. Maybe bullets that overreached their animal mark and struck a human. The other two were shot at distances that were deemed impossible by the court forensic expert. No bullet could be accurate, at that range. That's what the forensic expert said. I went to the private prison in Shelby and made my way to Deer Lodge, like everybody in Montana held accountable for their actions. I read the Bible, the most violent story I've ever known—an eye for an eye—and walked the yard when I could. I left when they told me to leave. It had all become one long night to me and that didn't change when I got out. Things didn't seem real to me anymore. My brother met me at my release, eight years and he was doing well, and after a month, we started to talk about money and work and the aspects of the normal world that needed to be attended to.

✳✳✳

My brother and I delivered a load of big timber to Lethbridge and a trucker up there put us on to it.

"Biggest storm ever," he said. "Going to wreck the whole Gulf Coast. Hurricanes, the real shit. Lots of work for loggers with their own gear. Big money in the cleanup. You boys headed south?"

My brother nodded. "We are now," he said.

When we got back into Montana, we stopped in a bar in Bozeman and watched the storm develop on the bar TV. Sat drinking and watching those hurricanes sow the seeds of the future for everybody in the Gulf. People abandoning their homes, running to stay alive. For some of those folks, the wind and water would change everything. They'd move, they'd live a life in a part of the country they didn't know existed, or that they hated. They'd be buried in cemeteries that didn't have any stones with their last name already on them, far away from family. The whisper from a voice can make a train jump the rail. And this was a lot more than a whisper. The endless piles of torn trees were sacks of dollars, to me and my brother.

We drove back to our woodlot and rented house and started sharpening saws and collecting equipment into the big pickup truck.

"Do you want to say goodbye to your girl?" my brother asked.

"Not really," I said. I'd been seeing a girl in town for three or four months.

"Okay," he said.

I stood next to the truck. "I don't have anything to say."

"Sure," he nodded.

We packed some guns too, the rifle and ammo, all in the lock box. Just in case trouble knocked and we wanted to knock back. The drive took us through Nevada and Texas. We stopped and drank with a couple of my brother's friends. Driving into east Texas, the disaster started to show and by the time we hit the Louisiana line, it looked like God had been pretty mad that day. Houses torn from foundations, boats in the streets, abandoned cars everywhere, no power, no sewer, no drinking water. We got some papers that allowed us to work, through a connection of my brother's, and we stayed in New Orleans—signed on to cut trees around high voltage at four hundred and fifty a day each, plus food and lodging. Anything we made on the side belonged to us and it was cash paid at the end of each day. It was tragedy for those folks, but it was a license to print money for the contractors. The whole city smelled, when we first got there. I thought of Sodom. And other things.

***

St. Gabriel only appears four times in the Bible. Some schol-ars of God say St. Gabriel is an archangel, on the same plane as Michael, and deals in vengeance and death. St. Gabriel is credited with having destroyed Sodom. Others say St. Gabriel is the angel of mercy, one of God's highest, maybe the highest, messenger. I don't claim to know. Somewhere it says that St. Gabriel never re-ally appeared, that all references to St. Gabriel are actually dreams that God had and St. Gabriel is mercy come to life through God's dreams and that mercy isn't what we understand it to be. Dying can be a privilege, I came to understand that in prison, as much as living can be its own gift. Mercy can be flowers, or making sure your aim is true. Dreams die hard. I know mine did. I don't imagine God's died any differently. Maybe St. Gabriel will appear again sometime.

***

I met her and it was like meeting life for the first time. She opened the eyes of my heart. In any other city she'd have been a model, not a dancer.

After, I asked her if she wanted me to go get some cigarettes. So she could smoke and go to sleep.

"Yeah," she said. "That would be nice." She smiled in the dark, hugging the pillow. She was all curves and so alive. Beyond beauti-ful. A for-real woman. We had talked for hours before this, about everything. She was without a doubt the most beautiful woman I'd ever seen. Inside and out. Her voice wasn't that sweet sickly Southern crap—she was Cajun, spoke her mind and had a good laugh. She lived like she meant it.

I put on jeans, a shirt and my light jacket and walked out into the New Orleans night. The fog was there, the storms had just ended. Crushed cars sat on Canal Street, but on Bourbon it was business as usual. I bought the cigarettes and a lighter and headed back.

She was gone when I got back to the room. No note, nothing. The sheets were still warm from her body, the pillow smelled of her. And I tried to take it like a good thing, that maybe she felt like I did and the possibility of getting closer was much more frightening than she could say. Or that she had a man to get home to get home to and leaving was polite—my karma had come back on me from Montana and I put the cigarettes in a drawer with the lighter.

***

The mess from the destruction went on and on. My brother and I burned through chains and gas and oil. We'd go out and check downed lines or move them with hot-line tools. Then we'd start cutting, so the scoops and chippers could come along and take care of what we left. When the humidity rose, my shirt was wet all day. The sawdust bounced off my safety glasses. We were cutting hundreds of years of growth. It was all the same to us.

***

She was at the room when I got back that one day. She was a little drunk, high. She had on a red top and jeans over those long legs. That didn't last. We fucked like champs and kept going. Beyond where we'd been before. She made my cock so hard it hurt and my mouth ached from being on her, everywhere. Hours. We smoked and talked in bed. Drank some beer. She was having problems in town, within the city. The cops were harassing her, her ex was harassing her. The guy she lived with turned out to be friends with dealers. The cops were watching her. They wanted to kill her, as revenge on her man. And she wanted to leave. She had children, two young boys, and wanted to give them a better life and she wanted a better life for herself. We came up with a plan that fit the hurricane. We made a hurricane of our own.

$$***$$

There is a town in Louisiana called St. Gabriel. It's a new town, only been around a couple years. After the hurricane, it was the morgue for all of New Orleans. The women's prison is in St. Gabriel too, they hold all the security classifications together under one roof. Women from Sodom, you might say, kicked out of New Orleans for their crimes. I doubt that anyone at the prison even knows who St. Gabriel is or was supposed to be. And the number of dreams that have died within those walls, countless thousands, even dying now. It could make your soul cry, if you were a sentimental person.

$$***$$

My brother didn't show two mornings later and when he hadn't come around in the afternoon, I went looking. He wasn't at the bar we hung out at. I finally walked over to the police station, about two in the afternoon and talked to them. They had grabbed him, thinking he was me.

"Who are you again?" the black cop behind the bullet proof glass asked me. He had the NOPD fatigues on and his gun sat smart at his right side.

"I'm his brother," I said. "I'd like to see him."

"We'd all like things," the cop said.

"Can I see him?"

The cop studied the sheet in front of him. "Lots of charges here," he said. People went in and out of the station house with a dazed look.

"What's the bail?"

"No bail," he said. "Just charges."

"What charges?"

He shook his head. "Felonies." Then he went and got the detectives.

***

They took us in a cop car and another unmarked car out to St. Gabriel prison. Nobody spoke on the way out. We drove around the facility and pulled up in a parking lot, near the edge of some trees. They had my brother cuffed. We walked out through the mud, until we could see something on the ground in front of us at the very edge of the woods, covered with some dirt and leaves. Half in the woods. It was a woman. In a red top and jeans. A large caliber shell had passed through her ribcage.

"Do you know her?" the cop asked. The detectives stood back, watching us.

"Not really," I said. It looked like her, but not if you knew her. Up close, like I did.

"She's been shot at long range. We think she was trying to escape and during the hurricane, someone had it in for her and shot her." He shrugged. "Or something."

"That's a good theory," I agreed.

"You wouldn't happen to know any boys from Montana, that have a reputation as long-shot artists, would you?" he asked with a New Orleans slow drawl.

"No," I said. "I honestly don't."

"That's funny," the one cop said. "Because after we ran your sheet and came up with some facts, we kind of thought it might have been you that pulled the trigger."

"I've never shot a woman," I said in truth.

"People change," the other cop said.

"Not that much," I said.

"We were looking for this woman, in New Orleans," the one cop said. "We were watching you."

"She was here," I said, pointing at the ground.

"You know," the one cop said, "during the hurricane, some bad folks in New Orleans disappeared."

"Must have got caught up in the storm," I reasoned.

"Certainly," the other cop said. "That stuff happens."

"This woman here," the one cop said. "This woman got caught by someone else."

"I don't know anything about it," I said. "I don't know why you have us out here."

The head detective walked over to the corpse and kicked it in the head as hard as he could. He watched me. "I've got y'all out here," he said, "because we think you were together and you're a killer. We have established that. What we haven't established is who this woman is. She was just printed the other day and that got destroyed in the storm. If she's the woman from the prison. On the other hand, if she's this woman we were looking for from New Orleans, the one hooked up with that dealer, then we can call that off, because we'd have done this to her anyways." He drew his foot back and kicked the head of the corpse again as hard as he could. The whole body moved off the ground a foot. "So which is it?"

"I know who it is," I lied. "I know her."

"Why'd you kill her?" the detective asked. "Did she owe you money? Drugs?"

"I didn't," I said.

He kicked the corpse right in the mouth and watched my face the whole time as he did it. "Does that bother you?" he asked. "I'm kicking your girl here." He stared at me. "Play tough guy like it doesn't bother you, but I'm going to kick her again."

"She's not feeling it," I said.

He brought his foot back and kicked the head of the corpse three or four times, hard. The sound was a loud wet smack. The body moved up and down. Mud and fluid mixed on his shoes and the gray cuff of his pants.

"This isn't the man we want," the detective said to the other cops. He motioned at my brother. "Uncuff him and let's go." He walked back through the mud to the unmarked car. I was walking behind him for a couple steps. He turned to me, his face white and puffy. "If that's her, and I think it is, you did us a favor." He kept on walking, toward the cars, alone.

One of the cops came forward with keys and uncuffed my brother. The cops walked back to their car and drove off, leaving me and my brother standing there outside the facility. After we walked for half an hour, we hitched a ride with a guy, back into New Orleans.

The hurricane raged through the night and day. An older man in southern Louisiana woke up with a straight razor under his bed, with a pink ribbon on it, like someone might use for a little girl's hair. His wife found her gas tank had been filled with pig's blood. A young man in New Orleans who lived with his dad found the locks to the house glued. A guy from Illinois, a DJ, woke up with his shit in the street, and broken ribs. There was mercy all along, no revenge, no vengeance. That's how you know a human did these things and not God. If it was God that had done them, the answer would all be the same. Death, death, death.

***

The work ended and we drove back to Montana. We hadn't made millions.

***

I ask myself that now, am I St. Gabriel? Is the mercy that I once had long gone and who will show mercy on me? What a privilege it will be to die. We create ourselves, or so we believe, and we become locked in, we become afraid not to meet the same person each morning in the mirror. I am St. Gabriel and I will stand accountable for what I do and will hold others to account. I am the highest of God's messengers and no Sodom will stand while I live.

***

Nobody asks a man why he drinks. Mixed in there with the private darkness of reasons, nobody wants to know the answer from the man who is already drunk. I was drinking to get a woman to come back to me, which is the worst reason of all. The cost of pain. When you see someone so bright, such a bright fire, a diamond, it stays with you and their image is on the inside of your eyelids when you close your eyes. I can still see her, she lights up the night of life. Who wouldn't want her back? Her smile alone could cure you of whatever disease had got hold of you. Oceans of booze couldn't put out that fire.

***

My brother saw her one time, in a bar, on TV, modeling in Milan. I was covered with sawdust and staggered in.

"She's coming," he said. "She'll be in the next clip."

I stared at the screen as it changed. It was her. She walked like a princess and a queen all at once, she fucking owned that crowd and that show and I had to look away. I was proud, so proud of her and all she had done and there was a plan that had worked.

✳✳✳

My brother knows better than to ever ask. You don't ask about stuff, because then you can't talk about it on the stand. He asked with his eyes, one night, late. We were standing in the cellar, throwing darts and doing laundry.

"Sure," I said. "Part of it was me. And part of it was her."

"It worked," he said.

"It got her a new life," I said. "She deserved that and more."

"Do you think she misses you?" he asked.

"Not in the way you might think," I said. "Like you might miss an old dog."

"You might be wrong," he said. "I miss my dog every day." He took his shirt off to put it in the wash and even his scars were healing from his trauma. His tattoos always looked amazing. He pulled a clean tee shirt over his head from the dryer.

I drank some beer.

"I really think you're wrong," he said. "She's going to come here and be with you."

"Fuck," I said. "I don't want to be with me most days. What would make her want to be with me?"

"Who else would protect her like that?" he asked.

I nodded. "But I would protect her like that and she doesn't have to be around. I'd do it anyway."

"Does she know you feel like this?"

I shook my head. "Look," I said. "I really don't want to get into all this. Somebody who has kids and is living a life, they don't need crap dumped on them. I can handle whatever I feel, regardless of the situation." I drank my beer. "What does it matter what I feel? I'm a grown man."

"What about being happy?" he asked.

"What's that got to do with anything?"

"Are you happy?" he asked. "Without her."

I drank some more beer. "I'm a big boy," I said. "I'm happy for her. That's all that matters." I shook my head again. "She's under enough strain without me being an asshole."

We threw some more darts and I walked upstairs and went to bed. It has been five years and she hasn't shown up. She won't. At first it was hard, but now it's the same. Sometimes, when I'm in a crowd, if we go to Spokane or all the way to Seattle, my eyes hurt and I have a headache. Because I've been looking for her, all day, among the faces. After an eighteen hour day of cutting and hauling big timber, even the work can't erase her from my mind. Thinking of her keeps me alive some days. Some people would call that sad. They don't know what I'm talking about it. I'm lucky.

***

When I wake up, I am someplace else in my mind. But she is always there. And I'm happy for her. She died the fake death and will get to live the real life. I will wake up in my coffin underground and be comforted. I'll wait for the hurricane to uproot me from my eternal rest and carry me off. To meet St. Gabriel, to whom I will show no mercy. Even if I am in hell, my aim will be true. Gravity pulls the bullet toward earth. There is friction, recoil energy, computed velocity, measured velocity, freebore travel, resistance, ratio of powder charge. None of it will stop me, it didn't stop me those nights in Montana when I had those five men in my sights and breathed easy and slowly increased the pressure on my finger until that hammer dropped. The cops of heaven can puzzle over the how and why and look for witnesses that don't exist. Maybe she is my St. Gabriel, appearing briefly and now only in my dreams. At least one of us made it out of the night.

***

If it weren't for her being alive in the world, I'd turn the gun on myself. Show myself the mercy I deserve. The chance to hear her voice keeps me on earth.

FUCK

KEN BRUEN

has been a finalist for the Edgar, Anthony and Barry awards and has won a Macavity Award and a Shamus for his Jack Taylor series. He lives in Galway, Ireland.

SPIT
KEN BRUEN

FUCK

Fuck

Fuck

I loved her.

That's the holy all of it.

I didn't ask for it, not like I woke up one morning, asked,

"Dear Jesus, let me fall in love."

Yeah, right.

I was thirteen years old at the time. I come from a family, what's the buzz word.......dysfunctional? Read fucked.

My mother was a shrill nervous woman and with good reason. My old man, a piece of work. I wish I could say he'd been a drinker, cover for him with what the Americans term *excuse abuse*.

No, he didn't drink.

He was simply one mean bollix. He liked to torture us, count the ways:

> Beatings
>
> Be-littlement
>
> Be-ratement

He was stuck on the B's.

More than enough for him I suppose, you find a letter that works, stick with it.

He did.

In public, Mr. Persona, the most charismatic, stand-up guy you could wish to meet, your classic psychopath.

He should have been a priest, he had all the ingredients.

What made him so?

The fuck knows?

And hey, it matters?

A toss?

You think finding the cause, the root, will ease the damage?

Dream on.

He fucked us but good.

I was just short of my eighteen birthday when he got lung cancer and the beauty of it is, he didn't smoke, his body was his shrine, he took real good care of his own self and fat fucking lot of good it did him.

Dutiful son?

You betcha.

I went to visit him every day, brought a mountain of grapes on each visit, big bag of those green suckers, plonked em right on his bedside table where he could see em. Before he finally gave it up, he grabbed my hand, gasped.

"I hate grapes."

I squeezed back, hard, said

"I know."

My mother, the tic under her left eye in full jig had said,

"You're a good son."

I smiled, said,

"Good, I want to ensure he gets good and dead."

She elected not to hear. You live with a tyrant for thirty years, selective hearing is but one of a line of fragile useless defences. We buried him on St Patrick's Day and thank God, it was raining, bucketing down.

Buried him cheap.

That night, me and my mate Johnny, we drank half a bottle of Jameson, six pints of the black and I dunno, cans of cider? I was delighted, like, really happy.

Fucking A.

Saoirse, the Irish word for freedom, the name of my obsession. More than spuds, the Irish love irony, even when they don't know what it means, especially then and her name, I wonder if that's ironic? It was certainly, fucking hell. I'd just turned thirteen when I first saw her. Standing outside Garavans, one of the oldest pubs. She'd have been fifteen then, wearing a black mini skirt, white T-shirt, black shiny boots and that Goth make up.

Man, I love boots.

Soft spot for Goths, too.

Soon as I began to pull in the wedge in America, making some real bucks, I bought me a hand made custom pair. Boots, not Goths, though they were certainly for sale.

Those boots, scuffed, beaten, worn to a thread, I ain't never giving those babies up.

Saoirse's hair was auburn, fell in ringlets to her shoulders. Thing is, she wasn't all that pretty.

But something.

Electricity in the eyes, attitude, a semi smile that danced around her mouth.

Her eyes were green.

I swear to fuck.

Green as shamrock. The key word there is sham.

What did I know? I was thirteen for Chrissakes. I do know, she smiled at me.

Open

Full

Radiant

Neon writ.

Cursed, blessed me, forever.

Then she turned away.

I was signed, sealed and delivered.

Maybe because of my horrendous home life, or my age, or chemistry or maddens, she, or the idea of her, got me through the next five years.

I learnt everything about her; I even knew her favorite color.

Red.

Figures.

I'd planned my eighteenth birthday, the day I'd make my pitch. You'd think five years would have given me plenty of time to get a decent rap together, a convincing spiel.

You'd be wrong.

She, of course, was twenty then, had developed in to a gorgeous woman. Hey, this isn't just my take, I'd hear guys going.

"That Saoirse, she's the biz."

I wanted to scream.

"*My* Saoirse."

She was studying business at The University. I'd watch her emerge from lectures, her hair caught by the wind, late winter sun on her cheeks and my heart was fit to implode. The delicious pain of demented longing, it was mighty.

Always, surrounded by a gaggle of girls.

No boyfriend.

If there had, I'd have waited for him, knifed him.

You think I'm kidding.

I already had the knife.

I'd been saving my money, I have a knack for cash, it just comes to me, and stays, unlike women. I had a part time job, in a fast food joint. You want to see the new Ireland, the real fruits of prosperity, see them eat.

Fucking pigs.

In the trough, true gutter snipe.

Oceans of fries and the greasier the better, triple burgers, with shite oozing from all sides, mage cokes and the manners of dirty mongrels. My old man loved one thing, his dog, a mongrel, named Eire. He ate with more delicacy than the new rich. I worked there four evenings a week, one of the reasons I hate people. The way you got treated by the *public*, leave the L out of that word, you got it down. I learned all I needed to know about ferocious barbarity, learned real well.

Bit I sucked it up, took the insults, the physical attacks, the flat out ignorance, the freaking condescension.

I simmered, whoa hey.

I had a higher cause.

When my old man croaked, I took Eire out the back, slit his mangy throat with my knife.

Felt good.

I asked as he did the death rattle.

"Fries with that?"

Day of my eighteenth, my mother bought me a cheap card and a cheaper shirt, said

"Things are a little tight, son."

Yada yada, what else was fucking new?

I threw them in the garbage.

I'd been buying me own gear, getting primed, getting set. Had me a black silk shirt with pearl buttons, black pre-washed 501s, black polished shoes.

Polished to a spit.

The piece de resistance.......see, me schooling wasn't a complete bust.......was a cream leather bomber jacket. Fucker creaked a bit so I washed it in the bath; put some fabric softner in there. Kinda worked.

I let me hair grow and had the gel ready to whip it into a cool frenzy. I was good to go.

The student dance was in The Boatclub. The bouncer was from our street so no problem there. Okay, let's get this out of the way, I better get this said:

I'm not real good looking.

Me nose is a little hooked and I have a thin mouth. But me eyes, they're the feature, big and blue, me sister said she'd kill for them.

I worked out, a lot, the Irish version, hurling. Go at that six days a week, you get lean and mean.

Me sister said women like guys with hard bodies.

I've only ever had one mate. Johnny Dunphy, a head banger, in every sense. Flunked out of school and was working in a garage. Well, he hung out there, dealt dope. New Ireland, we were awash in drugs.

Me, I don't do that shite.

Saoirse wouldn't like a druggie.

Only Johnny knew of me love. He used to rib me about it, till I put his head in the toilet. The hours before the dance, I was sweating like a cornered rat. Christ on a gate, me heart was hammering. I put on the gear, slathered on the gel, checked me own self in the mirror, said,

"Looking slick."

Almost believed it.

When I hooked up with Johnny, he gaped at me, went,

"Jesus wept."

I snapped.

"What?"

He blurted out,

"Danny, you look like a fucking ejit."

I blew him off. We were sitting on a bench near the canal. A year before, Johnny, high on E had gone into the water, strangled a duck, I laughed me arse off.

Headbanger.

We were swigging from a bottle of Jameson, Johnny had some other gig going, speed probably. I checked me watch, a Timex with a plastic strap. Took it off me old man's wrist when he first got sick, had said,

"Time's up, Pops."

Johnny, his eyes fevered, said,

"Danny, you're me mate, don't do this."

I shrugged him off and he said,

"She's a cunt."

I hit him smack in the mouth, broke his front tooth. I think he whimpered but he didn't call her any more names. He knew about the knife.

We got into the Boatclub around ten thirty. Jesus, it was packed, a punk band murdering, "*I never will marry.*"

Omen right there.

And then I saw her, sitting with her friends, shining in a low cut dress. My adoration hit DEFCON 1. I began to move. Johnny tried to grab me arm, I pushed him off, gritted

"F…u..c..k.. off."

She looked up as I approached and one of her friends whispered something. I was in front of her, and fuck, the band took that moment to have a break so my voice was audible, all

　　Down

　　　The

　　　　Line.

I asked,

"Saoirse, may I have the honor of the next dance?"

Cringe city.

And it gets worse.

I held out my hand, as I'd practiced a thousand times before the mirror, get that flourish just so, and wouldn't you fucking know it, the leather creaked.

Loudly.

She began to laugh, her friends too and she said,

"If you were the only prick in the hall, I wouldn't look at you."

I don't remember after that.

***

I'm twenty nine now and the years in New York have been tough. I've done good, real good.

See that watch on me wrist, that's a Rolex Oyster, you fucking better believe it. My knife is from Oklahoma, best blade I could have fine honed. I'm part owner in a bar in the Village and we pull down serious change. I did some very hairy stuff those early years but I didn't get caught, did get rich.

Johnny is out of prison, his six year stretch for dealing served in full. He's picking me up at Galway Airport. My mother's dead, I didn't go home for the funeral. Buried with my old man, she could never escape him, they deserve each other.

Not my problem.

Saoirse.......phew-oh, still have some difficulty saying the name, she was married and separated. She run a printing company, run it into bankruptcy. I've been negotiating to buy it through a solicitor in Galway. I'm going home.......To see her.

Being twenty nine and rich is fucking mighty. Don't let anyone shine you otherwise.

It rocks.

Am I happy.

Take a wild fucking guess.

Last panhandler I abused, he didn't seem too happy.

I'd bit down, got me a whole new plan, re-invented me own self. The old model sucked.

No biggie, trade the mother in.

I did.

You got the bucks, they got the surgery.

Nip and fucking tuck.

You betcha.

Got

>   Me nose fixed

>   Me teeth capped

>   Me hair styled (100 bucks a pop)

And learned to talk Yank.

How hard was that?

Harder than I thought.

Dropped, shite, bollocks, arse.

Adopted, crap, Jesus H. Ass.

Took a time.

Women.

Yeah.......well.

Used and abused.

Discarded.

A sound in my head of leather creaking.

I file them under,

>   "Disposable income."

My mother, her mantra,

"Unlucky in love, lucky in life."

You got that right.......*Mom.*

I'd been to Vegas, discovered a flair for roulette, blackjack.

Added to my pile.

In the bar game, you make connections. I made the dark and dangerous ones. The trick is, don't give a fuck.

I didn't.

I had no friends. You have a heart doused in hate, the fuck you want friends for?

See? See how I've learned the talk?

And walked it, with total sleek, sheer focus.

And

Hurt some, as George W. terms them, Folk?

Yeah, I fucked them over and good. It never, not once, cost me a moment's sleep.

One single time, Let the control slip, lost the plot. I've said, I don't do dope.

Dope for dopes.

And my drinking, purely social.

Couple cold Coors over a game, nothing major, I can go,

"Damn Yankees choked."

And sound like I give a fuck.

That one misstep, I dunno, I'd been putting down eighteen hour days, adding to the pile, flying way out on the edge and I got.......tired?

Maybe.

I certainly got careless.

Debbie, my manager in the Village pub, had been dropping hints and one evening I went to her apartment. She's a bottle of Old Grandad and I downed six?.......then a whole slew of Longnecks.

Green Day on the speakers.

And

I

Began

   To

      Share.

Oprah rules.

Spilled me guts, the whole Saoirse show. Debbie, weeping, moved to me, put her hand on my face, said,

"I'll make you whole again."

I put her in the hospital.

Had to call in heavy connections to make sure she went away.

Quietly.

I quit drinking.

I've been in Galway almost 2 weeks now, engineered a casual run in with Saoirse, she barely remembered me but was delighted with my dinner invitation. She still looked pretty damn hot.

I took her to a flash place on Quay St and after we sat down, I took the papers belonging to her company, placed them on the table. She was stunned, and I could see her mind working, I was going to give her the business back. Her face was glowing, she was on the verge of reaching over, placing her hand on mine, when I said,

"I have something for you."

She smiled demurely, and with all the phlegm, saved up for over ten years, I spat in her lovely face, I stood, put the papers of her company in my pocket, threw a wad of notes on the table, said,

"They say the fish is really tasty."

I've bought a new knife and we'll keep that for the next act, what is it Fitzgerald said?

"There are no second acts in American History."

Oh yeah?

LIBBY FISCHER HELLMANN

is the author of the award-winning suspense series featuring video producer and single mother Ellie Foreman. Libby grew up in Washington DC, but has lived in Chicago for thirty years. She is also the editor of *Chicago Blues*, a dark crime fiction anthology, which was released by Bleak House Books in October 2007. Her next novel, *Easy Innocence*, a stand-alone PI novel, will be released in 2008. She blogs at "The Outfit" (www.theoutfitcollective.com) with six other Chicago crime fiction authors, including Sara Paretsky, Barbara D'Amato, and Marcus Sakey.

THE JADE ELEPHANT
LIBBY FISCHER HELLMANN

GUS stared at the jade elephant in the window of the pawnshop, wondering if it could be his salvation. A soft translucent green, about ten inches tall, its trunk curled up in the air as if it was trumpeting the joy of existence. Charlieman, his fence, said that meant good luck. Charlieman was Chinese.

Gus folded his newspaper under his arm. Charlieman's pawnshop was pretty much the same as all the others. Tucked away in a building with an illegal gambling operation upstairs, it was a grim and dingy place. Faded yellow Chinese characters—who knew what they said?—covered the window. A shabby dragon sat above the door spitting imaginary fire.

Gus trudged down chalky cement blocks and pushed through the door of the restaurant. One of the few that hadn't fled to the suburbs, it had dim lights. That wasn't all bad—at least you couldn't see the yellowed napkins and the stains on the tables.

Pete was in the second booth, slurping his soup. The only other customers were three Asian men at a back table. The Chamber of Commerce claimed Chinatown was bustling with commerce, but much of that commerce was conducted by dubious "businessmen" in alleys or street corners or greasy Chinese spoons like this. Rumor was the mayor had slated Chinatown for urban renewal. Then again, that was always the rumor.

Pete stopped slurping and looked up. "What kept you?"

"Traffic." Gus slid into the seat across, wondering why they still came here at all. Habit, he figured. Inertia.

His partner grunted and went back to his soup.

"How is it?"

"Like always."

A waiter came over and offered Gus a laminated plastic menu whose edges curled away from the page. Gus waved it away. "The usual, Chen."

"You want egg roll or soup?" he asked, rolling his "r's" so they sounded like "l's."

Gus pulled his coat more tightly around him. The December cold had seeped into his bones. "Soup."

Chen nodded and disappeared through a swinging door that squeaked when it flapped.

Pete looked over. "So?"

Gus leaned his elbows on the table. "It was benign."

Pete cracked a smile. "Attaboy!"

"I was lucky."

"It's all that clean living." Pete laughed. "What'd the doc say?"

Chen came out from the kitchen, carrying a steaming bowl of soup. He set it down in front of Gus.

"That it happens when you get old."

"Who's fucking old?" Pete sounded defiant.

"You're pushing sixty, and so am I," Gus said. "He said I could get another in a couple of years. With the stress and all."

"Stress causes tumors?"

Gus nodded. "Said I should take better care of myself. Build up my immune system."

"Eat your vegetables," Pete snorted.

"That's what he said."

Pete took a bite of his egg roll and chewed slowly. "But hey. You dodged the Big C. Time to celebrate!" He twisted around. "Hey, Chen. You got any champagne in that lousy kitchen of yours?"

Chen's face scrunched into a frown. "Sorry. No champagne. Next door. I go?"

"Naw. Don't bother," Gus called out. He looked over at Pete. "It ain't worth it."

"You sure?" Pete looked like he wanted to argue, but then decided not to. "Well, at least have some Dim Sum."

"I don't—"

"Chen. Bring the man one of your fucking Dim Sum, okay?"

Chen disappeared into the kitchen.

"So you ready to get back to work?" Pete asked.

"Why? You got something?"

"I got lots of somethings." Pete grinned. "I was waiting to hear about you. There's this sweet job out in Barrington, for openers."

Chen brought the Dim Sum on a plate. Gus studied the puffy white thing, not sure how to eat it, then palmed the whole thing and took a bite. It was surprisingly good.

"There's this trader. Mostly retired now, see. Lives in a mansion, but they're gone most of the time. Snowbirds in winter, Michigan in summer, Europe in between. The place is empty. We get Billy to disconnect the alarm, and—"

"Not Billy! Christ. He's a maniac on wheels. Remember the last time? He nearly got us picked up."

"I know. But he's good with electronics." Pete made a brushing aside gesture. "So. You in?"

Gus shook his head. "I don't think so. Not now."

Pete frowned. "How come?"

When Gus didn't answer, Pete shrugged and poured himself some tea. He took a sip and made a face. "Bitter."

Gus smiled.

"What's so funny?"

Gus shook his head. "Nothing."

"Hey," Pete said. "There's something else we need to discuss."

"What?"

"I think we got a problem with Charlieman."

Gus shot him a look. "What kind of problem?"

"Well, you probably didn't notice, what with being preoccupied with your—your situation. But I got a feeling something's—well, he's just not himself. I think he's in trouble. I'm thinking he made a deal with the goddam devil. Surveillance. That kind of shit. So I found this other guy, but he's not in Chinatown, see? And I—"

"No." Gus shoved his bowl of soup away.

"What do you mean, 'no'?"

"Charlieman would have warned us. We've been working with him a long time."

"I don't know, Gus. He's different these days."

Chen came with their food: chicken chow mein for Gus, sweet and sour pork for Pete. Gus sprinkled crunchy noodles from a wax paper bag on top. For a few minutes, the only sound was the clink of forks on plates. They hadn't used chopsticks for years.

After a while, Pete blurted out, "Hey, man, what's the matter?"

"Nothing."

"Don't try to con a con. I know you twenty years."

Gus stopped eating. "You're right." He laid his fork across his plate. "When I was sitting in the doc's waiting room, there were all these patients there. Most of them were really sick, you know? You could—I could tell from their goddam faces."

Pete nodded.

"The doctor was over an hour late. I don't know why the assholes can't get their act together, know what I mean?"

Pete giggled nervously. "If we were that late, our asses would be warming the benches at Cook County."

Gus nodded. "I'm antsy, you know? I hate hospitals. So I take a walk down the hall. So there I am walking, and there's this pay phone at the other end. I walk past it and I see this woman on the phone."

Pete speared a chunk of pineapple.

"She was in a hospital gown, and she was crying."

"Fuck. I hate to see a woman cry."

"Me, too. So I turn around and go back the other way, but as I did, I sneak a look at her." Gus paused. "There was something familiar about her. I don't know. Something about her face. Her voice, too. I'd heard it before."

"Yeah?" Pete shook out a cigarette from the pack he kept in his shirt pocket.

"I walk away real slow, but I can still hear her, you know? Turns out she's talking to her insurance company. Asking them to pay for a new kidney. But they don't want to. She's begging them, Pete. Says she don't got nothing left. She's got to get some help, or she'll die."

Pete struck a match and lit the cigarette. "That's tough."

"She looked bad, too. Scrawny. Pale. All bent over." He sighed irritably. "I mean, the woman's looks like she's about to keel over any minute, and no one lifts a finger to help."

"Maybe her—what d'ye call it—maybe she reached her limit."

"I dunno. So, I'm just turning around on my way back to the doctor's office, when it dawns on me how I know her."

"How?"

Gus licked his lips. "We, pal. She was one of our marks."

"What?"

"You remember the job we did in the high rise downtown? About six months ago?"

An uneasy look came over Pete. "The one where the woman was in her bedroom and we had to—"

"Yeah. The one where you, and then me—where we scored the jade elephant."

"No, man. You gotta be wrong. What are the odds—"

"I'm telling you it was her. You were the one …" He paused. "… who took care of her, remember?"

"I remember." Pete frowned. "Hey, do you think that was how—?"

"I don't think anything. Except that she's gonna die because she can't pay for a goddamn kidney transplant."

"Shit. That's Twilight Zone stuff, you know?" Pete shook his head. "But we didn't make her kidney dry up. All we did was rip her off."

"You think?" Gus went quiet.

"Hey." Pete went on. "This ever happen to you before?"

"No."

"Me neither, but Pauly … remember Pauly?"

"We worked a couple jobs with him, right?"

"Yeah. So he's doing a job out on the North Shore. Something looks familiar. He can't place it. Then all of a sudden, he realizes he ripped off the place five years earlier. The same place. But this time, he trips a silent alarm and some guy comes after him with a shotgun. He got five to ten."

Gus kept his mouth shut.

"Hey, don't get squirrelly on me. God didn't put her in your path. It's just the way it goes. Her luck ran out. Yours didn't." Pete wiped his napkin across his mouth. "By the way Mike—the new fence— says he can get us ten grand or more for that elephant."

***

Pete did the job in Barrington the following week without Gus. He did another in Winnetka after that. Gus insisted he use Charlieman to fence the goods, but Pete wasn't happy. He wouldn't even go into the pawn shop. Gus handled the negotiations. While he was there, Gus scoped out the place, looking for tiny cameras, bugs, or recorders, but he didn't see a thing. The place looked like it always did: shabby and crowded with junk. He asked Charlieman how much he wanted for the jade elephant, but Charlieman said he didn't know. He was waiting for the right customer.

The next few weeks flew by. The city glittered with lights, music, and tinsel. Even Chinatown was decked out. If you walked down Cermak, you could hear a tinny rendition of "Silent Night" from somewhere. Pete convinced Gus to have lunch at a new restaurant in the Loop, but the waitresses were too young for the attitude they copped, and the food was too rich.

"So what's it gonna take for you to come back to work?" Pete asked over apple pie. "You were right. Billy is a fucking lunatic."

"I don't know, Pete."

"You still thinking about that woman?"

Gus shrugged.

"You think it's your fucking fault. You want to do something for her."

Gus looked over in surprise. "How did you know?"

"You always had a goddamn soft spot."

Gus shrugged again and finished his pie.

After lunch Gus bought himself a winter coat at Field's and started walking. He noticed the squealing kids and their parents in front of the department store windows. The Salvation Army volunteers shaking their bells. People gliding around the skating rink, sappy smiles on their faces. Why was everyone so goddamn cheerful? Come January, all the unkept promises would litter the streets like garbage. Now, though, the promise of hope and deliverance floated through the air. Gus fastened the buttons on his new coat.

He hadn't planned it—or maybe he did—but just before dusk he found himself in front of a condo off Michigan Avenue. It was prime property, the middle of the Gold Coast. That's why they'd cased it to begin with. They'd hit more than one place in the building, and truth was, it had been a good day. In addition to the jade elephant, they'd scored some jewelry and a roll of bills some idiot had stored in his freezer.

"Got us some cold cash," Pete had laughed afterwards.

"Everyone's a comedian," Gus replied.

Now, he peered up at a series of porches that jutted out from the building like horizontal monoliths. She lived on the eighth floor, he remembered. He counted out eight slabs. Light seeped around the edges of the window shades. What was she doing? He was surprised to realize he hoped she wasn't alone. That someone was looking in on her. He wondered how she got the jade elephant in the first place. Had she traveled to some exotic spot to buy it? Was it a gift? He lingered on the sidewalk, half-expecting to see some sign she had found a way to pay for her kidney. But all he saw were flat granite facings, slabs of porch, and light seeping around the window shades.

He took the subway and then the bus to his apartment on the West side. He turned on the tube to some tear-jerker about a lost baby and a frantic mother. Ten to one there'd be a "Christmas miracle" where they found the little bugger. A few minutes later, he snapped it off and pulled out a bottle of bourbon.

✳✳✳

The next night Pete told Gus something came up and he couldn't meet him for dinner. Just as well, Gus thought. He wolfed down a sandwich and a brew at his neighborhood bar. Then he went home, and dressed in dark clothes, gloves, and a stocking cap. He filled his pockets with a knife, picklock, and flashlight. Opening a drawer, he lifted out his .38 Special. He raised it to eye-level and sighted, then slid it into his holster. He belted the holster around his waist.

It was after midnight when he got off the Red Line at Chinatown. The Hawk was hurling blasts of arctic air that sliced through him like a blade. Halfway to the pawn shop, he heard footsteps behind him. He moved into the shadows. Three Asian goons swaggered down the block like they owned it. They probably did, thanks to an uneasy alliance with the Russians. The street was full of Boris's and Wan Chu's these days; Tony and Vito were just bench-warmers.

Gus waited until they were gone, then snuck into the alley behind the pawn shop. A lamppost spilled weak light on Charlieman's back door. The smell of garbage was strong. He pulled out his picks and was about to start working the lock when he noticed the door was slightly ajar. Curious. Charlieman never forgot to lock up. Gus put his ear against the door. He heard a faint rustling. Mice? Then he heard a couple of steps. Not mice.

Gus stuffed his picklocks back in his pocket. If Charlieman was working late, his lights would be on. So it wasn't Charlieman. Maybe it was one of the Asians? Charlieman had been talking about getting a silent alarm, but Gus always figured he was too cheap to spring for it. Still, he slipped out of the alley and went around to the front. He peered at the window. Damn! The jade elephant which usually sat in Charlieman's window was gone!

Suddenly the overhead lights snapped on, and a harsh fluorescent glare poured over everything. In the stark illumination, Gus saw Charlieman at the back of the store, aiming a gun at someone. Gus squinted and craned his neck. Christ! It was Pete! The jade elephant was in his hand.

Gus froze. He thought about banging on the window and yelling, "Hey, Charlieman, don't shoot!" He thought about pulling out his .38, but knew he couldn't get to it in time. How could he shoot his fence, anyway? Maybe he could buy Pete some time. Make a disturbance. Take Charlieman's attention off his friend. He started toward the front door, shouting, "Stop! Both of you."

Pete looked his way, astonished. So did Charlieman. Gus jiggled the doorknob. "Listen, this isn't right. Put the gun down. We can work it out."

Charlieman's gun hand waved dangerously from side to side. Wild Chinese exclamations spewed out of his mouth. Pete took the hint. He feinted left, broke right and, lunged toward the back door. He even managed to throw it open before Charlieman pulled the trigger. The flash of blue made Gus blink. Pete bent over so far his face nearly touched the floor, but he lurched through the door.

Gus ran back into the alley. Pete collapsed on the ground, still clutching the jade elephant. Gus crouched next to him.

"What were you thinking, pal?" he said softly. "Why did you do it?"

The only thing that came out of Pete's mouth was a gurgle.

Sirens whined in the distance. Gus looked up. Charlieman was at the back door yelling hysterically in Chinese and making big swooping gestures. Gus was back in the shadows, so he knew Charlieman couldn't see him.

The phone rang inside the shop. Charlieman backed away from the door. Pete lay curled on his side. Gus gazed at the jade elephant. By some miracle, the thing wasn't broken, but Gus could see streaks of red marring its green surface. Merry Christmas.

The sirens grew louder. The flashing lights were only a block away. Gus tried to ease the elephant out of his partner's hands, but Pete's grip was too strong. Gus had to pry back one finger at a time before he it came loose. Clutching it to his chest, he scrambled up and hurried from the shop.

***

The next morning, Gus wrapped the elephant in newspaper, stuffed it in a shopping bag, and headed downtown. He steered around an old woman hunkered down on the pavement with a black kettle in front of her and a hand-lettered sign that said "Need money for food." Everyone had their hand out this time of year.

When the doorman made him cool his heels in the lobby, Gus grew uneasy. He shouldn't be here. This was crazy. He was just about to leave when the doorman got off the intercom and pointed him to the elevator. The numbers on the car's panel blinked as he flew up, but the door was slow to open. When Gus finally stepped off, the woman was waiting for him in the hall. She looked every bit as pitiful as she had at the hospital.

He handed her the shopping bag. "This belongs to you. Merry Christmas."

She peeked into the bag then set it on the floor. "Well, I'll be damned."

Gus cocked his head.

"I remember you," she nodded. "And your partner."

Gus swallowed. "He's dead."

"Too bad." She said it almost cheerfully. A steely look came into her eyes. "But I remember what you did to me. The rope. The gag. And the rest of it. You almost killed me."

"That's why I'm here. I'm—well—I hope this helps." He looked down.

Silence pulsed between them. "I saw you at the hospital," she said. "While I was on the phone."

Gus looked up, surprised.

"Afterwards I went to the nurse to get your name. I even got your address when the nurse wasn't looking. I was going to call the cops, turn you in."

Gus fingered the button on his coat. "But you didn't."

"No."

"Why not?"

"I had a better idea." She eyed him curiously. "Why did you come here?"

"I told you. I wanted to give this back to you. It's worth a lot of money."

"You trying to turn over a new leaf?"

He shrugged. "Maybe."

She laughed, but it was a hollow sound, and something about it pricked the hair on his neck.

"So are we square?" He asked.

She didn't say anything for a moment. Then, "We will be."

Gus's felt himself frown.

"I've been thinking about this for a long time."

"About the jade elephant?"

"No." She slipped her hand in her pocket and pulled out a .22. "Did you know we have the same blood type?"

Gus frowned. "Huh?"

She grimaced. "Well, I'll say one thing. You saved me a trip to your place." She aimed high, so as not to damage his kidneys. "Merry Fucking Christmas."

DAVID BOWKER

is the Manchester born author of seven novels including *I Love My Smith & Wesson* and *How To Be Bad*. He is currently dividing his time between novel number eight and his work as a screenwriter, developing two feature films and two original sitcoms for TV.

JOHNNY SEVEN
DAVID BOWKER

HIS name was Johnny Seven.

You think the name is weird, you should have seen his eyes. They were real blue and bright, like the eyes on some kind of light-up action figure. First time I saw him, there was this silence, like that part in a western when the stranger walks into the saloon. The new kid was thin and not very tall, with longish fair hair. He had a tiny rip in the left elbow of his jacket, like his folks were on welfare or something. Pretty neat jacket, all the same. He sure didn't carry himself like he was on welfare.

We were all sitting down, waiting for the teacher to show. For a few moments, Johnny boy hung around in the doorway of the classroom like he'd rather be somewhere else. But then Griff came up behind him, put his hand on Johnny's shoulder and steered him right in. "This is Jonathan Severn and I'm sure you'd all like to welcome him."

Griff wasn't even our real teacher. He was some fucked up old man who they brought in when the real teachers were sick. He probably should have been in an old people's home. He was always telling us things that weren't suitable for middle school kids to know, like what the Germans did to the Jews in the war. Once he gave us all paper and crayons and asked us to draw a Martian pancake. The point was that no one knew what a Martian pancake looked like, so everybody had to use their imaginations. I drew a car crash with bodies on the road and blood everywhere. Griff said to me: "That isn't a Martian pancake." I said: "How the fuck do you know?" so he sent me to the Vice Principal.

It was unlucky for Johnny Seven that the first teacher he met was this senile old guy who wasn't even his real teacher. When Griff asked us all to welcome Johnny, no one did. So Johnny just stood there, hanging his head like he found the whole situation humiliating. He walked over to the only free desk, some of the girls smiling at him, then he sat down, not really looking at anyone, eyes straight ahead. Griff launched straight into his dull old routine. "Johnny, maybe you have an opinion about what took place today?"

"Took place where?" said Johnny. No sir, no nothing.

I laughed. Griff shot me a look that said shut the fuck up.

"You're from New Jersey and you really don't know what happened?" Griff just wasn't buying this.

Johnny shook his head, real steady and slow. The way he did it, you could tell he knew exactly what had happened that day. Griff knew it too. Suddenly there was this electric feeling in the air. Something different was happening. Everyone could feel it. Griff was doing what teachers always do. He was holding up a hoop for good little boys and girls to jump through. But the new kid just wasn't playing.

Griff looked around the class. "Anyone?"

Bugaski put up his hand. Bugaski always put up his hand whether he knew the answer or not, just so it looked like he was making an effort. Bugaski's report card probably says "This kid has got a name like one guy sticking it to another guy, he's practically a vegetable, but he sure as hell can wave his arm in the air."

"Sir!" said Bugaski.

At first, Griffiths ignored him.

"Sir, sir!" said Bugaski, wriggling and pleading like he was about to hatch a monster turd. "Sir, was it Bob Hope?"

"No," said Griff. "Come on. The news today. Someone must know. Anyone?"

Blank fuckin' faces.

"Come on. Something happened to someone associated with this state."

Anne Marie held her hand in the air. I like her, she's so nice you hardly even notice she's a whale. "Somebody Davies," she said.

"Hallelujah," said Griff. Real sarcastic. "That's close enough. *Jack David.* He was executed this morning. Anyone know why?"

"Was he a poor black guy that never did anyone any harm?" I said.

"Be quiet, Newton," said Griff. He turned back to Anne Marie. "Maybe you could tell us?"

"He blew up a library."

"Blew up a library?" said Warren Sherman, real shocked. "Really? They executed a guy just for blowing up a library?"

Griff sneered. "It had people in it, Sherman."

Even so …

This is how fucked up Griff was. I complained to the Vice Principal about him but she never listened. He should have been teaching us about algebra or some shit. Instead, he asked us whether we thought the US government having the power to kill one of its own citizens was good or bad. Bugaski put up his hand as usual and said, "Sir, sir, is it a good thing, sir?"

Griffiths kind of sighed. "Bugaski, this is not a quiz."

I said: "If you ask me, it's a terrible example to set to children."

"But no one's asking you, Newton," said Griffiths.

As well as being senile, Griff was a Christian. He was one of those weird Christians who hates the whole human race. He once told us wars were terrible things, but they were useful for keeping down the excess population. Guy like that, would he count murderers as excess population? I guess he would.

Kirsten Wells, dumb but gorgeous, held up her hand. "If Jack David didn't want to die for his crime, he shouldn't have planted the bomb in the first place."

Wow. Great fuckin point, Kirsten. A real sizzler.

Griff gave a nod, just to humor her. He was probably thinking he had to stay on the right side of her, in case the bomb went off and him and Kirsten were the last two people left alive. Dumb or not, a girl who looked like Kirsten could be pretty useful in a post-nuclear situation.

My dad already explained why Jack David did it but I wasn't really listening. It was something to do with protesting about the government. All I know is the whole senate ganged up on this guy. It wasn't just a state crime, it was something called a federal crime, which means you've insulted the whole of America. Like saying, "Fuck off America."

And now I was feeling sorry for Griffiths. All he wanted was for the new kid to throw him a bone but Johnny was sitting there like Whistler's mother. Griff tried again. "Five years ago in this very city, the Melton Library was blown apart by a bomb that David left in an elevator. Over two hundred people died."

Big silence. Suddenly the new kid sighed, like he wanted to get something out but didn't know how. "Okay," he said. "Okay."

"Yes?"

"I don't like talking about it, sir, but actually, yeah," said Johnny, all solemn and still. "I remember that day very well."

"Hmm?"

"I didn't want to say, sir. My mom worked in the City Library. We lost her that day."

Shit. The whole room was in shock. Griff's face turned purple nearly, and his mouth dropped wide open. Teachers aren't meant to have feelings, but now he looked like he was about to cry. "Oh. Oh." That's all he said. It's like he couldn't move, he was paralysed.

"I didn't want to say," said Johnny like he was about to cry. "You forced it out of me."

"I'm extremely sorry, boy," said Griff. He said it like he meant it.

"Wasn't just mom. We lost my dad that day," said Johnny. "And my big sister. They were only returning their books, too."

Griffiths stared, open-mouthed.

"Yes sir, Mr. Griffiths, sir. My uncles and aunts all got killed, too," said Johnny. "Along with the little dog who lived down the fucking lane."

Griff kind of rocked on his heels and his face went all pink. Then Griffiths dragged that kid out of his chair and damn near threw him halfway across the room. "How dare you! Get out!" Griffiths was screaming.

Johnny left like he was told. He looked real happy to be going.

"You shouldn't have done that," I told Griffiths. "Throwing kids is against the law."

That's all I said, but the way Griff turned on me, you'd have thought it was me who blew up the fucking library. "You too, Newton."

"Sir?"

"I said get out!" I get a real big blast of his breath. It smelled like he'd been eating dogshit with a mayonnaise dressing.

"Hey!"

"Don't 'hey' me, boy! Out!"

I looked at my friend KC, hoping he'd put in a good word for me; tell Griffiths I didn't mean to cause offense. KC kind of shrugged with his eyes like it wasn't really any of his business.

"What did I do?" I said.

"You're an idiot. Get the hell out of my classroom!"

In the corridor, Johnny Seven was smoking a cigarette. I couldn't believe it. "What is wrong with you, man? You're gonna get yourself expelled on your first day," I said.

He smiled at me and blew smoke in my face. "Let's hope so."

***

At lunch, Johnny wandered through the yard on his own, kids giving him a wide berth in case getting hurled across a classroom was contagious. Me and KC were smoking behind the wall. KC was a year older than me. His real name was Kevin Chester, but he called himself KC because he thought his real name sounded gay. He was fucking right.

Wasn't just his name, either. When he got drunk, KC was always dancing and taking his clothes off, even when there weren't any girls around. But if you reminded him of it when he was sober, he punched you on the fucking arm. KC switched schools and had to start the eighth grade all over because he wasn't achieving his full potential. His grades were so bad his parents were afraid he'd grow up to be President of the USA.

"Maybe we should talk to the new kid," said KC.

"And say what?"

"I dunno. Anything. Tell him you're sorry about his family blowing up."

"You fuckin' idiot. He was making all that shit up about his family. That's why Griff threw him out."

"Oh. Really? I thought he was just lying about the dog."

Kevin's dad drove a limo, and I don't mean he was no chauffeur. He worked for some big chemical corporation and smoked cigars and wore a smoking jacket in the home. When I first saw this smoking jacket I thought it was some kind of comedy robe. If I visited Kevin's house, his dad always shook me by the hand like I was an old friend and asked about my parents. Kevin's dad wouldn't have known my mom and dad if he'd driven over them in his fucking limo.

"You don't know what it's like," says Kevin. "Switching to a new school is the worst fuckin' feelin.'"

"Worse than what? Worse than having boiling oil poured in your ears?"

"Fuck you."

"Anyway, you did know somebody. You already knew me when you came to this school."

"Exactly, Newton."

"What's that supposed to mean?"

"Whatever the fuck you want it to mean."

"You already done the eighth grade once. You're familiar with all the fuckin' subjects. You said so yourself. What's so tough about that?"

Kevin punched me on the shoulder.

The last school KC went to was this Catholic place run by a bunch of real monks. Except instead of being all peaceful and holy, these were the kind of monks that stank of sweat and twisted guy's nipples when they stepped out of line. I told KC that twisting nipples was illegal. KC said that if it was in the Bible, it's okay for monks to do it.

Kevin got a lot of shit from his mom and dad, about how he had to work real hard to fulfill his dream. What dream? Far as I know, he didn't have a dream, apart from wanting to own a Harley someday. Kevin was a big tough kid with real muscles but when his dad told him he was letting down his family, he cried like a baby. I saw him do it once.

"You comin' round Maya's house tonight?"

Maya was allegedly Kevin's girlfriend. She was twelve years old, with no tits whatsoever. That kind of thing might go down well in Mississippi, but it looks pretty sick in New Jersey.

"Yeah. Okay."

"Her cousin's comin round. Mirabeth. Did you ever hear such a stupid name?"

"How old is she? Seven?"

This time, he tried to kick me. It was a pretty half-assed attempt, though. For an athlete, Kevin was getting a little porky. Every day, his lunchbox has about two million cookies in it. Kevin says this is because his mom used to be trailer trash and never had enough to eat as a kid. But her dad, KC's grandpa, worked real hard until one day, he became the trailer trash that owned the trailer park. Suddenly Kevin's mom found she could eat all the cookies she wanted. And now she made sure her little boy always had his fill of cookies too, so he wouldn't stand out in a crowd of Americans.

"You scared?" said KC.

"What of?"

"I dunno," said KC. "I just feel something bad is going to happen."

"That's right," I said. "It's called the rest of your fucking life."

✱✱✱

That night, KC called for me. We were going to hang out at the mall, spitting off of the balcony before going over to Maya's. On the way, we saw old Johnny Seven sitting on his bike outside a house with paint peeling off the front door. There was an old fucked-up pickup truck parked in the drive.

"Yo," I said. "What're you doing here?"

"I live here," he said.

A big freight train rattled by. The railroad ran past the back of Johnny's house. We had to wait until the train had passed before we could hear ourselves talk.

"Your name's really Johnny Seven?" said Kevin, with a big smile. "That's one cool fuckin' name."

"But it's not seven like the number," said Johnny. "It's got an 'r' in it." He spelled it out for us. "S-e-v-e-r-n."

"Oh. I prefer Seven," said Kevin.

"My uncle says Johnny Seven was the name of a toy you could buy when he was a kid. It was a plastic rifle with toy grenades that you could actually fire."

"Yeah?" I said.

"So your mom and dad named you after a toy? That's cool," said Kevin, who never listens.

"I ain't got a mom," said Johnny. "My dad raised me by himself."

We didn't know what the fuck to say to that. Then Johnny said: "That Griffiths is a real grade-A cunt, don't you think?"

"Yeah," I said.

"One of these days someone's going to shoot that guy in the head while he's begging for mercy," said Johnny.

It was a weird thing to say, all right. Kevin kind of stared. "Yeah. Like you'd fuckin' do it."

"I fuckin' would," said Johnny. "I'd do it just like that."

"You'd shoot a teacher? Yeah. Fuckin' right."

"Certainly wouldn't shoot a kid," said Johnny Seven.

"You're full of shit," said Kevin.

"The rights of children are sacred," said Johnny, not like a preacher would say it, but in the voice of a real person. "Any adult who violates those rights shall die."

We didn't know what to say to that neither.

So me and Kevin said goodbye to the new kid and cycled away real fast so it looked like we were on some kind of secret mission for the government. On the corner of Chatsworth, we spotted Wheelchair outside his house. It was like he was lying in wait. Except he was sitting, not lying.

"Oh, fuck, no," said KC.

We were so depressed we almost turned right round and went home again. Wheelchair was the same age as me. Shelton's his real name, but one day my mom accidentally renamed him by telling me I should see the person, not the wheelchair. I took a real good look at the person and guess what? I preferred the wheelchair.

All year long, Wheelchair sits at the end of his drive and accuses kids of all kinds of crazy crimes he's imagined. My mom says it's not Wheelchair's fault, the poor bastard can't tell the difference between dreams and reality. She may be right, I don't give a fuck. It's upsetting to be heckled by a cripple.

Tonight, Wheelchair gave us one of his old favorites.

"You're the kid who stole my boomerang!" he shouted, pointing right at me.

We stopped to look at him. Wheelchair wore glasses that magnified his eyes, so he always looked angry and sad. Maybe he was. Guess he had every fuckin' right to be. Thing is, some people in wheelchairs wish they could walk. I swear this kid wished everyone else was in wheelchairs.

"He never touched your stupid boomerang," said KC.

"I saw the bastard do it!" yelled Wheelchair.

"I think you're mistaken, pal," said KC in a reasonable kind of voice.

"Liar!"

"Anyway, when'd you ever even have a boomerang?" I said. "Bet you never even seen a boomerang."

I felt bad as soon as I've said it. Not as bad as Wheelchair, though. His bottom lip trembled and he glared at me like he wanted to kill me. Then he started to cry. Right away, I knew I'd committed a major sin. I'd made a kid in a wheelchair cry. KC stared at Wheelchair, dead serious. When we rode away, he said: "What the fuck did you have to go and say a thing like that for?"

"You were the one who said his boomerang was stupid," I said.

"Sometimes you're a real prick, Garrett. You know that?" said KC.

In my defence, Wheelchair isn't the easiest cripple to get along with. My kid brother Monkey, who writes compositions about what a swell guy Jesus is, went up to Wheelchair once and tried to make friends with him. Wheelchair was real grateful, so grateful he tried to pull Monkey's pants down. That's the trouble with the less fortunate. One minute you're trying to do them a good turn. The next minute they're pulling your pants down.

When we turned up at Maya's house, she was with her cousin Mirabeth. Name like that, I thought Mirabeth would be terrifyingly ugly. Mister, she was not. She was the same age as her cousin. Long dark curly hair and no tits, also like her cousin. A pretty face, though. I really liked her. Right away, I wanted to impress her so I pretended to fall off my bike. Mirabeth laughed a lot, so did Maya. I felt I was off to a great start.

Maya's mom and dad were out at the store with her kid sister, so we all went inside to listen to music. Except Maya didn't have any music, all she had was her mom's fuckin' Neil Diamond CDs. Me and KC were supposed to listen to this shit and act like we enjoyed it, just for the privilege of sitting in the same room as two girls. Except I didn't pretend, I said right away that in my opinion, Neil Diamond didn't deserve to live.

Mirabeth and Maya went off to fetch us some cokes from the kitchen. Then Maya came back to say that in *their opinion*, I was very immature and didn't deserve to be in their grown-up company.

"What?" I said to Maya. "You're kicking me out?"

Maya nodded. Mirabeth passed me my coke and shrugged, like it wasn't up to her.

"Seriously? You are seriously asking me to leave? What about Kevin?"

"Kevin stays," said Maya.

"What about my coke?" I said.

Maya told me to drink it outside. I waited for Kevin to take my side and say that no buddy of his took orders from a flat-chested moron but he just sat there same as fucking usual, sipping his coke like enamel wouldn't melt in his mouth.

I told Maya I admired Neil Diamond really, really admired his wig and the way he pretended he had a deep voice. But it was too late. The bitch said no, I was leaving anyway. She kept saying I was immature. I got my revenge by farting real loud outside the window.

By the time I'd finished my coke it was getting dark. I was sulking on the porch when Johnny Seven rode by on his bike. He saw me and right away slammed on his brakes *eek-eek-eeeek*.

"Hey," he said.

"How's it goin'?" I said. Feeling awkward because I hardly knew anything about the kid, apart from the fact that he was a little insane.

"What did you say to Shelton, man?"

"You mean Wheelchair."

"No. I fucking don't. I mean Shelton."

"Shelton Wheelchair. What about him?"

"What did you do?" said Johnny. "I just seen the kid, he was almost hysterical."

I told him everything about the conversation. Johnny leaned over and spit on Maya's drive. "He's a kid, Newton. One of our own. We've got to look after our own."

"Yeah. But he's crazy. He scares me."

"He's scared too, man," said Johnny patiently. "Shelton can't tell dreams from reality."

"How the fuck would you know?"

"Because I talked to him."

I doubted this. Far as I knew, Shelton's only topic of conversation was boomerangs. Johnny gave me a stick of gum. "Thing is, I don't want kids ripping on other kids. I don't like it."

"You don't like it? What the fuck's it got to do with you?"

"Just go easy on him," said Johnny. "I'm asking you as a favor."

"Hey, you're not the boss of the neighborhood. You only just moved in. You don't ask me a fucking thing."

Johnny just looked at me, like he thought I was better than this. I kept looking at him like I fucking wasn't. After ages had passed and we'd both turned into old men with grey beards and crap in our pants he said: "Listen, my dad's out looking for me. If he comes by, you guys haven't seen me? Okay?"

"Okay," I said.

"I appreciate it," said Johnny. Then he did a wheelie for about half a fucking mile.

A minute later, Maya threw Kevin out. They were getting a divorce. She'd asked him to kiss her, so he did. Then she accused him of kissing her with his eyes open and asked him to leave.

"Oh, that is fucked up," I said. "How was you supposed to find her mouth if you didn't have your eyes open?"

"Exactly," said Kevin. "Exactly."

"I mean a guy wants to know what he's kissing, doesn't he?"

We were standing in the road, debating about why girls are so full of shit. Then we heard a voice shouting: "Johnny? Johnny!"

I remembered what the new kid had said about his dad looking for him and told Kevin. We figured the guy calling out was Johnny's old man. He sure as fuck didn't sound friendly. I was still pissed at Johnny for lecturing me about Wheelchair so I yelled: "Fuck you, dad!"

I nearly cried with laughing at how Johnny's dad would think it was Johnny who said it. Johnny's dad made this big roaring sound like an animal in pain. Then KC joined in. "Dad, fuck off! You big ugly cunt!"

Now we were both creased up, cackling so hard we were nearly in tears. Then the guy started running and we could see right away that he was fast and didn't move like no daddy we'd ever met. We got scared and pedalled off. The wind was in our faces and we thought we were safe when we heard this big bastard's feet pounding the road behind us. Man, that spurred us on. Our hearts and legs didn't stop racing until we reached my house. When we looked behind us and saw he wasn't there we started laughing again, this time with sweet relief.

"Fuck you, dad," I said.

KC howled and so did I. Then I had an idea. "Let's go over to his house, maybe we'll see what happens when Johnny's old man catches up with him."

***

So what we did was climb the railway bridge and walk down the tracks in the moonlight. We were still pissing ourselves. KC or me only had to say "Fuck you, dad" and we'd crack up. Then we had to stop, bending over and holding our ribs, laughing 'til we cried. Finally we were looking down at Johnny Seven's house. It was as shittily painted at the back as it was at the front. We sat on the verge under the railroad track, staring straight across into the bedroom windows. All the lights in the house were shining.

Out of nowhere, I got this scared feeling. Coming here was beginning to seem like a mistake. "What if his dad looks out and sees us?"

"So what?" said KC. "This isn't his property. Right now we're sitting on railroad property."

To lighten the mood, I said "fuck you, dad" again but the joke had worn kinda thin. I told KC that maybe we should go, but he said we should linger for a few more minutes; see if anything "transpired." KC had a bit of weed and he knew how to make roll-ups, so we inhaled real fucking deep to give ourselves breathing problems in later life. I hoped it'd give me a real buzz for once but it didn't so I had to fake it. "Man," I said, pretending to lose my balance. "I am so high you wouldn't believe it."

"Damn right I wouldn't," said KC.

We were on the point of leaving when we saw Johnny Seven walk into one of the bedrooms. Johnny was yelling his head off at someone out of sight. Then a big guy in a vest walked over to Johnny and hit him in the face. Wham!

Not a slap but a real, grown up punch, like a boxer whacking another boxer. KC and me were so shocked that we started laughing. Johnny Seven dropped like a brick. Then Johnny's dad picked him up and hit him again. Hit him three times, holding him steady so he could get a real good aim. Now it wasn't funny anymore.

"Jesus, I don't believe this," said KC. "Do you believe it?"

"No way."

That kid must have got punched and thrown and kicked around that room a hundred times. KC got upset. I knew he would.

"Hey! Fuckin' cut that out!" he shouted. He picked up a stone and threw it at Johnny's window. I threw another. We both missed.

We kept on tossing those damn stones but missed every time. Johnny's dad didn't hear us yelling. He was enjoying himself too much. He just carried on beating up his boy. KC and me had to go home, we couldn't watch it anymore.

We started walking. "That's bad," said KC. His voice sounded strange. "That fuckin' sucks."

"Shit, you see the way his dad laid into him?" I said.

"I saw," said KC. "That is so wrong, man. My dad may have smacked me round once or twice, he never hurt me. That bastard was using his *fists*. Goddamn."

There was a train coming. Me and KC slid down the slope to get out of its way. The train whooshed past. It was a cold lonely feeling, seeing all the passengers through the windows and knowing not one of those motherfuckers knew about me or KC or Johnny Seven or would have given a shit if they had. To them, we were just a bunch of kids.

We watched the train until its tail lights snaked out of sight.

As we headed for the bridge I said: "So what're we gonna do?"

"About *what*?"

"Someone getting half-killed, that's what! Do we call the fuckin' cops or not?"

"Are you joking?" said KC. "What good would that do?"

"We witnessed a violent assault."

"We witnessed shit. We were spying, for fuck's sake. Things you see when you spy don't count."

"Hey, I'm shaking," I said. "Look at me. I'm shaking all over."

KC sniffed. Might have been snot, might have been tears. I didn't ask. "I hope that kid's all right," he said. "Because, God help me, if he dies, it's your fucking fault."

***

But Johnny Seven lived. A week later, he was back at school. His mouth was all swollen and his left eye was so bruised he could hardly see out of it. No one asked him how it had happened, not even the teachers. By now, both me and KC felt we owed Johnny something so in recess we went over to be nice to the kid. At first, he ignored us but we wouldn't let up. It became like a fucking mission with us.

We asked him to play catch. But he was so sore he couldn't raise the mitt properly. So instead we sit on the wall and talked. We didn't say anything about the terrible way Johnny looked and you could tell Johnny was real relieved that we didn't mention it. And we certainly had no intention of telling him it was our fucking fault he looked that way.

"I was thinking of going shooting after school," said Johnny Seven. "Wanna come?"

"Shooting who?" I said. "Griff?" The idea kind of appealed to me.

"M-h." Johnny shook his head. "Just trees and stuff. My old man collects handguns. He wouldn't miss one."

We were impressed but trying not to show it.

"What happened to your mom?" said KC. "She die?"

"No sir. She just walked out, man. My dad never wanted to go anywhere or have friends over so she kept getting depressed and finally she just left."

"Where'd she go?" said KC.

Johnny shrugged.

"What's it feel like, not knowing if you're ever gonna see her again?" I asked him.

KC acted all shocked. "Fuck, Garrett, what kind of asshole question is that?"

"S'okay," said Johnny. "Way it is, when you got a mom, you sometimes think you'd be better off without her. But when you don't even know where she is, it feels like you wanna hurl all day long."

KC nodded respectfully. "I bet it does. I bet it really does feel that way."

***

We met in the woods near the lake. There was a fucked-up old ruined house near the lake. It was called the Retreat, because that was its name when people lived there. The walls were half down and it didn't have any windows because so many kids had thrown rocks at them. KC told Johnny 'The Retreat' was an unlucky name to give a house, because retreating was what cowards did in a battle. Johnny looked at me and smiled. He could see that KC was pretty dumb but would never have said it out loud. That wasn't Johnny's style.

So Johnny took this gun, this police special with six chambers and he let me and KC hold it and said we could have two shots each. We got a rock and scratched the shape of a naked lady on the side of the wall, then we each took a couple of shots at her. When the gun went off, it was real loud, like thunder, so loud that we were sure someone would come running, but no one did. Johnny walked half a mile away. He fired twice and got the woman smack in the nipples. It was like he was Clint Eastwood or somebody.

"Where'd you learn to shoot like that?"

"We had a ranch in Oklahoma," said Johnny. "That's where my folks come from. We used to shoot at things all the time. I can drive a car, too."

"No fucking way," said KC.

Then it was my turn to shoot. The gun went off before I was ready and I didn't hit a fucking thing. KC laughed but he didn't do any better. I had one more shot and I fired it straight into the ground because I felt like it. Johnny said what I'd done was a waste of ammunition. "What?" I said. "But it ain't a waste to shoot at a picture of some tits?"

Later we went back to Johnny's house and he let us in, said his dad was out and wouldn't be back until late.

"Like how late?" I said.

"Who knows?" said Johnny.

"Wow," I said. "You could stay out until midnight if you wanted."

I could see KC looking pretty surprised. Me and him usually had to be home by ten, on the fucking dot, or we got grounded. And there's Johnny coming home to an empty house. The place was a fucking mess, though. There was this thick layer of dust on the TV and the kitchen looked like someone had been throwing soup at the walls.

Johnny took the gun back to his dad's room then got us some cold beer from the icebox. We couldn't believe it. It was real German beer. He got out a CD, someone called Martha somebody. "Listen to this, she swears her head off in it." It was a boring song, except at the end when this woman calls someone a mother fucking asshole. She sang it about six or seven times. Man, we rolled about laughing. When the song was over, we played again just to see if we'd heard it right the first time. After one can of beer each we were all pretty drunk.

Johnny got us another beer, even though he'd said we could only have one each. Then he put on another song we hadn't heard. It was some really old party record called The Monster Mash. On account of the song being about monsters, KC had the bright idea that we should listen to it in the dark. I knew what he was planning. I fucking knew. Sure enough, next thing he was asking Johnny if he had a flashlight. Johnny said sure. So KC asked Johnny to aim the flashlight at him while he did a dance to the record. In no time at all, Johnny was pointing the spotlight at KC while he flashed his big white ass in the dark. Jesus, it was funny. Johnny was laughing so much he was crying. KC wasn't laughing, though. His face was all serious, like he was concentrating on giving an artistic performance.

Then the light turned on and Johnny's dad was standing there. From a distance, he'd looked like the main villain in a gangster movie. Close up, he was just a normal looking guy, average size, ordinary hair and clothes and his belly starting to bulge, like any dad from anywhere in the world. He just looked at us. No expression on his face or nothing.

KC tried to pull up his pants, his belt buckle rattling. Johnny's dad walked over to him and pushed him. KC did this sort of hopping dance, still holding onto his pants. Then he fell over. Johnny tried to get up off the sofa, but his dad got to him first and held him down with one hand over his throat. I thought he was going to hit Johnny, but no. He just kept on squeezing his throat like he wanted to strangle him. I said: "Stop." That's all I said. Johnny's dad turned and slapped me on the ear so hard I could hear humming.

Now Johnny was turning red, trying to knock his dad's arm away. But he was too little and weak. He was making clucking noises in his throat. And what was really scary was that his fucking father still hadn't said a goddamn word. Both me and KC felt sure he was going to kill his own kid. We kept yelling at him to stop but he was like a maniac. The guy was so mad his forehead was throbbing.

KC was crying his eyes out. He picked up the shitty dusty old TV and used it like a battering ram, slamming Johnny's dad in the side of the head. Johnny's dad looked confused and blew out air like he'd just done ten pushups. Then he fell over. KC smacked the TV down on top of the guy's skull. The TV didn't break. The guy's head did. When he was lying down, all three of us started kicking his head and stamping on it. There wasn't nothing mean about it. We were just scared shitless of what the bastard might do if he ever stood up again.

When we'd finished stomping, it was pretty fucking obvious the guy wasn't much of a threat to anyone no more. He wasn't moving, his eyes were wide open and his tongue was hanging out. He looked like a dog I saw once that had been hit by a car.

"He fucking deserved it," said Johnny.

"He really fucking did," I said. Even my voice was shaking.

KC hadn't stopped crying the entire time. "You dumb fucking bastards," he kept saying. "Now we're all going to get lethally injected, just like that guy Griff told us about."

I was scared and trying not to show it. "They won't kill us. We're minors."

"They wait until you're eighteen and then they fucking do it," said KC.

"They won't do nothing," said Johnny. "Because they ain't gonna find out. My dad had no friends. He never spoke to nobody. Who's gonna know?"

"The body's gonna stink," said KC. "It fucking stinks already."

"There's a big old freezer in the garage," said Johnny. "We can put him in there."

"I ain't gonna cut anyone up," I said.

"We don't need to," said Johnny. "We just take the frozen stuff out and lift him in."

"Someone's gonna know," I said. I was shivering just like Scott of the Antarctic. "You can't live here on your own without someone knowing."

"This is America," said Johnny. This kid was calm as anything. I think he was even relieved. "Long as you keep paying bills, no one cares about you. I lived in lots of places, that's how it works. People only knock on the door if you owe them money or they want you to join their church. I'll keep going to school, just like normal. I'll pay the bills and sign checks while the money lasts out."

The more we thought about it, the more it seemed like the ideal solution. Even KC could see the sense of it. We wouldn't admit to killing Johnny's dad, we'd just pretend he was alive. It wasn't such a big lie, anyway. Most kids spend their entire childhoods pretending their parents are alive.

EXPLETIVE DELETED
SECTION FOUR

FUCK

MICHAEL O'MAHONY

escaped a life of North London drudgery by whoring himself all the way to California, where he lives with his wife and their profoundly disturbed cat. He'd love for this particular sentence to begin "When not writing …" but the sad truth of the matter is that when not supervising, assessing, or teaching customer service for a large corporation he'd rather not name, Michael occasionally finds time to pen a chapter or two of his first novel. And play video games.

EVERY OUNCE OF SOUL
MICHAEL O'MAHONY

I'M lying on my front in a rust-colored puddle, staring at the café just to keep my eyes open and focused on something. Tough to breathe down here. Tougher still when your lungs feel like they're shrivelling up, assuming the crash position and refusing your mouth's commands to let in a little air.

"You're fucking my *wife*," Nathan says, italics indicating exertion, indicating his boot in my side.

Something—denial, admission—gurgles up from my throat. Something else—saliva, blood—leaks from the side of my mouth. Hard to be sure, but I think my bladder just went.

"You're *fucking* my wife," Nathan says. This is repetition twelve, variation five. He stamps on my head, draws out the two syllables by extending his leg, grinding the side of my face into the gravel.

"Ai-aa," I murmur. There are no longer any consonants in my verbal alphabet.

Silence from Nathan. For a few moments there is no sound but my attempts to force oxygen through the blood and snot clogging my throat. Beyond that, distant and distorted, "Nutbush City Limits" on the radio in the café.

He rolls me out of the puddle and onto my back. I swallow and heave, my eyes trying to roll back into my head. I can't raise my arms. My hands are shaking. I'm still trying to speak, and I don't even know why. Nothing I could say would make any difference at this point.

"*You're* fucking *my* wife," Nathan says. New variation. He's making that sentence an art. I barely feel the accompanying impacts. The sky is bright grey, fading.

He's right, though. I *am* fucking his wife.

✳✳✳

The first time was at their place. Nathan, the import/export king, was away on business. Naomi and I were mellow on Glenfiddich. She was wearing a tight black blouse and a bright red miniskirt. When she bent to turn on the stereo, I got a flash of stocking-tops and white thighs and suspenders.

"Like that?" she asked, knowing what I was looking at without turning around.

"Yeah," I said.

Music filled the room and I burst out laughing. I was going to be seduced to the strains of Atomic Kitten.

"You've got to be fucking kidding me," I said.

"I like this song."

"At least play the original. At least."

"I don't have the original."

"But you have Atomic Kitten."

"Shut your mouth and show me what I do to you, Alex."

"Excuse me?"

"I want to see your cock."

I was drunk enough to forgo embarrassment, drunk enough, in fact, to undo my flies with one hand whilst casually sipping the drink I held in the other. I wasn't ashamed. She was the one with the terrifying record collection.

"Do you wank over me?"

"Sometimes."

"What do you think about?"

"Fucking you."

"How?"

I considered this. "You on top, so I can see your body."

"You've never seen my body."

"I'm seeing your body now."

"You're not wanking."

"Should I?"

Naomi hiked up her skirt, showed me stockings and suspenders and black silk panties. I put my drink down on the table, sat back and stared at her. I took hold of my cock.

"That's nice," she said, watching me stroke myself.

"Do you think about me?"

"When I finger myself?"

"Yeah."

"Yes."

"What do you think about?"

Naomi walked around the table and stood with her legs to either side of mine. In my head, I was drowning Atomic Kitten in a pool of Coltrane.

"I think about you slapping me and calling me a whore," she said. "I think about you forcing me to suck you off. I think about you fucking me hard from behind, pulling my hair."

"You have a gift for language," I said.

"I have many gifts."

"You're a whore."

"Tell me."

"You're a whore."

"I don't think you mean it."

"Maybe I need convincing."

"Then tell me what you want. I'll do it."

"Turn the music off."

"You're a very funny man."

"I don't think you mean that."

"I think you're afraid of me."

"Is that so?"

"That's so."

"Naomi?"

"Uh-huh?"

"Get down on your knees."

She smiled.

***

Nathan kicks me square in the bollocks and reality comes rushing back in a bolt of pain that races up into my chest before settling into my stomach. I curl up into a ball, gasping for air, vision blurring with tears.

"How many times?" he asks. "How many times did you fuck her?"

I have no breath to answer the question. Even if I could, he'd have to qualify it a little. Does he mean how many times did we meet up or how many times did we actually have sex? How many times did I fuck her? Well, that depends, Nath old buddy. Vaginal intercourse is one thing, but I'm afraid my cock's been in both her hands, her mouth, her arse, and—yes—even between her tits. Could we be a little more specific?

I almost laugh and my outraged lungs push out enough air to constitute a cough. My mouth fills with the coppery taste of my own blood. Christ, am I fucking hemorrhaging here?

Nathan crouches down beside me. "You're in a bad way, son," he says. He wipes my mouth with the backs of his fingers and holds them up, showing me a stringy red mess he then wipes on my chest. "Was she worth it?"

I look up at him. He's a vicious bastard, but he's not a hard man. He looks, with his smart suits and his stupid little glasses, like an accountant. Even now, knowing who he is and having a vague idea what he does, I'm not afraid of him. Nathan, for all the pain he's putting me through, for all the cold, jealous rage in his eyes, he's a wanker.

I only manage one word, but it's enough. He stands up. He seems almost sad. "Here's the deal, Alex. This goes on until she's not worth it or I kill you."

And as he looks around to make sure nobody's watching, as he pulls a pair of gloves from inside his jacket and slips them over his small hands, I realise that it's probably going to be the latter.

From the open door of the café, I can hear a tinny Elvis doing his thing, and as the point of Nathan's boot hits me in the stomach and pain shoves coherency to one side, I wish I was in Dixie.

Away, away.

∗∗∗

"You awake?" Naomi asked.

"What's up?"

"Nothing. You can turn the TV off if you want."

I rolled onto my side, leaning on my elbow to look down at her face. "You look good in this light."

"Not so old," she said, with a hint of a smile.

"You're hardly old. Fishing for compliments, maybe, but not old."

"So compliment me."

"Is this the flipside to the whore thing?"

"Do you want it to be?"

"Do you always answer a question with a question?"

"Why do you ask?"

I grinned at her, kissed her dry lips. "Can I ask a serious question?"

She nodded.

"Are you scared of the dark?"

She looked away towards the window. "I wake up and I don't know where I am," she said, frowning. "I don't know who I'm with." Her eyes came back to mine. "Does the TV really bother you?"

"It drives me up the fucking wall."

"Nathan, too."

"Ah-ha. The mysterious husband. Can we talk about him?"

"Let's not and say we did."

"Does he know you do this?"

"He trusts me."

"And if he found out?"

"I don't know."

"Import and export. Like trafficking?"

"Leave it alone, Alex. I really don't want to talk about this."

"Alright."

I lay back down, watching the light flickering across the ceiling, picking out patterns. I didn't react when I felt her turn towards me, the warmth of her body against mine. She stroked my chest and my stomach, pressed her mouth to my ear so I could hear her breathing.

"He has a small dick," she whispered, and I laughed a little. "He's clumsy. He has no idea how to please me."

"Why don't you tell him?"

"I've tried. He doesn't listen like you listen, baby." Her fingers curled around my cock. "He doesn't react like you react."

"I want to know you."

"I'm all yours. But not him, forget him."

"Naomi ..." I began, but the sentence and the thought behind it were lost, stolen by her quick, relentless strokes and the things she whispered in my ear.

***

"Alex," Nathan says. I'm lying on my side, just breathing, just trying not to throw up. I'm shaking uncontrollably, freezing cold. I'm wishing for oblivion.

"Alex," he says, and his voice is soft. "Answer me."

I raise my arm as far as I can. I give him the finger.

"That's something," he says. "That's something, son."

I gurgle some obscenity.

"Get up," he says. "Get off the fucking floor."

I roll slowly onto my front, get my arms underneath me. No strength there. My eyes are swimming in tears. I can't see him, but I know he's watching me scrabbling around in the gravel, covered in blood and dirt, crying. Motherfucker.

"What?"

I half-spit, half-puke a thin stream of blood. I cough up something huge and thick and dark red. I turn away from it, squeeze my eyes closed, dry heave until I'm dizzy. I get to my knees. I manage that much.

"It's always the skinny little fuckers that surprise you," he says. "Look at yourself."

I shake my head. I hug myself.

"You deserve this. For what you did, this is fair."

I look up at him. "I fucked your wife," I say. My voice is low, hoarse.

"You fucked my wife. I want to know if she was worth this."

I look around us. The only vehicle in the car park is his, the only building in sight the café. Nobody in there but a balding fifty-something who greeted Nathan like an old friend.

"Not this," I say. I try on a smile. Christ knows what it must look like. "Something a little more glamorous."

"Answer the question."

"You know the answer."

"Was she worth it?"

"Is she worth it to you? Is she worth anything to you?"

"She's a whore," he says.

"Yeah," I say. I cough again, wincing at the pain in my chest and throat, swallowing more blood. "Can't take that from her." I take a deep breath. I look away from the café and the car and Nathan, take in a vista of suburban decay dotted with occasional green. "Or me."

I keep staring right up to the point where his fist meets the side of my head and my only defiance is to put my hand down and keep myself upright. He grabs my hair with both hands, brings my head down as his knee comes up and it feels as though my face explodes. Down to the ground and everything's grey again, fading to black now.

* * *

Midnight-ish at Naomi's place and we were fucking to another terrible cover, Will Young choking every ounce of soul from "Light My Fire," while she moaned and thrashed beneath me, slapping the wall above her head, face red and glistening with sweat. I was listening to the music, channelling disgust to hold off my orgasm, arms and legs aching from being on top and thrusting as hard as she was begging me to for some fifteen minutes.

"I'm gonna come, Alex," she said, voice dropping to a dramatic whisper. "Fuck me. Fuck me with your big cock."

And I started laughing. I couldn't help it. I collapsed on top of her and buried my face in her shoulder, giggling uncontrollably, my whole body shaking with it.

"Alex?" she said, and I thought I could hear the surprise and hurt in her voice. She lifted my head and stared at me, all concern. I pressed my lips tightly together, tears in my eyes.

"I'm ..." I snorted. "I'm so sorry. Shit, Naomi ..."

Her eyes widened. "You fucking bastard! I thought you were crying!"

Mute, I shook my head and tried to kiss her only for another wave of laughter to hit me just as our lips met. This time she laughed with me, pressing her forehead to mine, holding my face in her hands.

"What the fuck, Alex?" she said, when the fit subsided.

"Fuck me with your big cock?" I said, stifling another giggle.

She shifted her hips, reminding me that the cock in question was still very much inside her. "I thought you liked it when I talked to you."

"I do." I lifted her leg and nudged her onto her side, lying behind her so that our bodies were tight together. "But you don't have to always be the whore."

"Don't," she said.

"What?"

"Fall for me."

I smiled at that. I kissed her shoulder as I began to move in her again, one arm draped over her hip, hand covering her crotch, fingers finding her. She tensed immediately, held my eyes as her breath steepened until each exhalation was a soft moan.

"Alex," she said. She reached back and grabbed at my waist, nails digging into my skin. "Alex." She bit her lip and her eyelids fluttered, her body still but trembling all over for a long, silent moment before the breath rushed out of her in a shaky sigh and she relaxed.

I kissed her neck and the side of her face. I brought my mouth to her ear. "Don't," I whispered.

"What?"

"Flatter yourself."

She turned and kissed me.

***

Consciousness returns slowly and reluctantly. Nausea swells and I swallow against it, spitting clotting blood and feeling missing teeth with a swollen tongue. A little effort gets my left eye open to find Nathan sitting a few feet away, his knees drawn up and his arms wrapped around them. My right eye is swollen shut.

"Was she worth it?" he asks.

I say, "Give me a fucking break," but what comes out is "Gimuhfuhbru."

"Last time," he says. He gets up slowly, reaches into his jacket like they do in the movies. I already know what's going to be in his hand. "Is my wife worth a bullet?"

And there it is. He really is some kind of fucking gangster, and he really is going to shoot me for fucking his wife. I work my jaw, clear my mouth. I remember Glenfiddich and Atomic bastard Kitten and the way she tasted that first time.

"Yes," I say.

Nathan purses his lips. "Hate this part," he says. He walks towards me, presses the cold barrel of the gun against my forehead.

There is no great moment of revelation. My life doesn't flash before my eyes. I don't think of my family or my friends. I don't even think of Naomi. I think of walking up to the café with Nathan what seems like a lifetime ago, having some idea of what was coming but no idea what I was supposed to do about it. I'd looked up at the roof then, where someone—the balding fifty-something, surely—had painted the word 'CAFE' in huge red letters, presumably so it would be visible from the motorway. As we went in and sat down, as I stared across the table and tried to read Nathan's expression, I kept thinking about how unstable that roof looked and what a bitch of a job the painter must have had. Nathan had sighed heavily, and just as he'd gone into his speech about how Naomi had broken down and confessed our affair, something had occurred to me, and I—undisputed master of the inappropriate—had smiled.

There is a dry click and then a long silence.

"She's always worth it," Nathan says. The hand holding the gun drops to his side. We stare at each other. "Every time."

He smiles and turns away, pocketing the gun. He's whistling as he walks to the car and gets in. Not once does he look back. He just starts the engine and drives away.

It takes me a while to get up. I'm a mess. Even once I've gathered the confidence and the necessary strength, the struggle to get to my feet and stay there takes a good ten minutes. I shuffle slowly and painfully towards the café, hearing Bowie and The Kinks and then—sweet fucking irony—The Bangles before, I slump against the doorframe and raise my head to find the balding fifty-something staring at me.

"Did you …" I pause to cough up more blood. He watches, horrified. "Did you paint that sign on the roof?"

He nods slowly.

"You missed off the accent," I say. "All that work, and you missed off the fucking accent."

RAY BANKS

has been a croupier, a wedding singer, dole monkey and various degrees of disgruntled office temp. His first book, *The Big Blind*, was the dahhhling of the critics, but nobody bought it. He's twice been featured in *Best British Mysteries*, and is creator of pseudo-PI Callum Innes who makes his novel-length debut in January 2008 from Harcourt. When he's not drooling like a boxcar hobo at a jug of XXX, he can be found loitering with intent at his website: www.thesaturdayboy.com.

MONEY SHOT
RAY BANKS

I'D thought about it.

Jesus forgive me, but I'd actually thought about it.

Mel Gibson in *Lethal Weapon*. Muzzle to the forehead, the temple, wedged between teeth. He'd lost his wife, same as me. Unlike Mel, though, my wife was still alive. At least I thought so. The flickering image of her on my telly kept her alive. That moan she'd make, hot breath in my ear as I beat myself into submission, the tears coming five seconds after I did.

Then I wanted to bite down on the barrel of a gun. Because there was no beauty left in the world once the semen started to dry.

My nights were spent like this. Too many to count, far too many to admit. I had a flatmate but I waited until he'd gone to bed. Daryl spent his days watching *Trisha* and old movies, smoking his weight in tack. Sometimes I'd join him for the movies, the old black and whites. Burt Lancaster shaking in his boots because *The Killers* were after him.

Daryl: "They don't make 'em like they used to."

And then he'd stick *Lethal Weapon* in the video. A lot of people forget, he told me, that Mel Gibson *is* the lethal weapon of the title. He's the nutcase. He's crazy. Look at him jump off that building; watch him try and get the stubbly guy to shoot him. He's fucking bat-shit. Look at him in his trailer with that gun.

The hollow point bullet so he'd be sure to take the back of his skull clean off.

"You know why I don't do it? The job. Doing the job ..."

Daryl: "Franco Zeffirelli offered him Hamlet because of that scene."

(Daryl was the one who got me the gun.)

Daryl: "You're not gonna do this."

Me: "You don't know that."

Daryl: "I know it. I know *you*. You're not that fucking mental. You're trying to draw a psycho pension."

Like a movie. He even pointed. I even turned away. The light from the telly cast dark shadows over my eyes, I'm sure. I lit a cigarette while he puffed on the joint.

I heard someone say: "God hates me. That's what it is."

And I said: "Hate him right back. Works for me."

Daryl said: "You talking to the telly again, mate?"

But I was already out the door.

I'd shaved my head. Did it as a ritual, like a monk. Had a Bernard Herrman accompaniment as I did it, watching the hair fall to the floor, my skull prominent in the stained mirror. I took a Bic to the rest, made sure I was clean by the time I'd finished. She wouldn't recognise me; nobody would. I'd spent most of my life with curtains in front of my face; now I had nothing to hide behind. I ran a hand over my head. It felt weird. And cold.

Most cities in the world, they have a porn district. There was a hooker pub up on City Road before they turned it into a media watering hole, but there was no real porn district. We didn't have pornographers in Newcastle. Something about the Geordie accent that put people off their wanking stride.

I caught the Metro into town, sat near the back. Fat girls on a night out further up the carriage, singing a song I'd never heard of.

Not that I would've recognised it, anyway. There was the clink of WKD and Breezer bottles, the high-pitched squeals after a dirty joke. There were plenty of dirty jokes. I pretended not to notice them, but I was watching them all the same. Thinking all of them naked and gagged and going down on each other. Thinking if they refused, there really was a gun in my pocket and I wasn't just pleased to see them. Screaming and lapping and shuddering all at the same time.

Fuck them.

I said we didn't have pornographers in Newcastle. That wasn't right. We did. They called themselves something different. They toted the monikers of "indie film producer," "adult entertainment CEO" and "erotica entrepreneurs." Like a turd covered in gold leaf.

I got headaches. Bad ones. Like when you have too much ice cream or milk and you have to close one eye if you're going to get any relief. We all have bloody thoughts. Morality's like some twisted fucking thing you never get to understand because no matter what you do, there's always someone waving a pamphlet, denouncing you as an animal. There was always someone, thought they knew better than you, lived more than you, understood the ways of the world more than you. What did they understand? They understood fuck all, just meshed their experience into some kind of bullshit ethos. The parents who despised corporations, booking their kids into a McDonalds party because they were too fucking weak to say no, had no way of explaining it. Fighting for multi-culturalism and crossing the street when they saw a gang of pakis coming.

I loved curry. Loved the pakis. Hated what they did to me.

This bloke I was going to see, he was a paki. I think. He looked like a paki, dressed like a paki, but he could've been Turkish, Somalian, whatever the fuck refugees we were letting into the country this fucking week without the proper papers. That's why they bombed us, I thought. They bombed us because they could.

It was the same reason the big smiling clown kept poisoning the kids, making them fat and useless. Because we were too scared to stop them.

Sometimes fear only gets you so far. Then you crawl out the other side angry as fuck.

And then you get a weapon.

Didn't take too much persuading. Daryl got off on the idea of playing a Leo Getz ("You get it? Leo … *gets!*") or Morgan Freeman in *Shawshank*, the kind of bloke, you want something, *anything*, he's the bloke to go to. He'll hunt it down, he'll be your finder.

I mumbled: "This is a real badge, I'm a real cop, and this is a real fucking gun."

And it was a weight against my rib cage, that recommissioned replica. Daryl knew this guy on the Leam Lane who sold them for a tonne apiece. I thought it was a bit steep at the time, but feeling the heft of the gun, I knew I'd spent wisely.

Daryl: "You want a proper pistol, you pay proper money. You want something to scare the fucker with, then you're better off with a replica."

Me: "I don't want a fucking replica. I want a real one."

Got off the Metro at Monument. I had to walk through the Saturday night orgies on the streets. Orca girls in tight tops that didn't cover a thing. Screaming, screeching in the shadows, like a feeding frenzy. The low humping noise of a dozen blokes in that same check-shirt-gold-chain combo coming up the street. Red faced, stinking of alcohol, itching to slap some cunt because he's looking at them fuckin' funny, like he's a fuckin' poof or a fuckin' nonce or something.

I kept my head down as I walked. Started towards the Bigg Market and the crowds got heavy, packed together. A sudden yell at my left and I saw this young lad get dragged out of a club across the ground. He was shirtless. The bouncer dragging him made sure he went over a pile of broken glass. Planted a fist in the lad's throat.

"I TELT YEH NOT TO FUCKIN' COME BACK, YA CUNT!"

Put my head down again, cradled the gun in my coat. The heavy throb of bass underfoot, I ducked into an alley, passed by All Saint's Church, lit up. Fucking incongruous to have a church here. I crossed myself, pushed down to the Quayside. There was a God. He was away on business, but he'd come back.

What was it? The meek shall inherit. Aye. The meek and the armed.

Up towards City Road now, where the office buildings jostled for attention with the council flats. Building new student accommodation up here, another push to get the undesirables out. Ship 'em off to the West End. Let 'em breed like the fucking pigs they were, then shut 'em in and drop the pellets.

A ratty woman with knock knees under a street light. She had a mobile pressed against her ear.

"I telt yeh yeh had to pick us up, didn't I telt yeh … ya fuckin' cunt, divven't … divven't LIE to us … yez're a fuckin' LIAR … a FUCKIN' LIAR CUNT … how, me fuckin' battery's gannin', it's gannin' … pick us up … yer not at yer mam's, I fuckin' knaa yer not at yer mam's … CUZ I PHONED YER FUCKIN' MAM THAT'S HOW I FUCKIN' KNAA … Aye … Aye … pick us up … pick us up … fuckin' … howeh, pick us up, ya cunt … me fuckin' battery … PICK-US-UP."

She pulled the phone from her ear and threw it against a partly-built wall. It smashed. She let out a noise like she'd been punched, started with: "Ahhhh, nooooo."

I passed her and she spun my way.

Her: "How, yeh gorra tab, mate?"

I shook my head.

Her: "Howeh, yeh got any spare change, like?"

She got in my way.

I smiled at her, showed her all my teeth. Nodded like I was going to give her something, like I was reaching for my wallet. Should've seen her eyes light up at that. Like, fuckin' hell, he's gonna givvus fuckin' NOTES.

I showed her the gun.

Took her a moment to realise what it was, still matching my smile.

When I clicked the barrel against her rotting teeth, her eyes took on the sheen of the newly-weeping. And I opened my mouth wide in a silent scream, felt my jaw click with the effort.

Hers wasn't silent.

But I let her run. It was funny. A heel snapped off and she almost went pocked arse over sagging tit. I laughed.

Just another cracked skeleton in this fucked up town, disappearing into the night.

And then I walked some more, made sure to replace the gun under my armpit. I knew I could draw easily now. Something that'd bugged me up till now. Because I needed to be swift when the time came.

God, my wife. Why was she my wife?

Hair: Blonde.

Eyes: Blue.

Same as an angel. Same as an angel was *supposed* to look.

Stood about five foot eight in heels. Had a walk to her that made the trousers tight.

She was my wife. I was bound to think that. But everyone thought that. Could turn a bender straight, make a dyke out of a cocklover. But she was an angel, too. You couldn't look at her and not see that. She wasn't about the fucking sex. That wasn't her. She was about love. Beauty.

And look what he did to her. Look what he made her into.

I found the place easily enough. Been by here enough times to know this was his office. I'd phoned ahead to make sure he was in, too. When I pressed the buzzer on the intercom, a gruff voice answered:

"What?"

"Here to see Harry Grace."

"He expecting you?"

"I phoned."

"Right."

The buzzer sounded again. I went in. Couldn't see much in the corridor. Might've been the giant with the square head blocking out the strip light. Looked like a huge clone of Tor Johnson.

Big Tor: "Go upstairs."

Me: "Right."

I went upstairs. Knocked on the door to his office. It smelled bad in here, like aftershave from the seventies.

A voice from inside: "Come in."

I did.

Set the scene, make it plausible. A huge office, like the entire top floor of the building. Like someone took an entire safari park and buckshot the fucking lot across the walls. Leopard print, tiger stripes, that dull yellow fur of the lion, the black and white zebra. The lot. Scatter cushions and a fucking glitter ball hanging from the ceiling. Along the walls posters of straight-to-video releases: *Airtight Bitch*; *Hot Fudge Sunday*; *Lesbos Lactation*. Bean bags. Somewhere a stereo plays classical music, throwing my synapses out of whack.

Sylvia Saint sitting on a bean bag in a yellow bikini. Except it wasn't Sylvia Saint. It was an older version of Sylvia Saint. Covered in downy blonde fluff. Looked closer and her fingernails were filed to points. Something wrong with her eyes, and they were cat contact lenses. Blonde hair scooped back to reveal two pointed ears and when she opened her kewpie mouth to hiss at me, she had fangs.

"Easy, Kitty."

Coming from the end of the office, waaaay down there. A massive desk, shining. Covered in leather. The man liked his animals. Loved skinning them, making them into decorations. Flash on Ed Gein and understand the whole fucking room.

"You come to audition?"

Every inch the erotic entrepreneur. Cypriot, I thought. Something not English, anyway, but he had a plummy accent that sounded like he'd learned the language from Charles Hawtrey. Had a belly on him, straining at his dress shirt. A Nehru jacket hanging on a stand behind him. Big cuffs, bigger cuff links catching the light and throwing it in my face.

Me: "No, I've not come to audition."

Him: "You sure? You look like the type."

"What's the type?"

"You."

Kitty hissed some more. Heard the rustle of the bean bag. Wanted to put that gun in her fucking face and pull the trigger. Wound up? Aye. Wound up like a fucking spring.

Me, squinting, my best Clint: "I've come about Liz Fairbride."

Him: "Who the fuck's Liz Fairbride? And what you packing there, son?"

"You what?"

"What you got? You able to rise on cue?"

"I'm not auditioning. Liz Fairbride."

"I don't know her."

"You know her."

"I don't."

Kitty growled.

Me: "Put a leash on your pussy."

Him: "Kitty. Stay put, love."

Harold Grace, all fifty-seven years of him, pulled himself around his desk and knocked on a cabinet. As he opened the top, music played and his face illuminated. He pulled out a crystal decanter filled with something yellow. "You want a drink?"

I shook my head.

"Amber Raines."

He poured himself a drink and turned. Said: "What?"

"Amber Raines. You made her change her name."

"Amber Raines." He sipped his drink. His lip retreated up his gums as he swallowed. "I know Amber Raines. She's the pisser."

I started unzipping my jacket.

"She was a good little actress. You sure you don't want to audition?"

"Getting comfortable. Go on."

"She was a good actress. Wasn't pretty enough to be a star, but she had talent in the watersports. Give as well as receive. She got off on it."

"No, she didn't."

"Nice tits. Nipples like tent pegs."

Kitty growled some more, ended it with a loud hiss.

Grace: "You like Kitty?"

Me: "No."

Another drink, another show of teeth. "Kitty's a star. *Feral Pink.* Big market for it. Kinkier the better. Some men ... Some men like their women *hirsute.* That's all real, all that hair on her. She grows it herself. I don't go for the fake stuff. Like my movies, they're all real tits. None of the silicone shite. Can't stand it. So you're a fan of Amber Raines?"

I shook my head.

"I didn't know her real name was Liz, like."

Keep talking.

He kept talking.

"Blast from the past, Amber Raines. Christ, what is she now? Like forty or something? But she was fucking good and a good fuck, know what I mean? What, you like the vintage shite? I got plenty of classic stuff for you. Thinking about—"

—thinking about pulling the gun now—

"—a line of retro-movies. You got all this coverage of *Deep Throat* and *Debbie Does Dallas*, people get these movies thinking they're gonna be real—"

—DEAD real DEAD—

"—hardcore stuff and it's all tits and arse, know what I mean?"

YOU KILLED HER

Me, softly: "You killed her."

Harold Grace stood there with his glass halfway up to his lips. A pause, then he drank. More teeth, this time bared like a wild animal.

Him: "Who are you?"

Wanting him to know.

Telling him now.

Me: "I'm her husband."

He spluttered. Laughed. HA HA HA. You're joking, mate. You're out of your mind. I didn't know Amber had a fucking HUSBAND. She got a husband, Kitty? You hear that? And Kitty made a noise like a cat laughing, a weird *choo-choo-huff* sound. And you're her husband. What are you, fucking twenty or something? And you're her hus—

First shot cracked like a bullwhip, like Indy Jones' whip, WAP.

Caught Grace in the whisky glass, smashed it, stuck him in that round belly. Blood in the hand that held the glass, blood flowering thick and fast on his dress shirt. Him wondering what the fuck just happened.

Second shot in the eye, right from across the room. WAP.

Didn't snap his head back like I thought it would. Harold Grace standing there, mouth hanging open, tongue rested on his bottom set of capped teeth.

Then he dropped.

And Kitty went wild. The rustle from the bean bag gave her away, but I didn't turn too quick—still wanted to marvel in that one dead eye looking at me—and she sank those filed teeth into my leg. Pain shook me back to the present, stench of piss in the air. The warm feeling of blood on my ankle. I looked down. There was Kitty. Screeching. I pressed the gun to her scalp and pulled the trigger. More warmth against my leg, but it wasn't my blood this time.

I kicked her crumbled head away, hobbled to the door as Tor Johnson threw it open and filled up the doorway. His eyes wide and bulbous, I stuck the gun in his nose and pulled the trigger. Muffled, but still loud.

Tor's head *did* snap back.

Fucking glorious. Finally.

I climbed over his body and took the stairs two at a time, both hands on the walls to throw myself down. Landed heavily at the bottom. On the bad ankle. Yelled. Partly out of pain, partly out of release.

Lunged my way down to the Quayside, hugging my open jacket around the gun. There was blood on me and I couldn't run, but I saw a cab and pushed a slapper out of the way to get to it. Her face turned in on itself and she grew a forked tongue, but I made the driver pull away before she could slam on the side of the cab.

Pulling away in a big car with lots of windows. Hearing the sounds of the night. Looking out of the side window like it was *Jurassic Park*.

"The point is … you're alive when they start to eat you …"

"You what, mate?"

"Nothing."

You're not her husband. How old are you?

Doesn't matter. I'm her husband.

She must be forty by now.

Well out of it. She's dead.

You killed her, Grace. You made her into this fucking beast.

And you made me into the same kind.

Just fucking shut up.

I paid the cab with some notes and some change that I managed to scrape out of my jacket. He saw the gun, I'm sure. I didn't care. He dropped me three streets away from my flat. I limped the rest of the way. Rain started to fall. It felt cold and good against my shaved head. Cleansing.

I got into the flat, bumped into Daryl.

Daryl: "You did it?"

Me: "Aye."

Daryl: "You're not trying to draw a psycho pension. You really are crazy."

I nodded and limped through to the living room. Daryl said he was going to bed. I didn't answer him.

Just went over to the video and put on a movie. One of Liz Fairbride's early works. My wife. That blonde angel, moaning just for me. And I wasn't old enough to be her husband, but maybe back then I would've been. I put the gun on the floor, sat cross-legged. Something white against the black blood.

Kitty's tooth.

I pulled out the canine and turned it in my fingers as my wife breathed. The slap of flesh against flesh, getting quicker now.

Then I flicked the tooth to one side, unzipped my combat trousers and wept silently as both me and my wife came together.

That was love. That was beauty even after the semen dried.

RUTH JORDAN

is the co-publisher of *Crimespree Magazine*. "Little Blue Pill" is her first short story and was inspired by an extremely long week at work.

LITTLE BLUE PILL
RUTH JORDAN

"GOD baby, you're the best."

"Only when I'm with you, Tom."

I began to slowly unbutton the shimmering silk. Minimalist black for the outer layer of date wear, but underneath it was hot pink.

"I love it when you take charge. Dance for me, girl."

I began a subtle swaying of the hips, accentuated by lacy boy shorts. Turned a few drawn out pirouettes so Tom could appreciate the entire view. Eye contact was made between us, Tom already on the bed taking it all in. I unhooked the bra, tossing it nonchalantly onto the floor and began to stroke my nipples, let my left hand wander south and make slow circles, spiraling inwards.

Tom's eyes turned into focused slits, his breathing audible now. He was mine.

"Are you ready for me, baby?" I was trying for Bacall.

His reply was a whimper. Christ, they're all the same.

I straddled him now, hand to zipper releasing his downfall. Rock solid and fully at attention, it quivered as I took him in, teasing at first, and then all of it.

"Baby, that's so good ... but you? What about you?"

"Don't worry love, you'll last all night," and with that I slid my hand to the bedside table that was a temporary home to my purse, wrapped a manicured hand around my newest sex toy and imbedded the number six scalpel into Tom's carotid artery. Life left quickly and Tom's body fluids flowed away. He stayed hard for me all night and I rode a wave of orgasms like none I'd ever experienced.

Looking down at the body that had been known as Tom, I tried to think it through. Knew then that I wanted to do this again, but boy was I fucked. Too busy planning last night's scenario, I hadn't planned how to get away with it.

My car was still at the restaurant where I started with friends. That was a plus. I met up with Tom two stops and three bottles of wine into the night. People knew that we were friendly but because of our jobs no one knew that we'd been sleeping together. We'd snuck away separately.

I was hoping we hadn't been seen.

"That's a crap shoot though, ain't it, Tom?"

4:30 a.m. now and Tom had volleyball at nine Saturdays. "Play it by the numbers, girl, and we'll be okay."

Fiber evidence: Victoria's Secret underwear, Anne Klein black shoes first taken out of the box Friday afternoon. Good there, fibers more common than a cold in January. The purse was more problematic. Someone might find something. A quick wipe down of surfaces didn't promise guarantees but it was worth a shot.

Looking down at the evening gloves I'd donned as part of the stripper's game, thinking back to the evening before.

"I buckled the seat belt, Tom, but you opened the door for me. Oh, and I flushed. You, my dear are the problem. I'm all over you and this bed. What can we do? Talk to me, baby."

Plastic sheeting in the garage, left over from a dry wall project. I wrapped him in one sheet. Duct tape really is helpful. Dragged him to the garage on another sheet, into the trunk.

"It's true about dead weight, Tom."

Vacuumed the now bare mattress. Put on a pair of Tom's sweats, donned a T-shirt. Paper towel and Dawn detergent took care of the visible blood and were stuffed in an empty grocery bag. Rummaging through a closet offered up a pair of slippers. Clorox wipes. Then I vacuumed like an Oreck salesman. Made my way from the side of the bed to the driver's side door of Tom's Focus, removed the bag and drove home in a stolen car with a body in the trunk.

Happenstance, an efficient 120 gallon water heater and an air compressor made it work. They found Tom's body in his car on Wednesday morning. The department was sure he'd been murdered at home. His nearest neighbors had been gone that weekend and there was almost no physical evidence. A few hairs that could belong to anyone and a couple of pink fibers that didn't match anything in his home. The theory was that someone had sought revenge. Probably from Tom's time in Vice.

Ecstasy, inner peace, adrenalin, power, knowledge. My new game was like acid without the melting walls. The flashbacks were better. They just weren't enough.

I set my sights on a great looking defense attorney. George Wolf had the greenest eyes I'd ever seen. Money eyes.

Flamboyant in court and self-assured in real life, he'd been through a divorce the year before. There was a party at my house and he stayed to help clean up. The dating was sporadic. George was involved in a high profile case, too busy for romance. We exchanged phone sex at the end of business related calls and promised a blow out at the end of George's case.

He got the client off. It was evident that the man had indeed raped his victim but police had played around with search and seizure a little too much. The jurors made everyone pay the price. I murmured congratulations and told George to come to me when he could, I'd have champagne waiting.

It was past midnight when George came through the door still high on the win.

"Before you start Trudy, I know the victim didn't get the justice she deserved but the department has to start respecting the laws they uphold … ."

I reached up to his lips, silenced him with my index finger, and walked him up the steps to the loft. Dim lighting, Sinatra and the promised champagne. George took in the setting and creamy lace for the first time. His eyes got hungry and he started to talk.

"Trudy, I …"

"We've talked enough George, dance with me, touch me, make love to me but no more talk."

I offered the blue aphrodisiac and saw the protest about to reach his lips.

"All night, George. All night."

This dance was more subtle. A few turns to Sinatra, the gentle kisses of adolescence and then frantic urges. Playing the submissive female that I knew George craved, staying in control only with the demanded silence. The irony of a speechless lawyer amused me. When George pulled the strap of my teddy down, I led him onto the floor. He tasted me then, still in the shirt and pants from a forgotten courtroom.

He was a good lover, not using his hands but wandering everywhere with his tongue. When he got to my center, I gasped. Knew he felt the power. They were all the same. He attacked with an enthusiasm I've seldom experienced. My excitement began to mount. Different than his.

Finally, from below a groan and a smile, I pulled him up to my mouth and tasted my sex. Brought us both to our knees and began to unbutton his Stafford special blend. Coquette now, leading us to our feet. Helped George out of his trousers and guided him over to the wine and the awaiting repose. A sheet scattered with rose petals. So easy. He never saw the ice pick coming. The bliss of the ride was sublime and I took all the time I needed to reach climax. This time I knew how not to get caught.

A couple of weeks later Tom's partner Don poked his head into my office to catch up. We shared abbreviated histories, promised to stay more in touch. As he was leaving, Don commented that he was glad Tom had had me for a friend. I returned the compliment and said we'd do drinks when I got back from my high school reunion. It seemed strange to be going back when everything was here now.

I had to change my M.O. for the reunion. No one ever forgets high school history. Lover number two took the humble offering and was dead by the end of the weekend.

I loved being alive. I wanted to share this darkness. Wallowed in not understanding myself. Rejoiced in being unique. Trying to analyze was fruitless. Books on criminal psychology have no definition for this.

Sometimes there was regret. No, that's wrong. In all honesty, the only thing I've regretted is that I've felt no regret. It eats at me sometimes. I know there are sensations left for me to feel. Still, at times this past year, I know I've been as alive as anyone has ever been. And now I'm not alone anymore.

Act 2 began on another Friday. I was daydreaming, ruminating, whatever you want to call it.

"I get my rocks off fucking dead guys, which is pretty sick."

"Talking to yourself, Trudy?"

"Hey, Don, no. Well, yes, but you don't want to know. What brings you here?"

"Margaritas, girlfriend. We're going to go out, swap war stories and drink too much."

We went for Mexican and the laughter flowed almost as fast as the tequila. Then shop talk.

"Two more dead girls, Don. Is it still being considered a coincidence?"

"It's not your problem anymore, Truds. Maybe one day, they'll find a link and the powers that be will have to admit you were right. For now, we have a bunch of dead sluts."

He read my eyes. Retreated quickly.

"Not what you wanted to hear. Sorry. How was the reunion?"

"Amazing. People who wouldn't talk to me then wanted to hear all about me now. Trudy the star. Reborn."

"You were hot shit in high school."

"For a time."

I looked at Don. Thought of him dead. I was sexually charged. He felt the energy. Shared it.

"We're out of here, Trudy. I'm going to take you on a ride."

The motel's name was a number. I had neither an offering nor a clean up plan, and hell I was horny. Don shut the door to the room, pushed me into a recliner.

"Right now you look pretty damned fuckable."

He yanked off my sweater. The buttons of my blouse flew across the room. Don turned me around and pulled up my skirt. Rammed me from behind, pushing my head into the chair's headrest.

I felt fear. Glorious fear.

Adrenalin pumped throughout my body and I began to thrust back. Thought to myself, "He cums and it will be over." But he lasted and just as his leg muscles reached that tell-all tightening, he pulled out.

"God you're a mess. We're going to shower now, clean you up."

He crossed the floor, still so hard.

Then I was in the cheap shower, handcuffed to the curtain rod, propped against the mildewed tile. Shit, I was sore. Sore and sober. Make that sore, sober and aroused.

He drew blood when he bit my nipple and I moaned. He took the coarse washcloth and wiped me down, cheap terry and hot water making my skin bristle. Out of the shower and onto the bed. It became interactive. Violent. My insides turned over from the lust even as I bit Don's shoulder with all of my might. The mutual battery lasted for hours until finally I came.

A grunt of satisfaction. Whose?

And then Don pulled out, cumming between my breasts like in a bad porno movie.

"Lick it baby, I want you to eat it all up."

And I did. Wanted to.

He dumped me at home that night without saying anything. I watched the bruises ascend to high purple and then recede to pea green. Finally they ebbed into the color of a winter sun and then were gone. I'd find myself massaging the newly healed skin, wishing the bruises back.

Victim number four was a necessary risk. Married with children, forensic pathologist Mike Johnson picked up my signals right away. He was flattered, no question. Balding, overweight, he took only tentative steps at first but when deer hunting season approached he invited me to his cabin, said he could buy venison for Christmas that year.

Afraid of male bragging and lack of alibi, I thought twice. Then Mike confided in me. He'd worked on both George and Tom. Found it curious; the similarities in the cases. When prodded, he plumed out like an oversexed pheasant. He had a litany of well thought-out similarities. They'd been killed with similar weapons in the same way. Both men had been scalded clean after death. Both had been drinking alcohol which suggested a social occasion and ...

"Trudy, they both had Viagra in their system. I'm going to work on this. I've been networking. I found thirty-two other unsolveds with stab wounds, but only one unsolved where a guy had taken

Viagra and consumed alcohol. That guy burned up in his car, in the middle of a cornfield."

"Mike, is it true about Viagra?" Couldn't believe I was saying this. I should do their commercials.

Mr. Personality responded, "I don't know. I never really want to last all night at home, but I have heard stories and testimonials."

"Mike, if I came up to the cabin could we …?"

And so this time, the victim brought his own sacrifice and burned in the woods.

Work. Fifty cases coming to the docket and then there was my special project. Eight girls dead in two months. This was bad. All those girls. Frustrated now, I pulled out an eight by ten that always made me smile. A snowy football game, contraband Budweiser, and Trudy young and confident with the only boy who ever knew the promise of her.

It was loud and smoky. Pool balls clattered while Randy Rhoades' guitar played to Ozzy's voice in the background.

"A shot and a beer, please, barkeep."

"Let me get that for you, little lady?"

"What do you think, Sal, are his intentions towards me honorable?"

"If they are, Trudy, it's a crying shame."

"Haven't seen you here lately, Trudy."

"All work, Don, no play."

"Drink. Now."

I looked at Don, hoping for sultry, knowing it came off as tired with too much mascara and settled for, "Salut."

Jameson's went down with a promise of warmth.

"One for the house, Sal!"

Cheers went up as AC/DC began "Have a Drink on Me."

Later, his place. Holiday sad for the single man but tonight it didn't matter. The dance began sweet. Harry Connick singing carols as the clothes disintegrated. This time different than last. Equals when our lips met. As strangers we explored. Don hovered over me and I wrapped my legs around him. Urging him inside. His hard-on wilted away.

"You asshole, who do you think you are?"

"Fuck you too, Trudy. I do manage to stay hard for most girls, you know."

"Prove it," and the game began.

I woke up having to pee so bad I almost didn't make it to the toilet. There was red in my urine. Scared of the consequences, I looked in the mirror. Don came in then.

"Christ, you're careful," were my first words. Don took in my mottled back, his fist prints on my arms and as he turned me around to inspect my thighs, caught a glimpse of himself in the mirror. I'd given as good as I got. He wouldn't be able to shower at the Y for a month.

"Trudy?"

This time it was slow because otherwise the pain would have been unbearable. Don looked up at me and the purity in that look made me grab onto him as if my life depended upon it. And then we both let go.

The D.A.'s office has a Christmas party. Attendance mandatory. Photo Ops optional. Don was here, playing Santa to underprivileged kids. He ignored me until the end. On my way out he grabbed me. Pulled me into my office.

"Ever been fucked in your office before, counselor?"

"Only by defense attorneys."

"Witty, but I'm not Tracy and you aren't Hepburn."

Don squeezed my cunt then, hard. It felt like heaven.

"I'm going to make you shudder with pain, Trudy. In your office chair. After you peak, I'm going to make you scream. Then we will begin again."

I was fascinated by this man. Briefly wondered if I'd found him before, would the ennui have ended. Would Tom still be spiking balls over the net on Saturday mornings and lounging in sweats on Saturday night?

Santa reached into his bag, pulled out plastic cuffs. Restricted all four of my limbs. Pulled out a video camera. Went to the tiny coat closet, nodded his approval at something inside. Turned around and pulled out a bottle of tequila.

"Drink up, baby. A toast to old times. Take this, too."

"What is it, Don?"

"Oxycontin. Beyond pain. We'll ride to the end of the world. I'll take a pill, too. We're in this together."

As he swallowed the little blue pill, I understood. I swallowed the pill, gently set upon my tongue, and knew I'd been absolved.

It's later now. The bonds are gone. And the razor Don used to do it? It's right here. The video rolled and there is plenty to keep both our offices busy for a long time. Sometimes there's more beauty in the end of a story than in the beginning.

REED FARREL COLEMAN

is the critically acclaimed author of three others in the Moe Prager series, and lives on Long Island with his wife and two children. He is the recipient of the Shamus, Barry, and two Anthony awards for his third installment in the Moe Prager series (and the precursor to *Soul Patch*), *The James Deans*.

PEARLS
REED FARREL COLEMAN

DRAW a line to connect the matching items.

Marilyn Monroe	Her favorite flavor
Leaving Las Vegas	Her favorite toy
Fuck	Her ambition
Pussy	Her favorite tragic figure
Pearls	Her favorite thing to do, feel and say

She would pull the string of pearls out of them one, two at a time. With each gentle tug, a moan, a sigh, a twitch—the quiver of an orchid as grains of pollen are removed. She loved the look of translucent white against wet pink. For her it was the feel, the friction. Finally, their muscles taut, pulsing with electricity, she would yank the remaining pearls out with a snap of the wrist. They would near explode as the twisted end loop was set free.

"Fuck me, fuck me hard!" she'd hear them scream, breathless, gasping for air, rubbing the wet pearls against their nipples. "Oh, fuck my pussy. Fuck it! Fuck it!"

It was the last voice she recalled, one of her clients screaming. Then the sun exploded with a burning, blinding light, a light so bright she could see through shut eyelids. But after the light came darkness. She dreamed of pearls in a sea of pink.

She woke up. *Was the sun up too?* It was impossible to tell. The room was cool, the lights low. She felt like a bottle of Chardonnay being brought down to the proper chill. She could not move. *Was she dead? In the ME's ice box?* The temperature was about right. But no, the refrigerator light pops off when the door closes. She knew that for a fact because her big sister had shoved her inside the big fridge her parents kept in the basement to store the extra food they never bought. Her sister had held the door shut while she sat there, a bundle of herself, cold and in the dark.

"Fuck you!" she had screamed at her sister when she was let out. It was the first time she had used the F word. She had thought it like a million bazillion times, but never said it. Like her daddy used to say, "You get arrested for what you do, not for what you think." Yeah, Daddy, like for coming into your little girls' room at night and fucking one while the other watched. Watching was harder, except the night her sister locked her in the fridge. She enjoyed watching that night. After her sister hung herself, she could not get over the shame of that enjoyment. There wasn't enough hot fucking water to wash that shame away.

She tried remembering her sister's name, her face. Nothing. Maybe she *was* dead. Fuck! This wasn't the way it was supposed to be. *Does everything just slowly slip away like a long greased rope between your fingers? Do the details of your life fall into the abyss, one aspect at a time?* She was determined that this couldn't be death. She had a plan for her death and this was pretty far the fuck away from it.

Leaving Las Vegas was her ambition. She was gonna kill herself one fucking drink at a time, but better than in the movie. Nicholas Cage, the dumbass with that nasally fucking whine, did it like by the bottle. She guessed that was due to Hollywood time constraints. When you've only got ninety minutes to drink yourself to death and fuck Elisabeth Shue, scarred ass and all, you gotta do it by the bottle. She dreamed about fucking Elisabeth Shue sometimes. Sometimes when she was pulling the pearls out of her clients' cunts, she fantasized they were Elisabeth Shue. Death would taste like vodka and pussy, Elisabeth Shue's pussy.

Her sister hanging herself was bullshit. Ninety minutes! It was over in like ninety fucking nano seconds. Coroner said she snapped her neck. What was that all about? You live how ever many years, endure all the shit life hands you and then snap, crackle, pop, you're dead!

Fuck that, big sister! No, she was going to enjoy her own dying. She'd surf the borderline and when she felt she was losing her looks and that she had become sufficiently tragic—see Monroe, Marilyn a.k.a. Baker, Norma Jean—she'd take that last drink. Her liver would do the big bang; her heart would explode; her face would suck into itself. For fuck's sake, it would be a glorious death. Though she was curious. She had heard that some men, when they were hanged, died with huge erections. When she got to the other side, she'd ask her sister, "Did you cum?"

But still, she couldn't remember her goddamned sister's name. Kinda makes for an awkward reunion in hell when you can't remember your fucking sister's name. *Don't I know your from somewhere? It's right on the tip of my tongue.* Wouldn't cut it. You were, even in hell, expected to remember your siblings. Hey, fuck on a bike, maybe not. Maybe that's what hell was all about, forgetting. Nah, it wouldn't be that easy. Hell would look and feel like her father's cock.

She gave up on her sister. The name would come to her eventually and, if it didn't, no biggie. She tried remembering her clients' names, one client's name, any client's name. The last client, the one she was fucking with the blue foot-long, the one screaming "Fuck it!" what was her … Nothing. She tried remembering their faces, any of their faces, any face, but they either looked like clenched fists or eyeless mannequins. What the fuck? This was crap. Enough of this shit. Time to move on. The wine was properly chilled.

She could not move. Her arms, her legs, her neck, her eyelids, her lips were just not in the mood. In her head she heard … *The shin bone's connected to the ankle bone. The ankle bone's connected to the* … What next, the fucking Hokey Pokey? She'd seen a bumper sticker once:

THE HOKEY POKEY-

IS THAT REALLY WHAT IT'S ALL ABOUT?

At least it didn't ask you to honk if you agreed. This was just stupid, she thought. What next, the Pledge of Allegiance, a Hail Mary, dirty limericks? *There once was an escort from* … Where was she from? Wherever it was, they spoke English there. The voice in her head spoke English. Well, it didn't have to be that autobiographical. *There once was a whore from Lahore who loved to get down on all four. She could drink and fuck and drink and fuck and drink and fuck and drink* …

She felt herself tiring. If her eyes weren't already shut, they'd have been fluttering closed. And she wasn't thirsty for a drink, only sleep. She felt herself relax for the first time in her fucking life.

***

The surgeon walked over to a bored looking detective sitting in the waiting room. He smelled like a thousand old cups of coffee and someone else's cigarettes. Even so, the surgeon didn't mind dealing with cops. They could be such fucking assholes, but they weren't family. They didn't need to hear his repertoire of false hope and comfort. They just wanted the real deal.

"Hey, Doc. So …"

"I got the bullet out. Looks like a nine millimeter. Bagged it for you."

"Thanks. It *was* a nine. Very good, Doc."

"You knew?"

"Yeah. If all my cases were this fucking easy, I'd stay on the job until I was eighty."

"What happened?"

"Woman found the vic fucking her 'partner' and decided she wasn't fond of the idea. Put one in the vic's noodle, twelve into her cheatin' 'partner', and swallowed one for good measure. Nice, huh?" The detective snickered.

"You'll have to excuse me, detective. I guess I missed the punchline here."

"Sorry, Doc. The vic had a blue rubber, twelve inch strap-on stuck inside the girlfriend. The EMTs had to like pry them apart. Good thing they carry crowbars with 'em."

The surgeon was right. Cops could be such fucking assholes. Said, "What's the world coming to?"

"I know what you mean, Doc. Time was you'd expect this shit with husbands and wives. Maybe it is time to put in my papers."

"Maybe."

"So what's the prognosis?"

"Who the fuck knows? Bullet went in pretty clean, but it did some damage along the way. She's in a coma. Could be there for quite some time."

"Hey, at least she's alive, right? The other two are history."

"That's one way of looking at it."

***

When she woke up, the world wasn't as cold, but it had gotten soft around the edges. She had dreamt of pearls in a sea of pink, but couldn't think of why. She lay back and enjoyed the buzz. There was fuck all else to do.

**EXPLETIVE DELETED
SECTION FIVE**

FUCK!

ANTHONY NEIL SMITH

was born and raised in Mississippi, and he currently lives in Minnesota. For five years, he edited the infamous online noir journal *Plots With Guns* and the later print anthology. He's the author of two novels, *Psychosomatic* and *The Drummer*, and his short stories have been published in many crime fiction and literary journals. He likes cajun food and blues guitar. He would be scared silly to run into most of his characters in real life. What awful, awful people.

FIND ME
ANTHONY NEIL SMITH

HOPPER Garland was a private detective who liked going to bars after work so he could impress college girls with job stories. His mentors in the business got drunk and laid all the time, so he had to keep up. Tuesday night in a too-bright college bar on Bourbon Street, the place was half empty, pop music echoing loud. The beer logo doo-dads were inflatable Saints football helmets and dinosaurs and palm trees. A big screen TV ran silent video of girls showing their tits at Mardi Gras. Beads draped everything.

Hopper chatted up a chubby blonde chick with frizzed hair, thick eyelashes and pink lipstick, an out-of-style look that big girls always pulled off well. A miniskirt and short boots, legs crossed with knees aimed at Hopper while they sat on two stools at the end of the bar. Her friends, a half-Korean girl with short hair and a pale brunette in thick make-up, wandered towards a table, but this one stayed.

Talking to her about divorce/adultery gigs, Hopper said, "I show pictures, phone records, video, and they'll get all pissed at me, like I should have worked harder or not at all."

"I'd want to know," she said.

Hopper tried to remember this chick's name: *Farrah, Farrah.* "You'd think, yeah. Me too. But so many times, no matter how nice or sorry I feel about it, they take it as I'm making fun of them."

"That's mostly it? You just track cheaters?"

"No. We find things, people. I'll do undercover sometimes, expose scams and shit like that. I never know, day to day. And that's good."

"You carry a gun," she said.

Hopper shrugged. "Got to protect myself." He didn't carry a gun.

He drained his plastic cup of light beer and signaled the bartender for another. Farrah sipped a banana daiquiri, still half full, her first tonight. Maybe she was interested in the story and the attitude, which he hoped would last long enough for her to work on a second drink and ignore that he wasn't the best catch in the bar and his glasses were too thick. Funny thing was how many good ones let him come home with them.

"I know someone you could find," Farrah said.

Hopper thought it was a come-on. "I can give it a shot, take a look."

* * *

In Farrah's dorm room a half-hour later, they were naked on her small metal frame bed, plastic mattress making squeaks, and Hopper licked Farrah's thighs. She moaned nicely, then squeezed her legs together a little and rubbed Hopper's hair. He stopped, glanced at her.

She said, "Will you really help find Cynthia?"

"Who's Cynthia?"

"She was my roommate, and she went missing over a month ago."

She rubbed his hair more. He worried about the rest of it falling out. He liked the rubbing. He was hard and wanting to be in her.

"Nobody cares about Cynthia. Poor Cynthia. No one's looking anymore," Farrah said.

"I can look into it."

"You mean it?"

"I said I would." He went back down and moved his hands under her ass, lifted her to his mouth.

✳✳✳

Later, Hopper sat on the side of the bed and stared across at the empty half of the dorm room. Cynthia's space was bare except for a small jewelry box on a bookshelf. Farrah, sprawled across her mattress, pressed her toes into Hopper's skin. She was awake but playing at sleep and he liked that they both knew it.

Hopper stood, slipped his glasses on, walked over to the shelf and opened the jewelry box. His eyes adjusted to the dim blue and shadows. He tilted the box towards the shaft of moonlight, nothing inside.

"Her parents took everything, but I kept that. I hid it," Farrah said.

He looked at Farrah, the sheet covering her breasts. She held pudgy arms over her head and made happy noises.

Hopper pointed at photos tacked to a corkboard. "Are any of these people Cynthia?"

"The one with us together at a party. It's the only one I've got."

"I have to borrow it." He took the photo, held it close. Cynthia was perfect but shadowed, small smile next to Farrah's wide-open mouth. The most important features were the eyes. Most people could adjust hair color, noses, chins, even wear colored contacts, but they couldn't change the way they looked at the world. "I'll need to talk to people who knew Cynthia. Friends, family, boyfriends. You've got numbers?"

"Sure."

"You knew her too, right? Friends?"

"On our way to being, I guess."

Hopper climbed into bed and straddled Farrah, held her wrists. He whispered, "I'll start with you."

***

The Korean-American girl with short hair at the bar was Cynthia's best friend, Divinity. Hopper found her working at the university library. They talked outside where people smoked and snubbed butts in the grass-patched dirt.

"I wasn't the last to see her. Farrah was, maybe. The cops checked with everyone," Divinity said. She was petite, tight-skinned and muscled, in a short dress, her tan like a glaze.

"Was she acting differently? Maybe she met someone new?"

"Every day she was different. Sometimes, she wouldn't speak to me, and then a few hours later would be fine and happy."

"This a mental problem?"

Divinity ducked her head. "Maybe she needed medicine. We didn't think about it that way. She was just her, right?"

Hopper stuck his hands in his pockets and nodded, watched a nearby flock of smokers breathe at each other. When he turned back to Divinity, she was checking him out, blinked and made eye contact, blushed. He grinned at her, guessing she was impressed—his sport coat too small at the shoulders made him seem wrestler-shaped.

"What did she like to do?"

"Dance. Hang in chatrooms, but she'd talk to the screen while typing. Oh, and she dressed up for *Rocky Horror Picture Show*."

"People still do that?"

"Once a week at the campus theater, yeah. She dressed like Janet, the virgin slut." Divinity sat on a stone bench. She rubbed her flip-flops together, tapped her fingernails on the stone. All flirt, no glam.

"Have you checked for her at the show?"

"I went a couple weeks ago, but I didn't see her. Everyone looked the same. They do it tonight. You want to go? Maybe something's changed."

Hopper thought it was a come-on. He liked this girl, even if she was one of those alternachicks he wouldn't usually go after, preferring Farrah's hairspray and desperation. He said, "Anything to help, right? Give me your number."

He jotted it down, but then she busied up beside him, hands behind her back, and said, "I can take lunch now, you know, or a break. I've got twenty minutes."

They walked to his Mazda, and he drove until he found an empty back parking lot behind an old warehouse. Divinity slipped her panties down her legs, reached over and undid his pants.

She leaned her seat back and said, "Come here."

He scooted over there, kissed her, climbed on top. It was so damn uncomfortable, him humping, her grunting, sliding down the seat. She clenched. Hopper was quick and he slid off to the side, holding her until they were ready to drive again.

He dropped Divinity at the library. She said, "Tonight, remember? Call and I'll tell you where to get me."

She slammed the door and walked away. Hopper put the car in park, closed his eyes and rubbed the sweat off his stomach, mouth-breathing until he stopped shaking.

***

Cynthia's parents lived in Covington, across the lake. Hopper called ahead, then went over in the afternoon, pinching the photo of Farrah and Cynthia to the steering wheel while driving across the long bridge, trying to figure out Cynthia by looks alone while trying not to see Farrah. She wasn't just a girl from a bar, an addition to his "I'm a Man" list. She was a client, and he cared about that. Fucking

Divinity felt a little like cheating. Maybe the girls would get together, compare notes. Maybe Farrah would hate his guts.

Glanced at Cynthia, then the road, then turned on 870 AM and listened to that doctor bitch rail against everything that kept Hopper employed—sex, lies, indecision. Glanced at Cynthia, the road, Cynthia. Not as perfect in daylight, sunken eyes, no make-up, straight brown hair strung across her face, but still magnetic in spite of it.

After finding the subdivision, Hopper pulled into Cynthia's parents' driveway behind a Jaguar. Upscale suburb, narrow houses bordering woods, the roads like marble.

Cynthia's mom stood waiting at the front door, smiling, more magnetic than the daughter. *They bloom*, Hopper thought. This was a woman in her forties with thin limbs, cut-off denim, a sleeveless sweater, and straight brown hair like her daughter, pulled back with a rubber band.

Hopper held out his hand. "Yeah—"

"Call me Mary, please, Hopper. I like your name, because it makes me more comfortable. You're just like I pictured."

"How's that?"

"Like movie private eyes, but less beat up." She took his hand, put her other on his back. "Come in, okay?"

Inside, it was all too compact, a door to the parents' bedroom off the kitchen, next to the door into the living room. Mary led him through, saying "Sorry about the mess. I'm cleaning. I clean all day." Her feet made sticky sounds across the tile floor in the kitchen and living room until they stepped on the carpet in the hall. She stood in a doorway and said, "This is Cynthia's room."

It was teenage girl all over, fresh and bright with a fluffy bed, posters *of Rocky Horror* and small mirrors with rock band logos painted on them hung on the wall. A small TV, a plastic yellow see-through phone, shoeboxes stacked in the closet under clothes that were too snug hanging on the rack. Mary stepped over to the bed and sat.

"We've only been here a year, and Cynthia started college this semester. She was so excited," Mary said. "Living at home would've been cheaper, but she wanted the whole experience."

"How old was she?"

"Nineteen in July."

"She come home every weekend? Was there someone she went with, a special trip?"

"She spoke about a guy she didn't like, but I could tell there was more to it. He worked on her car a couple times. I think his name was Clint."

"Where can I find Clint?"

Mary held her finger to her eye, rubbed, pulled, and rolled her thumb and finger together. Hopper knelt in front of her, hoping she wouldn't cry. Hoping it wouldn't turn into a TV show.

"Mary." He put his hands on her knees and then wished he hadn't. She grabbed his shoulders.

She said, "I don't know, and I can't guess, I'm tired. My husband, shit, like Batman suddenly, talking to the detectives when he gets home from work. He subscribes to true crime magazines now. He talks to the cops about Internet pedophiles."

"How does this connect to Cynthia?"

"It doesn't, because we gave up on finding her and just dream about her now. We take our minds off it anyway we can, and then you show up." Not teary yet, but intense. Her hands rubbing his shoulders now, the rough jacket itching his skin.

Hopper said, "I'm sorry. I was helping, I thought. Sometimes, we can find people."

"My husband hasn't made love to me since she disappeared."

On the vanity were little glass bottles of bright nail polish. A round brush with a black rubber handle next to a fold-up hair dryer. Mary slipped her hands under the jacket and rubbed Hopper's chest.

"Mary."

"It doesn't have to mean anything, please. But do this for me, and I'll talk to you forever. I'll tell you anything I can. Mother's instinct and all."

She inched her face close to his, opened her knees and pulled him closer. She hugged him tightly, kissed his neck. Hopper worked through his mind, *No, we can't do this, but I understand how you feel. I'm sorry. I'm so sorry.* In spite of her perfume and her warmth, in spite of needing Cynthia and wanting Farrah. He told her, "Okay," and thought about his list. In a college-rule notebook locked in his office file cabinet, bottom drawer, the bad ass private eye totaled seventy-five women in six years on the job. Three in one day was a first, a personal best. But he was so tired.

They undressed themselves quietly, standing apart. They stood naked in the light edging through the drawn blinds. Mary pointed at Cynthia's bed, the fluffy comforter and pillows. He wiped them away and sat. Mary pushed him onto his back, climbed on top. She grabbed his dick and pointed it into her. She was already soaked, like she'd been planning for this since he called. She rode him fast, not letting up. Things started to ache. Hopper held her waist tightly. He withstood it. It wasn't about him at all, and Mary let out low animal moans. When he came, he felt numb.

Nothing Mary said later about Cynthia helped him much, but she remembered where Clint worked. On his way out the door, she tiptoed and kissed him, a long deep kiss that felt to Hopper like a five-dollar bill.

✳✳✳

Clint was changing the oil on a PT Cruiser when Hopper stopped by. The guy was blond, tough-looking in a quarterback way, like he was only pretending the oil and grease on his clothes and face didn't bother him, but he really would rather be draped in designer jeans. Hopper climbed down into the pit beneath the main floor with him, the light dim and yellow. They had room to stand. Clint kept working while Hopper talked, the way people do on *Law & Order*.

"The bitch just dropped out. It's not like we were steady or anything. We fucked, we hung out, got drunk and danced sometimes. But even that all stopped a couple of weeks before she went missing."

"Before that, any clue as to what she was thinking? Acting differently?"

"God, I never noticed. Us together, we never talked seriously unless, you know, she danced with some guy I didn't know. We'd fight about it, yell some. But that was the booze talking. Hell, she danced with my friends, I didn't mind at all."

Clint wrenched something tighter, wiped his hands on a filthy rag. Hopper watched for nervous tics or shaking. He didn't see any. That didn't mean much, though.

"A real private eye, man? You're serious?" Clint said.

"Well, it's not like movies, but I like the job."

"You get beat up a lot?"

Hopper ignored him, studied his notes. "I've got to say that the answers you gave don't make me really confident. In fact, it's exactly what I would expect."

Clint stopped working. "What's that supposed to mean?"

"The first person to look at is the boyfriend, the husband. And ninety percent of the time, that's the right call."

Clint picked up his wrench and stepped closer to Hopper. "You think I had something to do with her disappearing?"

"Maybe."

"You willing to back that up?"

Clint didn't wait for an answer. He shoved Hopper, then swung with the wrench. Hopper blocked the blow with his arm, but it hurt and he dropped his guard. Clint swung again and clipped Hopper on the side of the head. Stars and ringing, stars and ringing. Hopper was on his knees.

Clint eased up, brushing Hopper's face with his legs, then he grabbed the PI's hair, lifted his chin.

"You look good down there, private dick. You know that? Nobody comes in here and accuses me of any shit. I didn't have a thing to do with it. You believe me?"

Hopper tried to nod.

"Let's see how much you believe me." Clint's other hand fumbled with his pants, unzipping his fly and dropping the grease stained khakis. He wasn't wearing underwear, and Hopper saw the kid's dick starting to move.

"Here's my private dick. You're going to suck it, gumshoe. Do that, and I'll know you believe me."

Clint slapped the wrench across Hopper's back. Not as hard as the first time, but it still radiated a dull ache everywhere. Hopper thought about headbutting the guy, or biting his thing off. But that would've made more trouble than if he just let it all go. He took Clint's penis in his mouth, easy and wet, his tongue working it the way he'd seen chicks do in porno movies. Clint let out low grunts, rustled Hopper's hair. His glasses fogged up, so he took them off. Hopper felt terrible, like a failure, but by the time Clint turned Hopper around and bent him over the tool cart, he thought it felt pretty good. He believed every word Clint said.

✳✳✳

Before going back to his French Quarter apartment, Hopper stopped by his older sister's house Uptown. She'd raised him, almost, their mother dying when they were fourteen and eleven, their father working most nights and sleeping days, only available for parent/teacher conferences, talent shows, and graduations, but still a fine man. Dead two years back, massive stroke.

Hopper was tired and he hurt all over. He sat in his sister's kitchen at the round table, everything cartoonish—big eyed cows and Precious Moments kids with straw hats and pilgrim suits or dresses. He drank milk from a blue tinted glass while Sister washed dishes, bubbles rising inches above the sink.

"I'm so tired, and it was just a favor." Hopper said. He left all the sex out of the story, especially Clint raping him, although his sister would disapprove of those *slut girls* too, for her own very personal reasons.

"But it sounds like you care. Doesn't that matter, you caring about it?"

"Caring won't find her."

"More so than not." She scrubbed a plate with a Brillo. She had big hips that faded to a slim neck, pretty thin face. Her hair was long and curly, reached mid-back, nighttime-dark, and she wore a long shapeless navy blue dress.

Hopper thought the milk smelled bad but not sour. Farrah had paged him six times in two hours, but he wasn't ready. She wanted to see him. A progress report that would turn into more sex that would turn into her telling him all the things he didn't want to know about her past. He could say, *Spill it, babe, and I'll be right back,* then take his clothes, slip out, never see her again. That felt wrong, too.

Hopper used to be a one-woman man and was engaged, but the closer they got to the wedding date, the worse it got. The last time they talked, she wouldn't open her screen door. Called Hopper a monster, a fuck-up, like her crap life could be forgiven, brushed aside, but when he mentioned his one dark secret—instant loss.

He said to his sister, "I love my job, but I hate my life. I'm still awful and embarrassed most days."

"You're one of the best. One day, the perfect girl will come along and you'll forget what things without her were like."

Hopper grinned at that, knowing she didn't mean it, and said, "Just what I need." He stood, brought the glass to the sink, and patted Sister's back. "I'm going to get out of here."

She said, "Not yet. You're not through."

He sighed, looked at her, the eyes sneaky, her nose tiny and crinkling.

"Not tonight," Hopper said. "I'm so tired."

"I can't take 'no' for an answer."

"It's been a long day."

Sister brought empty hands from the soapy water, spread them on both sides of the sink, and hunched her shoulders. "It doesn't have to be a big production. Right here, while I finish the dishes."

Hopper stepped behind his sister. He dropped his pants and lifted her dress, pushed her panties aside while she reached into the sink for another plate. He bunched the dress in his hand as he pushed into her, Sister moving her feet apart, and she said, "Go slow, Hopper."

✳✳✳

He picked up Divinity outside her dorm. She was dressed in a French maid's costume and a frizzy wig. She climbed in smiling and leaned over to kiss Hopper's check.

"I'm Magenta," she said, waving her hand like a fashion model in front of her costume.

"I know. I've seen it."

"Just once?"

"Many times. I dressed as the criminologist when I went."

"Oh." Divinity stared ahead, blank and maybe seething. "You could've said."

Hopper smiled. "One fuck, you assume you know me?"

"Stop that."

She sulked as they drove, the windshield misting up outside so Hopper kept the wipers on a delay. Water droplets streaking, then disappearing in the wind. At the theater, a small mob in costumes waited outside. Hopper parked, got out, walked around to the other door and opened it for Divinity. There was a cold wind but few jackets, everyone pumped, excited, seeing the same damn movie every week, Hopper remembering the songs and all the in-jokes even though it had been ten years at least. Divinity was happy again, took his arm, waved at friends, said, "You know what she looks like?"

"Who?"

"*Cynthia.*"

"I know who she wants to be tonight. Maybe I can see that better than you."

Divinity leaned her head on Hopper's chest. "Wishing."

When Hopper was younger, they had a weekend showing at a theater in Metarie, and he would go with friends from college. He was still living with Sister then, so he dressed like the criminologist, but what he wanted was Frank N. Furter in leather and fishnets, Dr. Scott in his wheelchair, a blanket hiding high heels and stockings for the floor show, or even Brad, a feather boa around his neck and face paint, against his will, singing "Help me, Mommy. I'll be good, you'll see. Take this dream away ..." But he had to settle for the one he could get away with.

Tonight, the Franks looked wonderful, the extreme Freddie Mercury outrage in drag, the Janets virginal, in ripped slips, maybe some girls too fat for the role, but still, the song from the film said, "Don't dream it. Be it." Eddies in biker gear, Columbias in glittering gold jackets and shorts, humpbacked Riff Raffs. Maybe thirty fans total, easing their way inside.

"It's a long shot," Divinity said. "But a place to start. She has friends here."

Hopper agreed, but really thought to himself that Cynthia was dead and rotting in a shallow grave or the Mississippi River. It had been too long. Instead of talking to these girls, he should really have started with the cops and the case file, but he knew from the start that there was no hurry. The coincidence of Farrah meeting a private eye in a bar wouldn't make things better. One theory that stuck with him was the idea that Farrah had killed Cynthia and now felt guilty about it, wanted to get caught. Still, he liked Farrah and would go see her tonight after the movie. He would bring Divinity along, too, and all three could fuck and fuck all night with the fucking, the girls saying "Fuck me," and Hopper fucking them and letting the girls fuck him and he would be fine with too much fucking if they were, because when it was over, they could put it out of their minds and spill secrets trying to poison everything. But *this* time, no poison. The antidote was that he didn't trust them and they didn't know him and they didn't trust each other. Hopper and Farrah and Divinity could listen and hold each other all night and say "You poor thing" and "I know how you feel" and not mean it.

Hopper examined the crowd again in his undercover role. Someone caught his eye. Dressed as Dr. Scott, the wheelchair-bound professor who knows Frank's secret, a mussed wig and round glasses, thick mustache, but familiar eyes.

The eyes. The same gaze as in the photo. In her costume, she really could pass as a man, but Cynthia was right there under their noses. Maybe she was tired of being who she had been, but she certainly didn't want to be found.

Hopper imagined he would slip over to her during the orgy scene, kiss her neck and stare into those eyes to be absolutely sure, and then say, "Your friends are looking for you. They miss you." Maybe not Clint, who only cared about himself, or Divinity and Farrah, both trying to drown out trouble with sex and masks, not that it was a bad thing to do that. It seemed to be his way as well. But he'd still say, "Your family and friends miss you."

Cynthia might tell him, "I don't know what you're talking about. Kiss me again." Or she might not. It didn't matter if she wanted to be found or left alone. When it was over, Hopper would point her out, maybe give Farrah a call to let her know he had done the job, and then go home alone.

He smiled down at little Divinity, her face morphing into character as they approached the theater door behind these colorful kids in cheap costumes. She repeated one of Magenta's lines: "I'm lucky, he's lucky, we're all lucky!"

Hopper said, "I don't believe in luck."

DELPHINE LECOMPTE

is a flemish poet and spinster.

THREE TEPID SHOTS, TWO DECAPITATED GULLS, AND A CRIPPLED TAXIDERMIST
DELPHINE LECOMPTE

THE cushion i'm sitting on is embroidered with four scandi-navian warriors who are ripping a fair bucktoothed washerwoman to pieces, my john is sitting opposite me, on a much comelier cushion, it's embroidered with three good-natured bricklayers who are wolfing down goat cheese sandwiches on a comforting half-finished brick wall, my john is a crippled taxidermist, i know this cos there's a complicated metal structure fastened to his left knee, and he smells of turpentine and road kill, "who crippled you?" i ask him to break the ominous and hostile silence, "my father" he croaks, "was he a taxidermist too?", "no, he was a vet," "what was his specialty?", "the cutting away of doberman brains," "doberman lobotomy??", "yes," "hmm," we fall silent again, the taxidermist gracelessly hoists himself up and staggers to his liquor cabinet, "do you want another martini?", "why did your dad cripple you?", "he was drunk, he mistook me for a rabid poodle and snapped my legs, when i yelped: 'daddy, stop it, you're mistaking me for a rabid poodle again!' he somewhat sobered up and drove me to a sinister north french hospital ...", "why was it sinister?", "don't fucking interrupt me," "i want another martini," "you'll get another slap if you don't shut your trap," "that rhymes!", the crippled taxidermist viciously punches me in my left shoulder blade and tweaks me by the right earlobe, "in the car park of the sinister hospital my father wagged his crooked little index finger at me and hooted: 'if you tell on me i'll throttle your precious budgie,' 'it's not so precious' i whimpered, my father dragged me out of the car and into the hospital, when i woke up i had a new set of parents and a golden retriever named twitty," "what a daft name," "i know," "let go of my ear … what were your new parents like?", "cold and conceited," "what was the golden retriever like?", "fluffy and conceited … strip off your clothes," i dolefully strip off my clothes, "what happened to your father?", "he went a little mad, one day he gutted the cancerous dachshund of a loaded spinster, he put it on his head, went into the waiting room and smacked up all the other loaded spinsters, he wolfed down their mink coats and their epileptic rabbits, he ended up in a drab secluded asylum in an east german fir forest, i visited him once, 'i throttled your precious budgie, it took me ten hours and 26 minutes to squeeze the life out of it, now scram, you bloody traitor you' he snarled, i always knew it was an exceptional budgie," "what was its name?", "tom," "after tom waits?", "after my geography teacher," "what was so special about him?", "he had ginger sideburns and big horse-like nostrils," "that doesn't sound very alluring, i …", "shut up, ignorant floozy … dance for me," i start to gloomily sway my hips, the crippled taxidermist pours himself a stiff shot of cheap bourbon without taking his greedy green eyes off me, he downs it, puts the empty glass on his chrome stereo and slaps me in the face, "you're dancing like a depressed squirrel" he snaps, "i am a depressed squirrel" i hiss, the nefarious john yanks my left arm, he drags me into his glum macabre workplace, there are two stuffed gulls standing on the floor, "were they related?" i point at the gulls, "how the fuck should i know?!", the taxidermist harshly pushes me down onto a sticky worktop, "do you know what these are??" he holds up big black shears, "why, those are big black shears! please don't gut me, mister," "oh shut up, i'm not gonna gut you, i'm merely gonna slice up your cheeks," "my buttocks??", "no," all of a sudden the ill-bred taxidermist drops the shears, he throws up seventeen pineapple cubes and nine grey quills, and then he passes out, i snatch the shears, i stab the taxi-dermist in the repulsive stark white chest, i rip off his prosthetic leg and force it down his throat, i decapitate the two stuffed gulls, i go back into the living room and get dressed, the telephone starts to ring, "now what?", "erm, is jack there?", "if by jack you mean the vile short-tempered taxidermist who named his budgie after his geography teacher who had horse-like genitals and ferret-like wits then no, he's not here, you've got the wrong number, meek bastard," i slam down the receiver, i pour myself another martini and turn on the radio, the telephone starts to ring again, "jack is dead, get over it already," the young male at the other end of the line starts to violently sob, "don't weep, he was cheap and graceless, not to mention dour and unforgiving," i slam down the receiver, i turn up the volume of the radio, but the smiths can't smother the shrill uncompromising sirens, i turn off the radio and scram.

HP TINKER

lives in Manchester where he has carved a niche for himself as the Thomas Pynchon of Chorlton-cum-Hardy. Born and braised in the North of England (circa 1969), his award-avoiding fiction has appeared in *Ambit*, *Dreams Will Never End*, *The Edgier Waters*, *Code Uncut*, among other places, and at *3am Magazine* where he is a semi-professional editor who writes about soup. Bravely, a collection of stories by HP Tinker has been published by bright new underground literary gunslinger Social Disease, circa September 2006. Recently, he tripped up in public. Currently, he is incapacitated.

ENTANGLEMENT
HP TINKER

... **A** *series of unexplained deaths rippling across a city paralysed by overly-ambitious copycat serial killers, bi-curious junkies, homeless Santas ... 197 exchange students killed in simultaneous unrelated coffee table incidents ... a travelling salesman mutilated in his bed surrounded by obscene cuddly toys ... art critics butchered amidst some of the countries most innovative new buildings ... a motivational dog-trainer garrotted in her car by a 5-inch child's lariat ... several hundred random business journalists killed by lethal injection ...* the city a vast amoral jungle of blue-haired gamblers and punk rock scholars ... out on the Sheik-infested streets a thousand tragically sassy beauticians, Rembrandt scholars who don't like Rembrandt, religious activists sexually haranguing timid agnostics ... the atmosphere of each day eerily in keeping with the vapid production values of the entire *Sussudio* period ... Q surrounded by photographs, articles, graphs detailing these sly, wittily constructed deaths: dismembered ex-girlfriends, decapitated nuns, disembowelled cardiologists, violently violated violinists ... Q pondering the dark methodologies at work, regularly raising both eyebrows simultaneously ...

***

... unshaven in blue underpants, organic cotton, knitted stripes—no logo of any description—Q squinting at cold black newsprint, reading about the death of a former chess champion. Several witnesses saw him fall "almost cheerfully"—after straightening his bowtie, tossing himself from the roof of the building … an ever-increasing grin widening across his face … on impact he was "practically having sex up against a tree for five to ten seconds."

Q circles the paragraph in bright red ink.

In some advanced technological epoch—Q thinks to himself—perhaps people will wonder why we bothered to circle such articles in bright red ink. Q filing away the latest of the latest unexpected demises … *a light-bulb salesman ripped apart by a gaggle of lions … renegade schoolgirls exploding into young pieces, their charred remains evenly distributed across the piazza …*

✳✳✳

"… my files cannot possibly take the strain of this increasingly worrying information," realizes Q. "Soon I'll be requiring an all-new filing system …"

✳✳✳

… cryptic messages arriving—from disparate loners: infertile child psychologists, lunatic travel agents, broken down housewives, fairly lethal sounding Hispanic 52-year olds … the latest: Mrs. A, a glamorous cripple in a dark suit, pale tie, gold shoes, legs splayed about a mile wide: "I must interject into your investigation in my customized wheelchair," she states earnestly, like Kate Bush. "My husband is listed as missing in the places where they list such things—and that's a distressing state for any husband to be in …"

✳✳✳

"… regarding your husband—"

A: "I fear he's gone, forever into the overbearing darkness, more overbearing darkness than I had personally bargained for. Having dreamed all my life of romantic trajectories, I now find myself in a full-length narrative of angry policemen, would-be assassins, pre-teen suicide bombers, nothing remotely romantic about it—"

Q: "The rediscovery of a missing husband rarely represents an enormous cause for celebration … but if you have any supplementary information that might shed light on your husband's disappearance …"

A: "Well, there is one thing—probably not important …"

Q: "No, please tell me. Even the smallest grain might prove central …"

A: "Well, people do say he bears an unnatural resemblance to Kris Kristofferson …"

***

… into his Dictaphone: "—as events turn ever more torrid, I am proud that I have not betrayed myself, not once—well, maybe once—but never twice and, in a corrupt and immoral age where inconsequential dialogue has become the order of the day, that seems important …"

***

… Q waking, the smell of maple syrup thick in both nostrils. In a city of fetid fragrances, the mysteriously saccharine odor rapidly hits local radio. One listener describes the smell as "oddly flavoured coffee", another: "rather like maple syrup". A well-spoken spokesperson from the Office of Emergency Aromas asserts: "We are fairly confident that the odor is no way dangerous and that citizens of the city can continue with their usual patterns of early morning business and communication …"

Stepping outside, a gigantic billboard overhead reads: "...
*THERE ARE SOME PEOPLE WHO WILL NOT FULLY
COOPERATE HERE ...*"

***

... an unexpected sight greeting Q along the angular carpet-
ing scheme of Mrs. A's apartment: an arm reaching outwards, two
fingers raised like a gesture, or sign—or salute; or symbol. Mrs.
A impaled on the far wall by several metal hooks. Dark scuffs on
the linoleum resembling less of a struggle, more a dance of death,
possibly the Foxtrot. *Why were murdered women often tortured and
mutilated horribly in this fashion?* asks Q. *As if simple murder wasn't
enough for them? Was the secret cousin of some rich and powerful people
involved? Who else would be up to the task of nailing somebody's wife
to a wall with so much obvious enthusiasm?* Recent events unusually
frozen on the face of Mrs. A in the form of a happy expression
... *but*—given the circumstances—*was there really anything to be
quite so happy about?* Q taking samples of her nightwear away—for
special analysis—under his jacket ...

***

"... even previously thick-skinned police sniffer dogs have taken
to contemplating their own mortality," Q notes, alone in his office
with cheap bourbon, sour conclusions, false assumptions, vague
deductions, a Dictaphone, some even cheaper bourbon ... the telephone spluttering in the ever-dimming dimness. Q picking up, as
is his custom. A voice answering like a deceased banker dredged
hissing from a lake, some time last May. "When an unhappily
married woman is unexpectedly crucified," advises the voice, "her
husband is generally called in for questioning ..."

***

... on a hunch, Q tracing the husband of Mrs. A to the Northern fringes of the Latino-Disco Crossover Quarter, where he is rumoured to be professionally dancing the *paso doble* under an assumed initial: "O". A largely colorful room crowded with the contours of humans; in the centre about thirty middle-aged bisexuals thrashing out symbolic acts of dance. Dubious dress codes at work: purple sequinned shirts, casual khaki slacks, Manhattan sandals ... an unusual man bearing a passing resemblance to Kris Kristofferson in a lime-green rental tuxedo ... a slim white cane sweeping in front of him, left to right, right to left, like the feelers of an insect socialite.

Q doubts the veracity of this disability, almost immediately ...

***

"... did you ever dance the *paso doble* with Mrs. A?"
Silence.

"Did you ever dance the *paso doble* with Mrs. A and then not contact Mrs. A for some time afterwards?"
Silence.

"Do you still dance the *paso doble* nowadays ... *with other people?*"

"O" smiles diffidently, the expression of idyllic contentment written across his face: "Sometimes," "O" admits, "I feel like a dead man. But I've made my choice. I have a certain life and I like my new way of thinking. I'm happier where I am today. I remain fairly confident of that ..."

***

... unperturbed, Q puts on his hat ... only when he looks down the hat isn't there anymore. Instead, in the place where the hat should be: no hat, a reduction in hat-based circumstance. Out in the street, noticing almost everybody seems to be wearing hats, wide-brimmed fedoras mostly, noting how hats are central to maintaining confidence during daytime detective work in the street.

As a consequence, Q feels hatless and alone …

***

… the corridor adjacent to his office: an incredibly angry look-ing young woman in a rhinestone kilt leaning heavily against an instant coke machine. Q wondering: *what is the source of the young woman's incredible anger? Were her parents incredibly angry through-out her formative youth? Does she have an incredibly angry young husband at home? Are her clothes incredibly angry clothes? What is the significance of the incredible anger of the incredibly angry looking young woman? What is the incredibly angry looking young woman really so incredibly angry about?*

"You are investigating these crimes not from compassion but from intellectual avarice," she tells him—incredibly angrily. "That may sound totally asinine—but that's never stopped me before …"

The incredibly angry looking young woman then invites Q to supper at her brownstone townhouse. Having already slept with more than five hundred young women during his investigations, Q welcomes this latest development …

***

"… you can disappear in this city," explains Q. "Its belly is death … you can become entangled in the everyday nuisances here, en-snaring you like a pop career you never even wanted."

"That's why this city needs you," she snaps. "Some people don't realise it yet. Others, however, are only too keenly aware …"

"… but"—Q flounders—"my masculinity appears to have become badly eroded, over time, to the point where I am starting to feel like I'm trapped inside a bad Phil Collins song …"

"How can you say that!?" she shrieks. "That implies there are *good* Phil Collins songs, which, as we both know, there are not …"

✳✳✳

… down in the square, a travelling carnival in residence: a procession of bearded ladies, Siamese triplets, marching penguins, fire eating gypsies, alcoholic strong men belittled by self-doubt … under the shadow of the big wheel, two men appearing like plain-clothed policemen, lingering across the street like plain-clothed policemen, blending in with their environment like plain-clothed policemen, smartly dressed in homburgs like plain-clothed policemen—Q suddenly suspecting that these men … *might … actually … be … plain-clothed … policemen …* as if to confirm the hypothesis, grabbed from behind by thick-set arms—thrust into a wall, gun pushed into the nape of the back.

"We have certain questions," they say together, nonchalantly waggling a subpoena. "Questions of a certain nature. Concerning a certain matter. Although we are not authorised to release any further information at the present time."

There is no struggle. Q not being guilty of anything—other than a cheap haircut and a sexual trajectory that had roused latent curiosities, perhaps—no need for a struggle. "I am not the person who crucified Mrs. A," Q informs them, forearms wrapped around his head …

✳✳✳

… beneath the ethereal lighting of the interrogation room, Q continues: "People are happily killing each other, cheerfully maiming themselves. And I am genuinely fearful for this city and any future implications for its general populous. Death is being interwoven, intimately connected on some level I don't understand. My findings have surprised me on many levels. I never knew there were so many deaths of a suspiciously transvestite-based nature, for instance …"

Chief Inspector S bends forward, removes the gilt-edged silver coffee spoon from his mouth with a confounded sigh and guffaws through a quick-fire series of shuddering jowls and crumpled face-skin: "So what is it you are trying to tell me exactly?" he says, voice incredibly loud, expression extremely close up.

"People are dying," Q tells him. "Some are vanishing. Others are being co-opted by the ghosts of the formerly living."

"Who are these people exactly?"

"I don't know."

"Where are these people now?"

"I don't know that either … but their lives form part of the wider investigation."

"And how wide has this investigation got?"

"At least twice as wide as it is long."

Droopy-eyed and sanguine, Chief Inspector S appears to be wearing a white turtleneck pullover and gold chinos, a prize Smith & Wesson half-cocked down the front of his pants like an utterly meaningful trophy. On his feet: a pair of tartan espadrilles tapping enigmatically to a soundtrack of smoothly-syncopated swing standards recreated by an authentic orchestra of recognised legal experts …

"Have you managed to reach any firm conclusions yet?" Chief Inspector S asks.

"Absolutely none," Q confesses, "of any firmness whatsoever …"

***

… more deaths …

Frozen motorcyclists. Electrocuted clergymen. Castrated hoteliers. Barbecued spouses. Casually skinned multi-storey car park attendants … Q occupying chairs, manipulating desktop toys, looking at women adjust themselves through digital binoculars—from high vantage points … slouching in gay revue bars, starting to feel like James Stewart at the end of *Harvey* … encountering an unusually tall man in heavy-rimmed sunglasses and yellow rubber gloves—in a gay revue bar—who tells him: "Come with me and you will find the answers you seek …" before sprinting unhelpfully in the opposite direction. Following a high-speed jog through the futuristic ruins of the city, Q tails the unusually tall man in heavy-rimmed sunglasses and yellow rubber gloves to a back street, down a side alley, through a sliding door, up dark creaking steps, into the grubby hallway of a communal spa which—Q guesses—is probably funded by an anonymous pervert millionaire for his own private purposes: the enjoyment of watching strangers conduct themselves nakedly, in private, via a two-way mirror system …

***

… behind the reception desk: a young Asian woman with the high-browed demeanour of Virginia Woolf, wearing a tartan turban.

"Who are you?" she demands in a refined voice, rich and plummy with strong overtones of Merlot. "You don't belong here. *What could you possibly want?"*

"Well," Q explains, "entanglement is weaving a path through time, very strongly, rather like an incendiary device … I do have some graphs and charts and other illustrative material to demonstrate this point … but outside of the investigation, my life is an empty canvas minus myself and prior to this I was desperate, down-on-my-luck, back against the wall, hand to mouth, mouth to hand, always questioning myself: *what am I saying? who am I? what is my destiny? why won't she answer my calls? has she rekindled her relationship with a former saxophonist?* because in essence, you see, I have been sucked into a vortex by all the beautiful absences in my own life, so many beautiful absences I couldn't possibly list them all, well, maybe I could, but it would take a very long time ..."

—only partway into one of the longest sentences he had ever attempted, Q notices the young Asian woman striking her turban violently against the hard, glossy edges of the reception desk. She pauses momentarily, gazes around, forehead glistening purple. Realizing she is still conscious, she repeats the action until almost completely concussed ...

***

... in the steam of the communal spa, the unusually tall man in heavy-rimmed sunglasses and yellow rubber gloves reclines on a long pinewood bench: naked except for a trilby hat now, his body improbably misshapen. The man signals with expansive homosexual mannerisms toward a half-raised portcullis framed by two portable cannons. Inside the gates: a stone-cold cold stone room, malevolent scarlet wallpaper, the smell of tepid piss, the ambience carcinogenic. Volumes of unread books line every wall, a dark archive of unremittingly obscure easy reading tomes. Over a grand piano, the vast imprint of a swastika, surrounded by a series of portraits, minor Scottish poets lounging indignantly in the semi-nude ...

***

... suddenly: the fearful drone of traditional bagpipe music ... 12 figures dressed as Judas Iscariot expressing a slight feeling of bewilderment via a Highland jig ... behind them, a gnomic man in sparkling jackboots and the habit of a nun. From inside his habit an epic pause ensues. Lowering the hood he reveals: the over-sized head of Princess Margaret. On her face a severe expression. Q having seen a similar expression on the faces of several other people lately. Friends. Family. Lovers. Lawyers. Paramedics. Magistrates.

There's another pause, not quite as epic as the last ...

"*My name is Herr Schmaltz!*" cries Herr Schmaltz, visibly demented. "*I have recently undergone a complete face transplant and—during the same procedure—had my colon medically revised. However, originally I came from Newark, New Jersey, where I trained to be a violist. But when I moved to Leipzig and became the world's smallest basketball player, they accused me of decapitating my nephew during a violent sex call ... then proceeded to arrest me for something I didn't do ... then questioned me about my relationship with a comatose futures trader ... then offered me cocaine, an incredible pay rise, and a part-time shot at redemption in the Scottish hills ... I quickly became very Scottish and having a head for business I quickly became a millionaire too ... now, having returned in partial disguise, I shall awaken dormant memories of love and crime and death ... and nobody shall penetrate the heart of my dark secret ...*"

✱✱✱

... dialing the emergency services at the bottom of the fire escape, Q briefly ponders the significance of the incident ...

✱✱✱

... that evening, staring down at his manual typewriter, drinking camomile tea. In front of Q: a blank page. Six months later, the same blank page still in front of him, an empty teacup in his hand ... the telephone spluttering in the ever-dimming dimness. Q picking up, as is his custom. A voice answering like a diseased hooker from a recent weekend in Amsterdam. "If it looks like a duck and talks like a duck and walks like a duck," the voice advises. "Then, in all honesty: it probably is a duck ..."

Q considers the words carefully, one by one, their residual meaning lingering in the upper reaches of the ceiling for several minutes afterwards ...

FUCK!!!

CHARLIE HUSTON

is the author of the Henry Thompson trilogy: *Caught Stealing*, *Six Bad Things*, and *A Dangerous Man*; as well as the Joe Pitt Casebooks, and various titles for Marvel Comics. He live is Los Angeles with his wife, actress Virginia Louise Smith.

LIKE A LADY
CHARLIE HUSTON

THE fucking kid behind the counter won't stop looking at her ass.

He gets it. She's a fine looking chick, a stone fucking fox, but she's his fox and he's getting sick of the kid staring at her ass.

Not that *she* minds. Pressed up against him, her arm wrapped 'round his waist, hand tucked in his back pocket, giggling and weaving on her high heeled boots. She never minds a little extra attention. She's a whore for it. She's a whore through and through. His whore. And she loves it that way.

Bombed on drinks they pounded at the flop, she teeters and knocks a few bags of chips from a display. They leave them on the floor and head for the beer.

He pulls open the door of the cooler and sees the kid reflected in the glass, his eyes still glued to the crescents of ass cheek peeking out from the bottom of her leather mini.

He slips his fingers through the plastic loops on a six of Coors tallboys.

—Fuckin' punk.

She works her fingers deeper in his pocket and gives his ass a squeeze.

—He botherin' you, baby?

He stands there with the door held open, watching the kid watching her butt.

—Punk's just about fuckin' you in the ass with his eyes.

She puts her mouth close to his ear.

—Easy with the hot talk, baby, you'll get me oily. Make me stink up my panties.

She giggles.

—If I was wearin' my panties.

She bites his earlobe.

—If *you* wasn't wearin''em.

He smiles and sticks out his tongue. She slides her lips over it, takes it in her mouth, and bobs her face back and forth on it a couple times, watching his face.

His eyes are watching the kid's reflection, the kid's reflection that just can't stop looking at his chick.

He pulls his tongue from her mouth.

—Fuckin' punkass.

She glances over her shoulder at the kid,

—Oh, he's OK. He's just curious is all. Just a curious little cutie pie.

He runs his tongue around his lips, licking away the cherry flavored lip gloss she just smeared there.

—What was that?

She's looking at herself in the cooler door now, running the wand from the tube of gloss around her own lips, reapplying it so she'll taste the way she likes to.

—Nothin', baby, just said he's a kid is all. Little cutie pie little boy. Still got pimples on him. He's just curious 'bout love is all. Can see it in his face. Bet you looked behind that counter, he has a boner just from watchin' us. Just from bein' 'round our love.

She drops the gloss back in the breast pocket of her fringed white leather jacket and flips her hair forward so it grazes the tops of her tits; nipples all but peeking out from the red bustier.

—No harm in his lookin' and learnin', baby.

He pulls one of the beers free of its plastic ring, pops it open, takes a long drink, wipes his mouth on his shoulder.

—What the hell is that shit you're talkin'? You like that punk?

She reaches for his beer.

—C'mon now, baby, s'not like that.

He pulls the beer away.

—Not like that? Sounds like that. Sounds from the way you're talkin' like you'd want that pimple-faced punk's hard-on up your ass. That's what it sounds like ta me.

She grabs the top of her bustier and pulls it upward, resettling her tits.

—Baby, my ass is yours. You don't like the way that kid is lookin' at it, stop bein' a pussy and do somethin' 'bout it.

She locks eyes with him. He drains the beer, tipping his head back slightly, but never taking his eyes off hers.

—Sir.

He crumples the can, drops it to the floor, opens another; all the time she stares at him, never blinking.

Crazy witch bitch never blinks it seems like.

His eyes are starting to feel dry. He kills another beer.

—Sir.

Still staring, motionless, like she could stay that way forever, frozen.

Freaky fucking whore, always fucking with his head, always pushing.

He drops the second can and tugs another free.

—Sir, I'm sorry, I'm gonna have to ask you to pay for those and drink 'em outside.

He blinks.

She smiles.

Fucking whore!

—Sir!

He drops the beers and does something about the fucking kid. Shows her who the pussy is.

And she watches her man, a warm trickle starting to run down the inside of her thigh.

***

—Oh no!

—Yes.

—I did not just fucking!

—You saw it.

—That. That is some fucked up shit.

—Some fucked in the ass shit.

—Who? Oh my God! Did he?

—Yep.

—Sheeeit! So who?

—Guess.

—Don't fuck with me just. Oh shit, no! Turn it off! Turn it.

—Too late.

—That is a sick fucker.

—Indeed.

—Who?

—Guess.

—No. Here. Just. Oh no, I'm turning this shit off, this is too. Oh fuck! Turn it off! Turn it the fuck off!

—OK, man, OK. Jesus fuck.

Hazelton touches the pause button, freezing the image on the monitor.

—Is it off?

—Yeah, yeah, man, it's off.

Sincere uncovers his eyes and sees the couple on the screen and the things they're doing, frozen, a thin black line rolling repeatedly up the screen.

—Fucker!

He covers his eyes.

—Turn it the fuck off. I got to sleep tonight. I got to kiss my kids.

The cigarette between Hazelton's lips jitters as he chortles, jitters and jumps away from the flame of his match.

He hits the power button on the VCR.

—OK, OK, didn't know you were quite so delicate.

Sincere peeks between two fingers, sees the monitor screen, blank and gray. He takes his hand from his eyes, wipes a trace of sweat from his forehead.

—Fucking delicate my ass, that's sick shit. Nothing to do with delicate. I want to screw my wife again some day, how'm I gonna do it with that shit in my head?

Hazelton gets his smoke lit on the third match.

—Still screw your wife? Fuck, who's the sick fuck here? That guy or you?

—Fuck you.

—Me, I'd rather have it like that guy than to screw my wife. Rather have it like his lady for that matter.

Sincere grins.

—Fucking-A, gave it to her didn't he?

Hazelton laughs, coughs, laughs, does both at the same time.

—That he did. Fuck knows how to treat a bitch that's for sure.

They high five.

Sincere plucks a cigarette from Hazelton's pack. Without asking.

—So?

Hazelton eyes him lighting one of *his* last fucking smokes.

—So, what?

Sincere blows a cloud.

—Who caught it?

Hazelton points.

—Thought you quit.

—Fuck, man, seein' something like that don't make a man need a smoke, he ain't human. Fuck do you care I kill myself a little more.

—Uh-huh. Well. Seven-fuckin'-fifty a pack, each one of those mothers is costing me about forty cents. So I'm wishing you'd quit, die, or take it up full time again and stop bumming my fuckin' Newports.

Sincere holds up hands, shakes his head, dips one of the hands in his pocket and tosses a crumpled single on the desk Hazelton is leaning on.

—'Scuse fuckin' me, didn't realize this was an economic issue. Keep the fuckin' change.

—Fuck off.

—No, seriously, keep the money, keep it all, consider the extra sixty cents a tip if you'll just tell me who caught the fuckin' gig.

Hazelton flicks the bill onto the floor.

—Borden. Fuckwad.

Sincere leans over in his chair, picks up the buck and stuffs it back in his pocket.

—The Whacker? No shit. Oh fuck. They laid it on her like all the other sick shit, didn't they?

Hazelton fingers a nostril.

—Nope. She caught it live.

—What? No shit. Picked up the phone and caught it?

—Nope. Bitch was in the area. Caught it on the radio.

—No shit. No shit?

—Better. She lives down there.

—Oh fuck.

—Uh-huh. Lives down there. What else?

—What?

—Shops there.

—No. Fucking. Way.

—Fucking drops in there, picks up her douche and whatever.

He taps the monitor screen with a fingernail, leaving a tiny smear.

—Knows the kid.

—That. That is fucked up. They let her keep it, she knows the kid?

—Sick shit like this …

Hazelton grinds out his butt on the steel top of the desk and brushes it into a wastebasket.

—Who the fuck else wants to deal with it?

—You gentlemen done with that?

The two uniforms turn around and look at Detective Elizabeth Borden, standing behind them, cup of coffee in one hand, other one held out, waiting.

They look at each other. Eyebrows arch.

Hazelton pushes away from the desk.

—Sure, sure thing, Detective. I was just bringin' it up. Thought best I take a look, make sure it was intact, the right tape an shit.

Sincere coughs into his hand.

—Yeah, the right tape.

She stands there, hand still out.

Hazelton hits eject and the VCR pops the surveillance tape from the deli gig.

—Here ya go.

He holds it out.

She waits.

He takes a step closer.

—Yeah, here ya go.

Places it in her hand.

—All set there, Detective.

She tucks the tape in her armpit, nods.

—Thanks.

Hand free, she reaches to her belt, draws her piece, points it at him and flicks off the safety.

—Hazelton, call me bitch, call me Whacker, whatever the fuck, don't mean shit to me comin' from a useless flatfoot like you; ever fuck with my evidence again, I'll fucking kneecap you.

She turns the gun on Sincere.

—You, fuckhead, want to have half a chance of going anywhere on the Job, stay the fuck away from this pathetic shitwad. He's a nose-picker. Nose-pickers finish fucking last.

She turns, slips the safety on and holsters her weapon, walking.

—Dead last, every fucking time.

And she's gone, out of the interrogation observation room before she can smell the stink of the urine spreading across Hazelton's lap.

***

Back in the room, he rummages through the plastic bag of half-pints they picked up down the block.

—SoCo. SoCo. SoCo. Fuckin'-A, you get anythin' but fuckin' Southern Comfort?

She's at the mirror, bustier pulled down, changing the piercings in her nipples, taking out the barbells and putting in the little jeweled pendants he bought for her this afternoon.

—I like SoCo. Janis drank SoCo.

Bottles clink as he spills them all onto the bed.

—I know you like SoCo. I can't stand SoCo. I asked you to get me some Cuervo.

She giggles.

—That rhymes!

He cracks the seal on one of the half-pints, holds it under his nose and sniffs.

—Fuck. Like drinkin' fuckin' perfume.

She turns, bustier still down, rotating her hips, singing.

—I know you like SoCo. I can't stand SoCo. I asked you to get me some Cuervo.

He picks up a tallboy, drinks half of it off, and empties the Southern Comfort into the can.

—Cute. Very fuckin' cute.

She dances closer, gripping the ruby red jewels dangling from her tits and pulling them out, stretching her nipples till they whiten around the piercing holes.

—I. Know. You. Like. So. Co.

She swings a leg over his lap, squats.

—I. Can't. Stand. So. Co.

She drags her crotch across his greasy jeans, leaving a trail.

—I. Asked. You. To. Get. Me. Some. Cuer. Vo.

She presses one of the jewels against his lips. He opens his mouth, takes it between his teeth, and bites down. She takes the beer can from him, swirls it, mixing the Coors and Southern Comfort, leans back, her nipple stretching further, a bead of blood appearing at either end of the hole poked through it. She places the beer at the stop of her tit, and pours. Most of it runs down the slope of bone white skin, down over her bustier, splashes in their laps, but some of it flows to her nipple and into his mouth. He drinks, nursing at her tit.

She yips, moans.

—Now baby, do it now.

He sucks, his eyes closed, knowing hers are open, always watching, and pulls the revolver from the front of his pants. The same one he used to do something about the kid.

She grabs the chain that runs from his left eyebrow ring to the gold hoop in his left ear and jerk on it. Beer and SoCo still pouring down her front.

—Do it.

He puts the revolver between them. She opens her thighs further. He presses the barrel between her legs.

—Unngh, baby, that's the spot.

He's chewing his way up the pendant, working it through his teeth, trying to get her bleeding nipple in is mouth while swallowing the trickle of beer and liqueur.

He pushes the barrel in. It slides easy on the leftovers from what they did after he was done with the kid.

—Baby. Ungh, baby. Do it baby, make me real baby, make it all real, baby. Let me hear it. Make the sound.

He's got her nipple now, the jewel rests on the back of his tongue as he bites her flesh and coppery blood joins the booze.

He thumbs the hammer of the revolver. It makes a loud click between them. She groans.

—Fuck me now, baby, fuck me all the way through, fuck my fuckin' brains out, fuck 'em right out the top of my head.

He fucks her, fucks her the way she likes it.

***

She freezes the tape.

She's watched it a couple times now.

At first, no real surprises. She'd been at the scene, saw the kid, saw the various fluids spread around. She already had a pretty good idea of the kind of thing that went down.

Sure enough, first viewing, just about what she'd expected. Guy goes berserk on the kid out of nowhere, put holes in him, then gets his thing on all over the place. Sick shit alright.

Second viewing, more of the same. Maybe looking more at the details. His piece. How he uses it. Not very well. Does it look like he's got another one stuck in his boot or something? No. Exactly how much time he takes getting off, like is he rushing to get out, worried about people coming it? Doesn't seem to be. Doesn't take him long to get his nut, but he doesn't seem to hurrying.

But it's that second time through she starts to see it.

Third time through, it's all she sees. The way he touches her hair. The way he wraps his arm around her. The way he cradles her and lifts her off the kid's body when he's done. The way he's always reaching out to touch her again the second he lets go.

Sick fuck, he loves her.

Her cell rings.

She looks at the window. TE AMO.

Fucking hell. Te amo, my ass. Fucker must have gotten into her phone while she was in the shower this morning and programmed that shit in. Fucker.

She answers.

—What?

—Hey.

—I'm working. What do you fucking want?

—Just. Sorry about that. Just fuckin' around.

She looks at the monitor, looks at the way he's touching her.

—Sincere, I could give a fuck. Do what the fuck you want. But Hazelton is a piece of shit. Got stuck with him as a partner, bad luck. You want to hang with him when you're not on patrol, your fucking business. But it's not gonna help you with shit.

—I can't shine him, got to work with him and shit.

—Whatever you say. Why the fuck did you call?

—Gonna see you later?

—Fuck do I know? I have work to do.

—Should I call?

—Do what you want.

—I'll call.

—Fine.

—Cool.

She starts to close the phone, stops.

—Sincere.

—Yeah, babe?

—Don't fuck with my phone. Don't fuck with any of my shit. Ever again.

She hangs up.

Fucking Sincere. What was she thinking fucking Sincere? She knows. She knows what she was thinking. She was thinking about the way he showed up at the precinct, all cock of the walk. She was thinking about all the girls in uniform and on traffic and in secretarial, and they way they all got wet over him from his first day. The way they all groaned when they saw his wedding ring and sighed when he flashed pictures of his beautiful mulatto babies and winced when they saw his pale skinned, model thin wife come by to meet him for lunch. She was thinking of how they'd all kill each other for a crack at him, but none of them thought they had a chance. She was thinking they're all dumb cows who couldn't see all that shit was bait on his line, the chum he used to draw the scavengers so he could reel them in before tossing them back.

She did it because she could. Now it's boring. Because he acts like a man, has all the trappings of a man, but he's not. He's a baby. And he still pulls that cock of the walk shit in public, still acts the *macho* around her when they go out for a drink. Puts on a show for any guys around, any audience he can play to.

And he's hanging with Hazelton.

She should have done it. Should have kneecapped the fucker right there. Fucking with her evidence. Fucking with her case. Should have put one in his knee. Got the useless nose picker off the force.

She thinks about how it might have gone down. How she could have manipulated Sincere into taking the hit. Hazelton said something about her. Sincere and she are having an affair. Sincere freaked and shot Hazelton. With her gun? No. Besides, it only works if Hazelton is dead. There's a fucking idea. Hazelton dead.

She looks at the screen. The way he holds her tight. Tender, even with the things he does to her. Yeah, he loves her.

She hits rewind.

—Borden.

She turns to the door of the video room. It's Hazelton. In clean pants.

He holds out a sheaf of faxes.

—Got the prints. He's got a record out of California.

She takes the papers, flips through them.

Vacaville. Over and over. Vacavile. Fucking psycho prisons. Put a revolving door on the things. Manson almost busted out of that place. Was building himself a hot air balloon. Jesus.

Hazelton is still there.

She looks up.

—What?

—We got him.

The VCR whirrs at a higher pitch, clacks to a stop, begins to play automatically.

—Got him?

He brings his finger toward his nose, sees her watching it, steers it away.

—Not got him like got him, but fuckin' got him in our sights.

Black and white images on the monitor flicker at the edge of her vision, the kid alone, flipping through a magazine while he talks on his cell. No idea what's coming his way.

She knew the kid. Fucking everybody making like it's a big deal. Fuck does she care she knew the kid. Just another Pakistani

American working the graveyard at his parents' deli over summer break. Kid was nothing. Just another teenager checking out her ass.

—Got him where?

He rubs the bridge of his nose, just dying to dig inside it.

—A flop on Bowery. Just about the last one. Like five blocks from where it went down.

He points at the screen, where the kid is making change for an old man buying a half-gallon of milk.

—Five fuckin' blocks.

—Who got the ID?

—Clerk at the flop. Some guys.

He scratches his nose harder.

—Some guys at the scene. The security system, had a backup, a second fuckin' VCR. Some guys dubbed the tape. Had it, what they call fuckin' rendered, digitalized. It's been on YouTube for a few hours.

She picks up her cold cup of coffee.

Hazelton shrugs.

—Hey, fucked up, but it, you know, the guys who did it, this isn't what they were, but it worked. Clerk at the flop is a member something called sickvideo.com. New stuff goes up, he gets a email. He gets a email, checks the new sick video, sees this shit. Fuckin' technology, huh?

The guy and his lover come into the deli.

—So where's the ID?

Hazelton laughs.

—Clerk sees the video, ID's the guy right there. Calls 911. Says this guy checked in this afternoon.

—Hazelton, is the ID any fucking good?

—Hey, fuckin' clerk says the guy checked in. Says a guy looks like him.

He points at the monitor.

—Checked in this fuckin' afternoon carryin' a fuckdoll that he was talkin' to. You think the ID is good?

She looks at the monitor, watches as the guy turns a corner toward the beer, the sex doll tucked lovingly under his arm knocking a few bags of chips from a display as he heads for the cooler.

She turns the VCR off.

—Get your partner. Meet me on the street. You can give me a ride over.

—You want some fuckin' help?

She looks at him, six-four and two-fifty of beefy Irish cop. Talk about a guy she never should have fucked. Jesus.

—Hazelton, guy's a nutjob. We need any help?

He nods.

—Fuckin'-A right we don't. I'll get Sincere.

He walks away, nostril filled with his finger.

She takes a sip of cold coffee, tastes blood on her lip. She looks at the blue and white cardboard cup. The cup she filled from the pot at the deli. Sees the tiny drop of blood just under the rim. Kid's blood. She wipes her lip. Turns the cup. Drinks from the other side.

***

He kicks his jeans off his ankles, goes into the can and takes a leak. Nice thing about wearin' her crotchless panties, don't even have ta take 'em down to fuck or piss.

She's still face down on the mattress, the thin, gray sheet unsprung from the corners, revealing the cigarette burns on the ticking.

He left the revolver inside her while he pushed into her ass. It's there still, she's squeezing it with her pussy muscles, he knows she is. That's what she does. 'Course, it's not as good for her when the barrel's cold, not as good as when he put it in her smokin' hot from doin' something 'bout that kid, but she still likes it.

He flushes and goes back in the room, grabs one of the half-pints and flops next to her.

She turns her face to him, hair plastered to her skin with sweat, smeared makeup, spit, cum, and tears.

—Baby, that was a keeper.

He cracks the half-pint.

—Wasn't it though.

She lifts her ass a little off the mattress, the heavy revolver danglin'.

—Wanna get that for me so's I can have a tinkle.

He sips the SoCo, not mindin' the sweetness at all now.

—Sure, Doll.

The door splinters open. A big fuckin' cop comes through the wreckage, 9mm first.

—Fuckin' hands in the air! Hands in the fuckin' air!

A lady cop's just behind him. Another blue's out in the hall.

Doll's frozen, not movin' a twitch. Then she smiles.

—*Do it, baby.*

He goes for the revolver.

The big cop's eyes go wide.

—No! Fuckin' no!

He's pullin' the revolver from Doll's twat. She fuckin' moans as it slips out.

The big cop's finger whitens on the trigger. There's a booger under the nail.

The lady cop trips the big cop as the 9mm goes off, the round punching a hole in the thin wall and probably going through four or five more and out to the street, she's around the big cop, her own piece out, swinging it downward, chopping the barrel on his wrist, makin' his hand go dead, bringin' her piece right back up and slashin' it across his nose and puttin' him down.

***

Borden tells Sincere to stay in the hall, keep the tenants away from the door. Not that he argues, not that he wants to be in the reeking room with smeared walls and carpet and the doll covered in jizz and KY and dry blood and years worth of little black bicycle tire patches. Such a fucking baby.

She stands by while Hazelton slams the guy against the wall, punches him in the kidneys a couple times, and pats him down.

—Sick fuck. Fuckin' sick fuck. Draw down on me, motherfucker. Lucky fuckin' fucker. Lucky she was here. Woulda died there was no bitch here ta save you.

Borden watches him shove the guy into the room's only chair. He doesn't cuff him. Wants him to do something so he can knock him around some more. Do some serious damage. But the guy just sits in the chair, staring at the doll.

Hazelton snorts.

—Sick fuck's clean.

—Check the doll.

He looks at her.

—What the fuck.

She holds up the bagged revolver in her hand.

—The doll had what appears to be the murder weapon hanging out its snatch when we came in, Hazelton. Why don't you see if there's another fucking piece on it just in case.

He flips her off.

—Fuck you, Borden. That was bullshit you pulled. Fuckin' sick fuck was goin' for a piece. I had a shot. That shit was clean. Could have fuckin got us both fuckin wasted, you fuckin' bitch.

Through the open door she's sees Sincere's back stiffen.

—He's a spazoid, nutcase, Hazelton, shoot him in the face and he'd have probably shot you five times before he kacked. Disarm the suspect whenever possible. That's the way we do it on the police force. What you garbage men do, I don't know.

—Fuck you, bitch.

He moves to check the doll.

She shifts a couple steps closer to the guy.

And he's watchin' the big cop, watchin' him move closer to Doll.

—*He's gonna touch me, baby.*

The big cop grabs her by the arm and flips her over and starts groping her.

—*He's touching me, baby. He's hurting me, baby!*

The lady cop is close to him, back to him, his revolver in that plastic bag, dangling loose from her fingers, right in front of his face.

The big cop is pawing her, pulling at her skewed clothing.

—*Don't let him touch me, baby, don't you fuckin' let this faggot cop touch me, you fuckin' pussy!*

He grabs the revolver, it slips easy from the lady cop's hand and he goes to kick her legs out but she falls before he can even touch her and he wraps his hand around the plastic wrapped revolver and his finger is around the trigger and he pulls it and the bag pops loud but you can't hear it and the back of the big cop's head has a little hole in it but the front of his head has a big hole and most of his face is on the wall.

And Borden drops and rolls when the bag is yanked from her fingers, rolls and comes up next to the bed, piece out by the time the guy is pulling the trigger, sex doll in her arms by the time Hazelton's face is hitting the wall, gun against its head by the time he's hitting the floor.

—Don't fucking move or I'll blow her fucking head off!

The guy has the revolver on her.

She jams her gun deeper into the side of the doll's head, denting the rubber.

—Fucking drop that gun or I will blow your bitch's head all over the fucking room, cocksucker! Drop! Drop!

Doll's eyes are on his, open, unblinking, always unblinking.

—*Shoot her, baby! The bitch's got nothing'! She can't touch us! Fuckin' shoot the bitch!*

Borden tightens her arm around the doll's neck.

—I'll choke her and shoot her and fucking kill her fucking dead! Drop the fucking gun!

Sincere is in the doorway, piece out, but pointed at nothing, staring at the stain on the wall that used to be his partner's face.

Doll starts to whisper.

—*Baby, she can't hurt us. All she can do is make it real. All she can do is make us fuckin' real. Go for it, baby, make her make me real. Make us real. Baby.*

He starts to cry.

Borden is shaking her head.

—No, no. Uh-uh, no fucking way. No one's gonna fucking die. Drop that fucking piece, man. Drop that fucking piece and you can have her. They'll let you be with her, man. You'll go away for fucking ever, but they will let you have her with you. You fucking love her, you fucking love her and you can't live without her. Take her, man. She's yours. All you got to do is drop the fucking gun.

He's crying. Crying. Cuz she's lying so much. They won't let him have her. They won't.

Doll is singing.

—*Crying cuz she's lying. Crying cuz she's lying.*

She stops singing.

—*Baby, do it. Make it happen for me the way I like it. Do it for me, baby. Make it real for me, baby. I love you, baby. I really fuckin' love you.*

She winks.

He puts the gun in his mouth and makes it real.

***

Sincere won't stop fucking sobbing.

She stands with him in the hall while the EMTs move around the room not even pretending that they can raise the dead this time. She whispers in his ear, tells him it's OK, he's gonna be OK. Tells him how sorry she is, tells him Hazelton shouldn't have pushed her into the guy when he got pissed, shouldn't have pushed so the guy could get the gun, tells him shit happens. He cries and cries.

More uniforms are filling the hall, pushing the tenants back into their rooms. Crime Scene cops will be here soon, acting like they're on TV.

She ignores them all and keeps whispering to him about how it happened and how he couldn't do anything about it.

She gives his shoulder a squeeze.

—Go down to the car. Get out of here for now, man. Nothing you can do. Go down to the car.

He nods, sucks air, stops his tears for the moment, and goes down to the car.

By the time they go in and they separate them for their shooting reports, he'll think he saw it, he'll remember Hazelton calling her bitch and losing his cool. He'll be just so fucking sure Hazelton called her bitch and pushed her right into the sick fuck. Sure that's how the guy got the gun.

By the time they get cut loose, it'll be morning and he'll be numb and empty and need someone and his wife and his kids will seem like enemies and she'll seem like his best friend.

So she'll take him home and pop his cherry for real, teach him a lesson about who the real bitch is between them. Make him like it that way. Like being the bitch. And as soon as the shoot is cleared by IAD, she'll cut him loose.

Fucking cock of the walk.

She goes and stands in the doorway.

One of the EMTs has a digital camera and they're all taking turns snapping pictures of each other with the doll.

She looks at the guy, sprawled in his chair, dick hanging out the front of the red panties, top of his head off.

Jesus.

Jesus she would have liked to get him in one piece. Would have liked to get him alone in the interrogation cell. Would have liked to ask him, what's that like? Loving like that? What your secret, knowing how to be with her? Knowing what she wants?

She looks again at the pathetic doll, so tenderly patched.

Sick fuck, that's for sure.

She turns and heads for the stairs.

But at least he knew how to treat his girl like a lady.

JOHN RICKARDS

writes books and things and is young enough to have been to Star Wars in utero. Probably. His parents have never really said. When not writing his bio, he can be found at johnrickards.com, usually making obscene remarks.

TWENTY DOLLAR FUTURE
JOHN RICKARDS

IT is night when the ghosts come for Abdi. He stands, as he has taken to doing, on the low pile of rubble behind their house. From the top of the mound of stones he can see the stars above mirrored by the waves on the distant sea, as if the edge of town is the edge of the world and there is nothing beyond it but the void. He stands there when the ghosts come so that he will not wake his sisters. So that if they do wake, they will not see him cry.

His mother, reaching out to him as she calls his name. Sometimes in her soft voice, a voice he only knows from dreams he was so young the last time he heard it for real. Sometimes she calls to him in the dying screams she let out giving birth to little Aisha, his youngest sister.

Yusuf and his parents, all burnt and broken. Black, staring holes where Yusuf's eyes were. Everything pinched and cracked just as it was when they found them. Yusuf's father was a big man, but this had not mattered to the militia.

Abdi's own father, blood soaking his shirt around the bullet wounds. Wordlessly mouthing something he cannot understand, some word forever frozen on his lips.

Other faces, people he never knew. Never had the time to know. Seen briefly through windshields or walking in the street. No names, but accusing faces. Blood, bullet wounds. Rape and murder. People say it is the way of things, but these ghosts ask Abdi why they died, why they suffered. They plead with him and paw at him, afraid and confused.

His father again, this time as he was before it all went so wrong. Standing tall and wise as he always did, working to provide for their family. He stands at the base of the rubble and holds out the twenty-dollar bill for Abdi to take.

Abdi knows all too well what the money means. He cannot forget the first time his father gave it to him.

***

"Take this to Jama," he said, pressing it into Abdi's hand. "He will know what it is for." The money would have taken his father almost two weeks to earn. He must have arranged something very important with Jama, a trader, and Abdi was thrilled to be entrusted in this way at twelve years of age, even if all he had to do was take the money across the town. He took it and wedged it deep into one pocket.

"Good boy," his father said and patted him on the head. Abdi trotted out of the door, into the dusty African sunshine.

His good feeling lasted until he ran into the militia. Half a dozen of them, lounging by a burned-out building with walls pock-marked by gunfire. He didn't recognise them, men of another clan, and he felt fear clench his throat and his heart pounded in his ears.

"Hey, boy," one of them said as Abdi tried to pass by on the far side of the street. "This is a checkpoint. You think you can walk through here without permission? There is a tax for walking this street. Security costs money. Keeping the streets safe costs money."

"Of course," Abdi said. This was the same militia bullshit he had heard so many times. "But I do not have any. I'm sorry. I am just going to take a message to Jama in the market. I have no money."

The militia man scowled, and his friends gathered around Abdi. "You are not willing to pay for security and safety? Who would not pay for this? Maybe you are a thief or a criminal. Maybe we should arrest you. Maybe you do not want the people here to be safe and secure."

"No, no. I'm just poor. Please."

"Let's check this 'poor' boy. I don't believe him and I don't like him." The man leaned in close and stared hard at Abdi. His breath reeked.

Abdi struggled, but the militia held him pinned while their leader checked through his pockets. The man yelled in triumph when he found the twenty dollars and waved it in Abdi's face.

"You filthy liar! You try to keep this from us? The rich boy does not want to pay his taxes?"

The blow came out of nowhere. The man slammed the butt of his Kalashnikov into Abdi's chin. Pain seared through his head and he could taste blood and dust as he dropped to the floor. The kicks the man followed up with hammered into his ribcage, but he could hardly feel them. His head swam with agony and he could do nothing more than lie there until the man picked him up and threw him across the street.

As he crawled away, trying to wheeze as quietly as possible, all he could think about was that his father's money was gone. He had failed his family, and perhaps now they would face hunger and hardship.

***

"Their militia are nothing but pigs," Hassan said. He was a friend of Abdi's, at thirteen, a year older than him. Two years before, his father and three other members of his family had died in a fire at a refugee centre. "They should be taught that they cannot act that way."

It was Hassan's idea to take the money back. They would steal the money back from another trader, one from the same clan as the militia, and then everything would be equal. Hassan's older brother, Osman, who had been a member of their own militia, would help them. Bring them guns and knives even though Hassan thought they could do it without any fighting, so long as they were quiet.

Osman looked up from flicking stones into the dust and nodded. "This is right," he said, with a voice like flat rock. "We don't make a sound, and we can take what we want. And if they do find us, we will be able to fight them."

And Abdi again agreed, because he couldn't face going home to his father and admitting that he'd failed him.

Hassan laughed and patted him on the shoulder. "That is good! Maybe we will even find something for ourselves there."

Abdi knew then that some people value children as fighters for their ferocity and bravery. But he also knows, now, that children do not think like men or plan like men.

When the three of them reached the trader's home and climbed in through a window, they were thinking many things. Imagining what might lie within. Worried, perhaps, that the trader would be less rich than they thought. Abdi certainly was. This could all be for nothing. But none of them expected to find his guards in the building.

Osman had not even reached the stairs when a burst of AK-47 fire cut him to pieces, the bullets shredding his body like paper. As he fell, he turned towards Abdi with a look, it seemed, of surprise and shock. He said nothing. Made no sound at all. His brother Hassan, though, screamed with horror and anguish. The guards fired again and bullets crashed into the walls around the two boys.

They chased Hassan and Abdi into a small room at the back of the building. Hassan, sobbing the whole time, turned and fired wildly through the doorway behind them. Abdi heard someone scream in pain, and someone else yell for them to cover the back. He scrambled through the narrow window.

"Hassan! Come on!" he hissed. But he did not wait for him. Instead, he ran away into the bushes before the guards could come around the outside of the building. Only once he was safe, out of sight in the dry scrub, did he hunker down and turn to look for his friend.

Hassan was still half in, half out of the opening when they caught him. Abdi heard them shouting and silently willed his brother to move faster, to break free, to run. Then he heard the gunshots and he buried his face in the dirt. When he looked back, Hassan was hanging limp, his blood washing the stones.

He stayed, staring wide-eyed at the scene, for a moment. Then he ran from the house. There were tears in his eyes and his heart was wedged like a stone in his throat.

Abdi still didn't know if the guards saw him running and recognised him. Or if Hassan was only wounded when they shot him and they hurt him so he would give up their names. It didn't matter in end, not really.

His father was dead by the time he returned home.

He found him executed, shot three times in the doorway to their home, punished for what they had done. Abdi's world ended at that moment. He felt as though everything he had or loved or dreamed was suddenly gone, and he was empty. His sisters were hiding in a closet. The men who did it arrived in a car, they said. Abdi's father would not let them into the house, even though they had guns and he did not. So they killed him where he stood.

Little Aisha clutched his hand. "Is father hurt?" she said. "When will he be better?"

Abdi could do nothing but stare at the man lying dead on the floor. His father. The man who had raised him for so many years on his own. All gone.

"Abdi?" Aisha said, voice choking. "Why won't he stand up?"

His other sisters, Hamdi and Habiba, led her away as the tears began.

The next morning, the leader of their militia, Osman's former commander, came to the house. He told Abdi that he would need to earn money to support his family, but that the clan would not fail them, so long as he did not fail the clan. He would join the men on the roadblocks. He would carry a Kalashnikov and protect their people. He would shoot their enemies and the rewards would be shared by all.

Or he and his sisters would starve.

***

They are all there now. Abdi's father. Hassan. Osman. And, at the back, another man. One he knows he will never see in this life. A kind, tall man, standing with his arms around his wife and three children, all healthy and strong. That they are all smiling is no comfort to Abdi, for he knows that the man is himself in a future he can no longer have. That his actions have destroyed everything he might have been as well as everything he was.

So Abdi stands there in the night, the ghosts all around him. And he does not fight them and he does not run from them. He stands there, a twelve-year-old man, a soldier and a killer, wishing that his father would speak to him and tell him that this is not his fault. That he does not blame him. That his life will change and he will never have to touch a gun again. That he could somehow give his father back that twenty dollars and stop any of this happening.

Then, he stands there, crying in the dark.

NATHAN SINGER

is a novelist, playwright, composer, and experimental performance artist. He is the author of the critically acclaimed and controversial novel *A Prayer for Dawn*. His written work has been published across a wide spectrum of print media, from academic journals to underground indie rags. Several of his plays have been brought to life on stage, including the theatrical adaptation of his second novel, *Chasing the Wolf*. He currently teaches writing at the University of Cincinnati, and is completing his fourth novel, *Blackchurch Furnace*.

THE KILLER WHISPERS AND PRAYS ... OR LIKE A SLEDGE-HAMMER TO THE RIBCAGE
NATHAN SINGER

I don't think he's being forthright with us, Sergeant ...

"No, I don't think he is. Are you getting excited, fella? Is this turning you on? Do you think this is a game?"

This isn't a game. This is war. Somebody told him wrong ...

"Somebody told you wrong, Habib. Oh, and he whispers and prays. The killers all whisper and pray. But you see, Achmed ... I'm sweet and nice. It's the *corporals* who are mean and tough. And the corporals have your little baby boy in the other room. And they have garden shears and a long, hard Maglite. Do you know what those shears will do to his little toes? Do you know what that rod will do in his little bottom? Shhh shhhh shhhhhhhhhhhhh ... none of that now."

Is all that screaming going to help him, Woyzeck?

"The screaming's not helping you, Haji. Pose for your glamour shot."

Smile and say Jihad ...

"Just like the sheep at the slaughterhouse back home."

Tell us all about it, Frannie.

"Hang them by a chain, alive and terrified, by their back feet. They roll in one after the other. Slit one throat, slit the next. It all drains into a bucket."

Message coming in, Sergeant. OPEN FIRE!

***

When Frannie came marchin' home again/ Hurrah! Hurrah!/ She was pale, gaunt, vacant and thin/ Hurrah! Hurrah!

***

I was discharged. And given special duty. There are terrorists and rogue agents operating on our very soil. I had to work under cover of midnight. Equipped with a customized rifle I would shoot diamonds into their throats. No trace. No serial numbers. Just hard cut diamonds right to the throat. I walled them up in the paneling at the neighborhood grocery store. The walls are packed with them now. Sometimes they weren't fully dead, and I'd hear them trying to scream as I walled up another. But they couldn't scream. Not really. Not with diamonds in their throats. There are hundreds. You can smell them rotting when you shop for produce. Special Ops. Not sanctioned. If I'd been caught I'd have been on my own. The pay was slimmer than I thought it would be. But I'm a proud soldier. I serve one master only. The one most high. I used to pretend that there was no God. But I'm not blind. Even in the roaring midnight I'm not blind. Oh Lord, make me an instrument of your justice ... And a channel for your righteous genocide. Wind. And rain. They've put out the sun. I could love this cellar life. Where spiderlets devour their own mothers ... Twilight is my cloak and salvation. And the killer whispers and prays. I am still. Centered. My head is gravel, my teeth are arrowheads, my eyes are sand packed tight pounded clear and sharp into brittle liquid windows into your forever nothing. I am where chaos goes to die, dragged

kicking and wailing, baffled and grief-struck into its own annihilation.
I suffer neither the fools nor the wise.

   I don't suffer at all.

***

"So today's the big day, huh?"

Second lieutenant J. Rogers packed his duffel with the few personal items he'd left lying about. He was an intruder in this meager efficiency and he knew it. He liked the feeling. Pulling a Camel Red out of his shirt pocket, he watched Marie pace about, shoeless, plain and simple, as she straightened second-hand lamps resting on cut-rate end tables. *No smoking around the baby, idiot.* He dropped the cigarette back into his pocket.

"Not the time," Marie said distracted, furiously tossing odds and ends into available drawers: pens, lighters, loose change, an old, worn copy of *The Unfinished Works of Georg Buchner.* "Not the time not the time." With a slight shudder-breath, she bent over and picked a piece of condom wrapper out of the stained carpet. She slid a cleaning bucket under the dining table.

"She's my friend too," said J.

"Come on, J. Please."

"We're probably closer, in fact. We were in combat—"

"You know what? That's great and that's awesome and I'm all about it ... but not today."

"I'm gonna be around, you know."

"Hey, fantastic—"

"So what? Do we meet for the first time next week? How we working this?"

"Oh god ..."

"Well?"

"Please!!!"

"I just want to do this right. That's all." Quite to his own surprise, J found himself filled with the sudden urge to go into the bedroom, pick up the baby and tickle him. Kiss him one last time. And at once, he was not so keen to leave after all. "Marie … look … You've got to realize … she's not the person you know any more. That person is gone forever."

"You don't know," Marie replied. The finality of his tone chilled her, and she absently gritted her teeth. "You didn't know her before."

"No, but I know her NOW, and you don't."

"You don't know." *Ohhh yes …* "Stop it."

"What?"

"I said stop." *Up a little higher.* "You can't touch me like that any more."

"You don't like it?"

"I didn't say that." *Just a little lower.* "I said *don't*. Let go."

"All right. I'm out." But he stood still. "Can I just see Christian for a moment?"

"Why? He's not your son."

"HE'S NOT HERS EITHER!!!"

Get a grip, soldier!

"Okay," she said, cool and direct, "Do you really want to have that talk with me now?"

"No."

"What I thought."

Say something, you fuck! Don't let her slip away this easy!

"You're not going to have any sort of … safety net, you know. No protection. No benefits. And she's not going to be able to take care of you."

"I can take care of myself."

"Yeah, and that's another thing. Does she know about that? Does she know how you've been *getting by* in her absence? What do you think she'll think? Huh? Will she be as understanding? Or forgiving?"

"Oooooh, you've got some big brass balls throwing *that* in my face. You wanna talk about dirty money? How've YOU been earning a paycheck the past couple of years, lieutenant? Let me see your hands, is that blood? Yeah. *Honorable.*"

"You're not going to tell her, are you." He laughed. Cold.

"Why would I?"

"It's just going to be our little secret." *Our little secret.* "Well ... yours, mine, and every miserable pathetic hunchback in town who's got the itch and the scratch, right?"

"Fuck."

"I'm leaving. It's been real nice. How much do I owe you?"

"Goddamn ..."

Asshole!

"I'm sorry, Marie. I'm so sorry. That was wrong and I didn't mean it. I didn't mean to hurt you."

"I didn't mean to hurt *you.*"

"So ... I guess ... I'll meet you, or whatever, in a week or two."

"Can't wait." And as he left, she whispered, "Goodbye."

***

And Frannie sings:

Run away, run away, run away, run away from me. Run away, run away, run away, run away from me. I don't trust myself when I'm like this. I don't like myself when I'm like this. Run away, run away, run away, run away from me.

***

Master Sergeant Francine Woyzeck entered her own apartment as if she'd never been there before. Tossing her satchel onto the couch, she surveyed the scene scanning for a trigger of tangible memory. *A little.* She sat down and opened the satchel, more out of habit than necessity just then. She pulled out her medicine kit and bag of toiletries. A few magazines. A butterfly knife, some length of rope, and a couple of black burlap hood sacks—*OH FUCK!* Those last items quickly went back into to bag and zipped up twice. She scanned the room again. *Nothing much.* No less alien than the barracks from which she just came. *Ahhh ... home again ...*

"Fran?"

From out of the adjacent bedroom Marie walked with naked feather footsteps. This moment she'd waited for for so many months was now here ... and at once she secretly prayed for *just one more dress rehearsal, Dear God.* No dice.

"Hm."

Fran stood before her still and on display. Same pretty girl, love of Marie's life. Auburn hair and hazel eyes like cool, shimmering lakes. Funny and silly and ticklish around her calves and heels ... now strangely hard like pewter. Angular and pointed.

"Hey baby ... Wow ... um ... So ..."

"Yeah. Hey there you."

They hugged. Stiff. They stopped.

"Doing ... good?"

"How's ... stuff?"

"Stuff is ... yeah. Feeling well?"

"It's ... you know."

"Totally."

"It's been a ..."

"Couple. Maybe ... a while. A little."

"So ... it's good to ..."

"It's ... it is. Yeah. God, you know, I thought it was going to be a little tough, and I THINK it is a bit rough but, but, but I think that, yeah, you know, it's quite a thing, right? Isn't it? Don't you think so? Yeah? Sure. I mean, how often are you just like FUCK, you know? It's crazy, uh huh, all the things that can happen in such a short time and, you know, things pass through your head that are *really* over here and then there's this OTHER stuff and you're thinking HOLY SHIT, you know. It's just such a different scene but all in all it's good, right. Things are great and it's all pretty great. Great. Yeah. Good stuff. Good ... stuff ..."

"Yeah ..."

"Fran?"

"Yep."

"Was it ... lonely?"

"Little chilly here."

"Fran?"

"Yup."

"Wake up now."

"I should ... uh ... maybe this isn't the right time."

"Oooooh no you don't. Not again."

"You're free to go on, Marie."

"You're free to stop now."

As Fran turned toward the door, Marie grabbed her arms with both hands.

"Let go, goddamn it."

"No."

"Marie!"

Instinctively Fran raised her fist and Marie screamed,

"Don't you DARE hit me!" Like a cougar, Marie jumped onto Fran's back and sunk her teeth hard into her lover's neck. Fran howled in pain and they both tumbled to the floor in a heap. "See," Marie chuckled, wiping her wet lips across the back of her hand, "you're not dead after all."

"Aggggh, let me go!!!"

"Not a chance."

"I changed my mind," Fran spat. "I don't want you any more."

"Tough shit."

"LET GO OF ME!"

"Not happening."

"You're fucking hideous!" snarled Fran. "You make me sick!"

"Bummer for you." Marie, grabbing the upper hand, pinned Fran to the floor at both wrists. With her knees she forced Fran's legs open and slid between them.

"Get away from me!"

"Nope."

"I put a bullet through a baby's heart!" Fran growled, thrashing, gnashing her teeth, her watery eyes so red her tears resembled blood.

"Sure you did." Without thinking Marie began to slowly grind her pelvic bone into Fran's.

"Collected, fuckin', eyeballs … and teeth!"

"F … fuh … fascinating."

"AAAAARGHHH!" Fran's aggressive thrashing gradually transformed into a futile squirm, and Marie pressed and pushed and rubbed harder between her thighs.

"You're wasting … your energy."

"FUUUUUUCK!!!" Fran screamed, absently joining in on the grind as the two of them began to slither and pulse against one another.

"Yessss ma'am …"

Just as Marie thought she might climax, Fran crumbled and collapsed inward, sobbing. Marie cradled her tightly in her arms, *shushing* and rocking like only a skilled mama can.

"I d-d-don't … want, *sob*, want to hurt you!"

"Shhhhhh. You won't, sweetie. You won't."

"I was … afraid … I'd, I'd, *sob*, lose you."

Marie smiled and brushed a few rebel strands of hair from Fran's damp checks. "But you're the beautifulest girl I know."

"Marie, I'm …"

"Shhhhh. I know, sweetheart. I know."

"It's just like … yeah …"

"Yeah …"

"Just …"

"Now, missy, howzbout you tell me the *truth*."

"It was … boring and lame and no big deal and I missed you every day."

"See, that wasn't so hard, was it." They giggled softly. They kissed. Warm and familiar. Marie held Fran's head to her breast and mouthed silently, *Love you … love you forever'ndever.*

"Say somethin'?"

"Nah."

"Okay …" Fran exhaled deeply and looked Marie directly in the eyes. "I'm ready now. I want to meet him."

"Really? Are … are you sure?"

"Y … Yes."

"I don't think you are."

"I AM. I'm ready."

"'Kay." Fran remained sitting Indian-style on the floor as Marie exited to the bedroom. She returned with a cooing gurgling bundle swaddled in a thin, aqua-colored wrap. "This …" Marie said by way of a grand introduction, "… is Christian. Here, hold him."

"Oh, I don't know."

"C'mon. You're his mommy too."

Marie handed the bundle to Fran. Fran could not help but be startled at how light and shapeless the baby was. Without much to go on, Fran had been imagining this child as the round, rosy cherubic infants one is likely to see on television commercials hawking fruit juices and rash salves. But this *Christian* here, with his ashen skin and skeletal, claw-like little fingers slashing randomly about, was nothing like those creatures. His tight, thin lips snapped aimlessly, like a vulture chick hungrily awaiting mother's vomit. At once the baby's head fell backward and his mouth gaped open, his eyes blank like a rag doll's corpse.

"OH NO!" Fran panicked. "OH GOD!"

"It's all right! It's okay. See?" Marie instantly righted the small boy's head in the crook of Fran's arm and he returned to his gurgling and lip-smacking. "See? He's alive. See?"

"Jesus ..."

"Yeah."

"Tiny."

"Wave for Mommy, Christian."

"Does he breathe okay?"

"It'll get better. See? That's better already. I've been waiting for this for so long."

"He's got your mouth."

"He loves you already. He loves you already."

***

My head is a thousand pounds of gravel. I walk spiders on a leash. I cast a shadow at midnight in pitch black with screaming indigo splashing across emerald eyes overflowing. I leave the quick wailing in my wake. Baffled and grief-struck. Tear ducts like choking deserts. Ducking shrapnel tearing throats coated with mother's dust and blood. I have no fear. I have no shame. I'm not proud of what I do but ... I'm proud to do what I can.

***

"Woyzeck?"

"Huh?"

Second lieutenant J. Rogers entered the squalid apartment bold and unannounced, without so much as a knock. Fran had, just moments prior, been rooting through the couch cushions in desperate search for spare change or at least a loose cigarette. No dice.

"At ease, sergeant."

"Well HOLY SH—"

"Shhhhhhh … Baby's sleeping." Indeed he was, in a thrift store pumpkin seat next to a small but mighty space heater.

"Right, right. How you been, Rogers?" They embraced forcefully. "With your big ole head start. Fucknut."

"Eh, you know. What'd I miss?"

"Sand."

"Goddamn, I miss that sand."

"Love it."

"I brought some home. I store it in my jockeys."

"For safe-keeping."

"Totally. Right next to my ass. Only way I can sleep."

Fran nodded, smiling.

"Look at you, F.W. You and your little family. Settling in I see. Nice."

They went on to catch up about the state of the war in bland, businesslike terms, never discussing anything beyond day to day soldier grunt work. The subject of their commanding officers came up briefly, which quickly devolved into language such as "necropederast," "cretin rat fuck" and "jizz mop," followed by a round of hearty laughter.

"So, F. Tell me straight. Holding up okay?"

"Like a steel rod."

"That's what she said."

"Dude ... that doesn't even ... make any sort of sense." Thunder crashed hard right outside the window. "Fucking hell!"

"Rain's been killing me," J said. "Like needles out of a cannon. For weeks. And I'm out there at the docks drowning in it. I've heard there's hail coming. Greaaaaat."

"So you're working these days."

"I'm solid. Doing well. Money in my pocket. Money to burn."

"I'm a little concerned."

"You're not working? You've been back for a while now."

"I can't ... get it together."

"Huh. No problem for me."

"Sooooo ... what are you saying?"

"I'm just saying, you know. Maybe I could help—"

"NO."

"Well, you'd better hop to it, F. You got these angels to look after. They're counting on you."

"I'm not ... at my best. But I'm good."

"How does labor suit you?"

"What? Oh ..."

"Huh?"

"Labor. Never mind. I thought ... never mind ... Labor. Yeah, I'm fine for lifting and shit."

"You'll be good, Ef Dub. You're pretty strong. For a woman."

"Yeah ..."

Another thunder crash and Christian began to fuss and whimper, never actually waking. J looked over to him with a warmth that betrayed his *official story*.

"Cute kid ya got there. I love babies," J whispered to no one in particular. "They suit me."

"Yeah ..." Fran replied. "Me too."

"I could at least make some calls for you."

"That'd ... be great."

"Hey, I'm not trying to—"

"You're not stepping on my toes. Got a cigarette?"

He pointed at the sleeping baby with a disapproving scowl.

"Right," said Fran resigned. "Thanksamil."

"Anything I can do to help. Call on me tomorrow. Or I'll call on you."

Suddenly the baby let out a shriek, and Marie came running in from the bedroom wearing nothing but an oversized flannel shirt. She picked him up in one swoop and began bouncing him to the beat of a song no one else heard.

"Shhhh shhhh shh shhhhh ... it's okay ..."

"Marie." J said stiffly. "Hello. Again."

"Hi. Uh ..."

"You've met, right?" Fran interjected.

"Well ..." Marie squinted. "Maybe ..."

"Yeah, cuz, remember," J stammered. "I brought you the thing? The thing?"

"Oh ... yeah."

"Yeah. Remember, Fran? I was heading back home and you weren't sure when you'd be, well anyway, you gave me, the, the package—"

"The anklet." Marie remembered.

"The anklet. Right."

"Uh huh," said Fran.

"Right. You asked me to bring the anklet, and give it, yeah, that one there."

Marie held up her otherwise bare leg to show off the anklet in question and J pointed at it as if it wasn't plainly visible. Fran stood quietly, perplexed by their behavior.

"So ... yeah."

"Right," J smiled, relieved. "Good to see you again."

"Ditto," Marie replied.

"I've heard so much."

"Yeah …"

"Oh, and this must be Christian, yes? How doin' there, buddy? Huh? How doing? He's adorable." The baby cooed and chortled. J looked up at Fran and said, "Yours?" And the silence was radioactive. Finally he continued, "So I'll see you tomorrow, Fran. Marie, my pleasure."

"All mine," Marie said as J made his exit. Marie kissed the baby's belly. "All mine," she said again and the infant giggled and belched. Marie placed him back in his pumpkin seat, and he nodded off immediately. Marie wrapped her arms around Fran. "Aaaaaall mine. Chilly?"

"Little."

"Feel my feet."

"They're cold."

"They're soft. They haven't touched anything but this floor in a million years."

"That's a long time. Well, get dressed. Go have fun. I'll watch him."

"Um … No … that's okay honey. I'm fine here. Hungry?"

"Nah."

"Tired maybe? Need to lie down a bit?"

"Uh uh. You've got to be freezing."

"You should warm me up."

"Yeah. GAAAAAA! God, your toes are ice!"

Marie giggled, "You're gonna wake him."

"Don't want to scare him."

"Don't worry."

"He should be fatter. He's not fat enough."

"He's happy, Fran. He's really happy."

"Are you happy, Marie?"

"I love you."

"I'm sorry."

"I *love* you."

"There's a draft."

"It's warmer now."

And with that they fell to the couch and made love ...

"Marie ... I ... love ... you ... back."

"Oh ... oh ... OH GOD!"

"Shhhhhhhh! You're so loud."

"I can't ... help it! You make me crazy. Oh sweet Jesus ... My my my lordy ..."

Naked and sweat-drenched, the rest of the world dissolved around them. As if flashed back in time, Fran was, briefly, once again herself.

"Marie ... oh ... yes ..."

"Don't p-penetrate me. All I need is ... oh yes, *riiiiiiiiight there* ..."

All at once Marie came to a shuddering, bucking orgasm and squealed with delight.

"Shhhhh ..." Fran giggled, covering Marie's mouth with her hand.

"Too long" Marie gasped. "It's been ... too damn long ..."

"Hey, how do you think *I* feel?"

"You feel ... pretty good to me."

"You're silly."

"Be silly with me."

They lay together, silently, breathing hard and listening to the leaden rain smash against the asphalt outside. "You think you're hard," Marie said finally. "But you're not. I think you're as soft and sweet as hot butterscotch."

"'Kay."

"I'll bet you didn't hurt anyone at all."

"You got me."

"Damn right I do. Wanna go outside?"

"It's raining! Real hard!"

"Let's go be naked in the rain."

"Oh, Christ."

"It'll be good stuff. We'll splash our bare feet in icy puddles. We'll freeze our asses numb."

"Freeze our assets?"

"Then we'll come in and get warm again."

"Sheesh."

"Aw, whaddaya 'fraid of, soldier?"

"You are too crazy."

"I'm just crazy enough."

"Goddamn … you're so pretty when your cheeks are flushed."

"Honey dripper."

"I could live in your smile. I could swim in your eyes."

"See? You're why I'm crazy."

"I'm addicted to your skin."

"Oh my …"

"You're my heroin."

"You're mine. You're *my* heroine, Soldier girl."

"Do you understand how bad I—"

Marie suddenly burst into tears … "If you ever, *sob,* leave again I'm going to …"

"I'm home now, sugar," Fran said, soothing. "I'm home for good."

"Tell me how it was," Marie cried. "Please."

"You got my letters, yeah?"

"Oh. Yeah. *Wish you were here.*"

"Heh heh heh."

"Too crazy ..." she sniffled.

"Home now. For good."

"I'm thinking of cutting all my hair off."

"Don't do that."

"Maybe I should grow it out long."

"No, I like it like it is."

"I need a change. I want a ball gown."

"Yuck!"

"And a sparkly neck-thing."

"Necklace."

"If you insist."

"What, and a pumpkin coach? And glass slippers too?"

"Nope. No shoes. Never. Rings are good, though. *A-hem.*"

"For your toes?"

"Toes OR fingers. *A-HEM.*"

"Subtle."

"I'm so sleepy."

"You're gonna drive me poor. More so."

"Not even, *yawn,* a plastic ring?" With that Marie fell deep into sleep. Fran covered her with an old, knotty afghan and walked over to the window to watch the storm. The hail had begun. Tennis ball sized, they pummeled the poor unfortunates caught out in it, and crashed through windshields, setting off car alarms for blocks. The wail of sirens increased as more and more lethal chunks of ice made their destructive descent. Fran turned back to find the baby wide-awake in his seat, eyeing at her with sharp, calculated appraisal.

"You need a plan, soldier," the baby said matter-of-fact. "We're hungry."

"Um ... well ... I could mercenary," Fran replied. "I don't know much, but I know how to kill."

"Plan plan plan, Fran."

Fran instantly felt awkward standing naked before an infant boy and quickly slid into a pair of jeans and a T-shirt.

"Nobody will fucking hire me."

"Tell us about it, Frannie."

"I do get sick on occasion. And dizzy. And I'm falling."

"Your feet are flat on the ground."

"But I'm still falling."

"All scooped out?"

"Hollow. Like a stone cave."

"Poison in the sand. It's creeps up inside."

"Sand. Air. Sky."

"Do tell. Tell us about *over there*."

"Pretty boring. Nothing much to say."

"Tell us all about it."

"Lots of sitting around. Meet the locals. Rebuild. Good things."

"Tell us about the *torture*, Frannie-belle."

"There are lies in the spires and the magic lies. All the magic lies. All of it. All my magic lies. All my magic lies … every one of them. This is where all my magic lies. This is where you will find all my magic lies …"

"Tell us a little story about the *torture.*"

"There was no torture."

"Tell us about the dogs."

"There was no torture."

"Pigs and dogs sniffing on the mezzanine. Pigs and dogs sniffing on the mezzanine. Thump, what was that? They're not coming, are they? Thump thump thump."

"All of it … lies … still …"

"Tell us about the black burlap hoods, Frannie-belle. The rape and the dogs and beatings and the torture and we laughed laughed laughed laughed laughed, didn't we laugh at the blood and the sodomy, Frannie-belle? Didn't we laugh at all the burning babies?"

Fran giggled, "Some corpses keep hard-ons ..." She put her face in her hands, horrified with herself. But she laughed again at the notion.

"No one blames you."

"Do they blame that brain-dead fascist who sent us down there?!?!"

"Nope. Him neither."

"It'll make us murder. It'll make us meat. Make us monsters all ..."

"Buck up, sergeant."

"The past has passed. It's gone now. Gone."

"Are you home now, love?"

"I gotta be pretty for her now. And strong. And strong for you. The past is the past and I'm hanging it on a nail in the hallway."

"You'll take care of us then? Strong and tough and all of that?"

"And all of that."

"Not like a *daddy* I hope."

"NO."

And once again the baby let out a shriek. Instant rage, the little figure shook and turned a deep shade of crimson, forcing out a scream to push his tiny lungs to their splitting point. Marie awoke with a sigh.

"Ohhh, will he never sleep?!?!"

"Why's he so loud?" Fran asked, gripping her head in agony.

"Jesus, Fran. Could you take him for a while?"

The baby fixed its razor wire eyes on Fran and hissed, "Take us with you, Frannie-belle. Teach us how you work. Should we follow the turkey buzzards?"

Marie bounced him shushing, oblivious.

"I ... can ... take him," Fran offered.

"Never mind."

"Marie ... We're gonna do better than this. I promise."

"I know."

"You yourself could sell, Frannie," the baby hissed again. "Bodies do sell we've learned. Hungry."

"I think he's just hungry," Marie said, squeezing her left nipple to express a bit of milk.

"Hungry," the child continued. "And we sleep and live in shit. You're still a pretty little kitty, Fran, and boys pay top dollar for sweet meat. Poor girls whore, love."

Fran paced, considering the infant's proposition. "I don't know if ..."

"He's just fussy," Marie said.

"I need a physical," said Fran. "But I'm good to work. I'm seeing a doctor tomorrow, then I'm good. I'll make you happy, Marie."

"I ... am. Already."

"You're good," the baby taunted. "You'll *make* her."

"It's too fucking loud in here. I gotta step out for a cigarette."

"We don't have any more."

"Somebody does."

"MOMMA!" the baby cried out, reaching for Fran. Fran backed away slowly toward the door.

"He doesn't want you to leave," Marie said, small.

"I'll be right back."

***

"Hush, now, baby you don't have to cry/I'm here and I'll always be by/Hush, now, you'll always be in my arms/Safe, warm, protected from all harm/My love/My baby my love/My love/My baby my love …"

Marie sang as she changed Christian's diaper and wrapped him up tight in his receiving blanket. J entered the flat quietly and stood watching and listening. He smiled and thought to himself, *this could be your life.* And a shot of anger jolted through his body. Finally,

"Beautiful," he said interrupting the song.

"OH! J," Marie turned with a start. "Hi. Thanks for coming. I wasn't sure if you would."

"Hey, I'm always happy to help a damsel in distress. Especially if I can help her out of *dis dress.*" There was an excruciatingly long pause until Marie realized it was a joke. "Um, just kidding." She giggled obligatorily and set Christian in his seat. "Soooo … how was the big welcome home?"

"No big deal."

"Yeah?"

"Oh yeah. You know. She rode in on a white horse, lifted me off my feet, carried me off into a green field and we made mad passionate love in the tall grass."

"No shit."

"All day long in the warm sunshine."

"Well I'll be damned."

"Yes you will."

"But see, I don't remember the sun shining for a month of Sundays."

"Well it did. And she's aces with Christian, too. Like a pro."

"Good. Good to hear. So where is the missus?"

"Out."

"Thank heaven for tiny miracles."

Another horrible pause, and J thought that maybe he should just stop talking altogether.

"She's just out … you know … doctor and job and alla that."

"That's a full bill. I walked that road already. I'm clean now, and healthy. And working. Frannie will, too, I'm sure."

"Of course."

"Fran's one of my favorite people, you know." Marie nodded absently. J continued, "She's who I want in my corner. But I wouldn't want to cross her."

"Yeah. Look, let's cut the *happily ever after* bullshit."

"What? It's not great?"

"It's ... not."

"It's not all roses and soft music and long walks in the moonlight?"

"It ain't Paris. It's just not. I mean ... we're good, but ..."

"But ..."

"So, just 'but.' Dot dot dot."

"So what can I do to make it better?"

"What can you do?"

"I want to help you."

"I couldn't ask—"

"You called. I came. I want to be here for you. So name it."

"I just wanted to ... talk to you. I miss talking to you."

"That's it?"

"Yeah."

"Quit playing." He simply couldn't take this stupid two-step any longer. Urgently he said, "She's not well, Marie. Let's be honest. She's not going to be able to come through. You're gonna starve. *He's* gonna starve."

"I don't think—"

"Somebody's gonna have to work. Cuz she won't. She can't."

"Maybe this isn't the time."

"I love Fran. You know that. But I just don't think Fran—"

"Fran Fran Fran. She's all over your lips." He moved in quickly to kiss her. "Don't!"

"Okay, fine. Maybe this was a mistake."

"Wait. I miss you. I … care about you."

"But you LOVE her!" He seethed.

"I do. Oh god, do I love her. Like a deep cut."

"Like a sledgehammer to the fuckin' ribcage."

"It's fatal."

"Goddamn …"

"I'm being honest, J. Do you want me to lie?"

"Maybe a little," he replied, small.

"And you're right. If she can't take … Well, maybe it's about me taking care of *her*. So I will take care of her. If she can't provide for me … for *us*, then I have to. Somehow."

"So it would seem."

"I just need a quick bit of cash to get us on sturdier feet. Fran doesn't have to know. She *can't*. Then we'll be good from there."

"So," he said coldly. "Go make that money. You know what to do."

"I'm innocent."

"Uh huh. I'll take that bet."

"You want to wreck my innocence?"

"No games, for chrissake."

"Just keep it quiet …"

"Everybody's got needs …"

"Business …"

"Sure. If you say so."

"Just a fine bit of business."

"Just fine."

"Nobody's hurt."

"Everybody wins."

"You shouldn't … touch me like that."

"You want me to stop? Tell me to stop."

"Sssssssssssssssssssssss …"

"Tell me to leave and I'll leave. Go on, Marie. Tell me to leave." Without warning she lunged, biting deep into his chest. He yelped like a dog as the pain shot through him, and he picked her up and threw her hard against the couch. Tearing each others' clothes away, they fucked fucked fucked fucked FUCKED FUCKED FUCKED. *FUCKED.* Hard, rough, deep. Savage.

"Don't you miss this? Huh? You miss this cock?"

"I don't … I …"

"Shit … slow down …"

"No. OOOHHH!!! DEEP! Deeper than that! YESSSS!!"

Marie climaxed wildly. The soldier did not. They fucked harder.

"Come on," he panted. "Wait for me."

"No."

"Baby watching?"

"Shut up. OOOOOOOOOOOH YES!"

"Not … working for me."

"Yes! Works for me."

"Goddamn it. I'm trying—"

"Try HARDER. Oh Jesus! HARDER! OH GOD!"

"Here, turn around."

"NO!"

"Turn around!"

Frustrated, J flipped her over onto her stomach and began pounding into her from behind.

"NO! Don't fuck me like that! I'M NOT A BOY!"

Marie buried her face in the cushions wailing as J continued to slam into her, finally grunting out a brutish orgasm.

"YES!!! Oh yeah ... Holy ... fucking ... Jesus ..." He rolled over, panting. Marie refused to remove her face from the cushions, treating J instead only to the sounds of wrenching sobs. "Hey. What's wrong? Don't cry. Come on, Marie. Stop crying!" No response. He stood up, fidgety and nervous. He quickly began to throw his clothes back on, never once having the nerve to look over at the silent infant watching it all. "You're not going to ... tell anybody, are you? ARE YOU?!" He grabbed her hair roughly and she let out a shriek of pain. "Sorry! Sorry! Come on. You hear me?! Sorry. I'm sorry. You won't tell anybody. You're not going to. I know you won't. Come on, please don't cry. I wanted to help you. Come on. Shhhhhhh. Shhhh. Please stop crying. Here." He pulled out his wallet and began raining down bills all around her. No response. Just the sobbing. "Come on. Take it. I just want to help you! Take the money, Marie. Here, take it all. Take the goddamn money."

After dumping all the cash from his wallet, J fled the apartment in a panic. Silence followed. Finally, Marie lifted up her head. Not sobbing. Not a bit weepy. Not even blotchy. Perfectly fine. She smiled self-satisfied, counted the money happily, and sang to herself ...

"Hush now/baby you don't have to cry ..."

***

It's hard to see in this light just how glum and dreary all those faces are. Drones and worker ants marching off to feed and gang fuck the queen bee. Clomping down the sidewalk with granite feet. It's a pity. What? No, I don't do that sort of work anymore. Yes, I'm desperate, but the answer is no. What? Speak up, you're cutting out. What's that? Come on, do I have to walk you through it? You tie 'em tight behind his back, push him to his knees, put the hood over his head, and slit a wide smile from earlobe to earlobe. Then just let him drain out into the tub. Easy as cherry cordial. There's no mess if you do it right. Well, get clean.

***

Fran entered freezing and soaked. No employment found to-day. The storm outside had gotten even more severe. Winds up to one hundred and three miles per hour. Piercing rain. And hail grown to thick daggers of ice. Fran herself watched a man's face lacerated open by such a jagged chunk as this, his cheek ripped asunder exposing his white teeth like a bloody, wailing skull. She thought to tell Marie about it, but decided instead not to say a word, lest it upset her.

Once inside Fran found only the baby, alone in his pumpkin seat. His talon-esque little hands waving absently in the air as if conducting an unseen and unheard orchestra.

"She whored while you were gone, you know," he said. "Babies need bottles, Frannie. She let strangers do all sorts of things to her. In your bed. In her hair. Poor girls only serve one purpose, my dear."

"The past is behind us now, baby-love. Sunny days on the horizon."

"Not the past. Today! They ate her skin right off her bones. She swallowed their poison. Babies get hungry and poor girls *get by somehow.*"

"Get bi?"

"And get bought."

"It's … all passing away into nothing. I'll have forgotten it all soon. Bright times ahead. But …"

"But?"

"It's always cold here."

"Are you sleeping, Fran? Wake up. They're dripping with her as we speak. Sopping. *Drenched*. RIGHT NOW. On your best day you'll NEVER be the mercenary she is. We'll eat now. We may be just fine. There are some women in this house who know how to work."

"No."

"How are things today, Fran?"

"Not true."

"Going well?"

"Wrong."

"She points her feet toward the heavens and earns her daily bread."

"You're wrong. The past is … hanging … in the hallway."

"What has *he* got that you haven't, huh?"

"He? Nothing. Nothing good."

"Oh, but what a busy little beaver she can be."

"She's all I have."

"And not even yours."

"SHE'S ALL I HAVE!!!"

"You've got talents. Gifts."

"I don't know much … but …"

"Skills. Training. Expertise. *Experience*."

"I'm falling. Odd sky today. Imperial violet."

"Lamb's blood."

"Even the sun is cold. Everything's cold here. She's all I have. I can't stop falling! There's even a damp chill about the sun. SHE'S All I … !"

"Hang them on a chain. One right after the other. Slit and spill. Slit and spill."

"Not true. Not real. Everything's fine."

She ran from the flat, outside the crumbling complex, into the screaming wind. The storm had eased slightly just there, but Fran knew there were corpses not but a mile from home crushed by falling hail the size of Volkswagens. Heading into a blind run, she ran smack into Second lieutenant J. Rogers.

"Rogers …"

J stepped back, unsure as yet of what she knew or didn't. She appeared distracted and upset, but not particularly *at him*. He offered her a Camel and a light. She took it and breathed in the smoke hungrily.

"Say there, Ef Dub. Uh … Fit as a fiddle?"

"Fit to be tied."

"Odd sky today. Hepatitis yellow."

"Thank God I'm not a sailor. Have you seen the hail?"

"No."

"Impossible."

"Hey F, if you're a little low—"

"Can't even afford a plastic …" she mumbled to herself.

"Fran?"

"I like your ring."

"Huh? Oh. Yeah."

"How much for it?"

"It was my great-grandfather's."

"She's got tiny fingers," Fran mumbled again to herself. "I could have it cut smaller, though."

"Not for sale."

"Everyone's for sale."

"Huh?!"

"Every*thing*. I mean every*thing*."

"So … uh … How's the old doc then?"

"Bearing glad tidings of course."

"Ill news?"

"I got no love for uncertainty."

"Dizzy? Vertigo."

"Devoured alive from the inside out. I'm rotting."

"You can still work. I work."

"Poison. In my blood like sludge in a river. In my tears. In my …"

"It was all in the sand and the air, Woyzeck. I have it too."

"At least I can't pass it to *her*."

"Oh …" *Shit* … "Yeah … well you can still work."

"Sure. Sunny days ahead."

Standing out in the cold and the wet, J felt his nervousness subside. Replaced with a burning rage.

"Or maybe … you … can't. Maybe you haven't got what it takes."

"What?"

"Maybe you're lacking the necessaries."

"Say again?"

"Maybe you're *under-equipped*."

"Fuck you." Fran flicked her lit cigarette at his chest.

"Would you even know how?"

"I … I'm …"

"Oh, I know you're tough like a cheap steak. I know what went down over there in the dust. I heard the screaming. Poor little babies. They suit you, huh? I know what you did. Or rather, what you *let happen*."

"I … need a moment—"

"Cuz when you can't do the job, F, there's always someone waiting in the wings to finish it off for you."

"Your hands are just as bloody—"

"Hey, I'm just the trigger man, darlin'. The boy with the *gun*. It's the bullets' fault, not mine."

"It's just—"

"You can toss and turn all you like. I sleep like a newborn all night."

"You've got a lot of fucking nerve—" Suddenly J grabbed Fran's wrist and twisted it behind her back. "AAAAGH!!!"

"You've got a lot of what you don't deserve," he growled through clenched teeth. Hot spit spraying out against her cheek. "A lot of what you can't handle. A lot of what rightly belongs to one better suited. You cunt."

"Don't sleep, maggot," she hissed. "I live in the pitch-black."

"Stop by any time, sergeant. We'll have a drink. Compare notes." He twisted her arm higher between her shoulder blades. She winced in pain, but was determined not to cry out. With his free hand, J began to run his fingertips over her nipples, and trail down her stomach. "Don't you just love it, Woyzeck? Don't you just love the way she claws your back when you hit that sweet spot just right? Don't you love how she always wants it deeper, deeper, *deeper*? Or ... did you not know about that." He let go and she fell to the cement kneecaps first, rubbing her sore shoulder, refusing to look anywhere but down. "Take it easy, Fran. I'll be seeing you. Again and again. Some sunny day." And away he strolled.

Fran lay on the cold, paved ground feeling it throb with the violence and death that surely was taking place not but a few miles away. The sharpened, pointed metallic rain began afresh, and she felt the little pin pricks slashing tiny cuts into her face.

"No." she said to no one at all. "I won't. I can't." She put her hand to her ear. "Shut up. I said shut up!" She began smacking herself in the head as hard as she could, desperately trying to *chase it away*. "SHUT UP!!!" She began to sing. "Run away, run away, run away, run away from me ... I don't like myself when I'm like this. Run away from me ..."

***

As Fran crawled back into the apartment, she was greeted by the sound of Marie singing,

"Hush, now, I'll always be here for you/I love who you are and not what you do/ Hush now, and know if ever you're scared in the night/just look and I'll be your bright light, my love/My baby my love ..."

Christian sat still in his little chair, suckling happily on a bottle of milk. Under the table upon which the baby and his pumpkin seat rested was Fran's satchel: her special compartment opened. Unzipped twice. The baby gave Fran a tiny wink and resumed sucking away.

Marie entered, radiant. Gorgeous and feminine in a brand new dress, make-up, jewelry.

"Still in your bare feet though, I see," said Fran.

"Of course," Marie chirped.

"You can get to hell without shoes."

"Am I a bad girl, my love? Am I as lovely as sin?"

"Do you hate me? Is that what it is?"

"What? You're the beautifulest girl I know. I LOVE you."

"Yeah ... Still need a ring? Or what?"

"Everything I do is for you."

"For me ..."

"For us. I want what's best for *us*. And I do what I can."

"DO YOU THINK I'M AN IDIOT!?"

"NO!!! But ... I know you're not well, Fran. You hear things that aren't there. You think things that aren't true. Your eyes play tricks."

"But I'm not blind."

"Sweetheart, I—"

"Even in the roaring midnight I'm not blind. Do you hear a snare drum?"

"It's just the rain and the furnace. Fran, please think for just—"

"I'm done thinking. My head is a thousand pounds of gravel. I walk spiders on a leash. I cast a shadow at midnight. In pitch black. With screaming indigo splashing across emerald eyes overflowing ... my love."

"Fran—"

"I leave the quick wailing in my wake. Baffled and grief-struck. Tear ducts like choking deserts." Fran slid her satchel out from under the table with the tip of her boot "There are lies in the spires. And all my magic lies."

"Fran, don't look at me like that. Oh god ..."

"Ducking shrapnel, tearing throats coated with mother's dust and blood."

"I love you, Fran. Please—"

"No fear. No shame." Grabbing Marie's wrist she said, "I whisper and pray—"

"OW! Fran, PLEASE! Let go! You're HURTING me!"

"Oh Lord, make me an instrument of your justice."

Fran forced Marie to her knees. She reached into the satchel and grabbed the rope and butterfly knife.

"Oh god, NO! PUT THAT AWAY!"

"It's only kindof sharp."

"Oh god ... no ... think of the baby, Fran!"

"Cold in here, darling?" Fran asked as she slid a black burlap hood over her lover's head.

"Please don't put that on me! Fran please!!! Take it off!!!"

"And dark? Wind and rain have put out the sun. Stay on your knees. I could love this cellar life. Where spiderlets devour their own mothers." Marie thrashed and screamed, muffled by the hood. Fran tied her wrists tight behind her back. "Be quiet," said Fran, irritated. The baby looked on intently as Fran slid the cleaning bucket from under the table. "Twilight is my cloak and salvation." In one clean slash Fran slit a half-moon from Marie's left ear to her right. "Oops. I think I penetrated you, hon." The body slumped forward, gushing and spilling right into the bucket. "I am still. Centered. And all that hot blood drains out."

Fran stood up, silently crying. Yanking off her boots, she began to sweat and shake. "God, it's so hot in here. And sticky. Need to scrub clean." She peeled off her shirt and pants. "It's getting worse!" She tore off her undergarments. "Boiling! Wash clean. I'm boiling alive!" From there she fell to her bruised, gashed knees and, using her shirt as a rag, soaked up Marie's blood, *washing* herself with it all over her body. "Wash ... clean ..."

"Fran?" J said as he entered the apartment, his boldness his undoing. "Marie?" The baby laughed.

"My head is gravel," said Fran.

"Fr—" Catching the scene, J stopped short in horror. "Oh Jesus ..."

"You're free to stop right now," Fran said, pointing the butterfly knife directly at him. "You think I won't catch you? You think I won't eat your skin right off your bones? My teeth are arrowheads, my eyes are sand packed tight, pounded clear and sharp into brittle liquid windows. Into your forever nothing."

"Fran, I can—"

"I am where chaos goes to die, dragged kicking and wailing, baffled and grief-struck into its own annihilation. I suffer neither the fools nor the wise. I don't suffer at all. Come here and you live."

"Wait—"

"COME HERE NOW AND YOU'LL LIVE."

"Is that ... Marie's? Oh my god, Fran. It's all over you. You're dripping with her."

"I'm drowning."

"You're drenched in her. MARIE! NO!"

"You pumped your poison into her. You put your disease in her. But we're going to get clean. Thump. Do you hear that? Are they upstairs? Thump thump."

"It's not real. No no no …"

"They're not coming, are they? Pigs and dogs sniffing on the mezzanine. Pigs and dogs sniffing on the mezzanine. Thump, what was that? They're coming for us. Thump thump thump. They're coming for us both."

"Fran, it isn't real. It isn't real!"

"Take you shirt off."

"It isn't real!"

"TAKE IT ALL OFF!" Crying, J peeled off all of his clothes down to his tube socks. Fran muttered, "All the magic lies. Make us murder. Make us meat."

"Make us monsters all," whimpered J. "God, God, please god …"

"We're washing clean."

Dabbing the rag into the bucket again, Fran smeared blood all over J's skin.

"AGH!" he groaned. "It's freezing cold!"

"Boiling. This is where all the magic lies. This is where you will find all the magic lies. Put your hands out in front. We're just the same," she said as she pulled his arms forward and tied a bit of rope around his wrists. "Don't squirm! You squirm they burn your wrists. You know that. We're just the same. Soldiers. It's all we know. Kneel down. We're praying and scrubbing clean."

"Oh god … oh god!"

"Quiet. Whisper. Keeps your prayers quiet. Hold out your arms." Fran removed Christian from his seat without so much as a peep, and lay him across the soldier's out-stretched arms. "Take him. Hold him, like a big, strong man."

"I can't! I can't hold him like this!"

"I don't think he's being forthright with us, Sergeant," the baby said with a smirk.

"No, I don't think he is."

"Take him back!" J screamed.

"Don't drop him. Don't wake him."

"He's awake now!"

He began to sob as she covered his head with another black burlap hood.

"Buy the kid a hobbyhorse, daddy."

"I can't breathe!"

"It'll get better. It's better already." The storm continued to rage outside as snow mixed with rain and hail. Bullet shots were heard as no doubt hoarding and looting had begun. Such is the end of things. It gave Fran a great familiar comfort. But the messages trying to get through to her from her commanding officers were muffled, and loaded with static.

"Woyzeck? Sergeant Woyzeck? Do you read?"

Master Sergeant Francine Woyzeck, naked and drenched in blood, simply resumed her duties like a good soldier, following the last command given. Should any more terrorists or rogue agents be delivered she had more hoods, more rope, her knack for improvisation, plenty of hard-cut diamonds ready to be shot.

"What's the word, lieutenant?" She asked the baby as he rested steadily upon the soldier's shaking outstretched arms. The soldier's moaning muffled by the burlap.

"They're coming, Woyzeck," he replied solemnly. "Pigs and dogs. Thump thump. They're on their way."

"I await your word, sir," she said, reaching for her specialized rifle, eyeing the window, eyeing the door.

"The time is now, soldier." The infant bellowed, "OPEN FIRE!"

ACKNOWLEDGEMENTS
JEN JORDAN

EXPLETIVE *Deleted* came about over a rough session of editing and layout for *Crimespree Magazine*. Jon Jordan's enthusiasm and Ruth Jordan's story, "Little Blue Pill" (and her mordant sense of humor) sparked an idea that only a late night with crime fiction cohorts like them could produce. Sarah Weinman, Kevin Wignall and Ben LeRoy made the idea a possibility. Alison Janssen gently prodded its actual existence.

Others have held me steady along the way: David Thompson of Busted Flush Press, Ken Bruen who doesn't know no, Dianne Jordan, Andrea Carroll, John Connolly (who listens to me kvetch with the patience of a saint) and my Mommy, who read to me every night.

Thank you Red Bull for allowing me to work until my eyes bled.

And the biggest thanks go to everyone who has a story between these covers. No one hesitated to say yes and, for some reason, every one took the theme to heart. There is a little fuck in us all, isn't there?

—*Jen Jordan*
September 2007